# MY ROOMMATE
## IS A
# VAMPIRE

# MY ROOMMATE IS A

## VAMPIRE

### JENNA LEVINE

BERKLEY ROMANCE

New York

BERKLEY ROMANCE
Published by Berkley
An imprint of Penguin Random House LLC
penguinrandomhouse.com

Library of Congress Cataloging-in-Publication Data

Names: Levine, Jenna, author.
Title: My roommate is a vampire / Jenna Levine.
Description: First edition. | New York: Berkley Romance, 2023.
Identifiers: LCCN 2022056153 (print) | LCCN 2022056154 (ebook) |
ISBN 9780593548912 (trade paperback) | ISBN 9780593548929 (ebook)
Subjects: LCGFT: Romance fiction. | Vampire fiction. | Novels.
Classification: LCC PS3612.E92389 M9 2023 (print) | LCC PS3612.E92389(ebook) |
DDC 813/.6—dc23/eng/20230112
LC record available at https://lccn.loc.gov/2022056153
LC ebook record available at https://lccn.loc.gov/2022056154

First Edition: August 2023

Printed in the United States of America
3rd Printing

Book design by Daniel Brount

*For Brian, who always makes me laugh,*
*and who is always up for adopting just one more cat.*

# MY ROOMMATE
## IS A
# VAMPIRE

# ONE

### Roommate Wanted to Share Spacious Third-Floor Brownstone Apartment in Lincoln Park

*Hello. I seek a roommate with whom to share my apartment. It is a spacious unit by modern standards with two large bedrooms, an open sitting area, and a semiprofessional eat-in kitchen. Large windows flank the eastern side of the apartment and provide a striking view of the lake. The unit is fully furnished in a tasteful, classical style. I am seldom home after sundown, so if you work a traditional schedule, you will usually have the apartment to yourself.*

*Rent: $200 per month. No pets, please. Kindly direct all serious inquiries to fjfitzwilliam@gmail.com.*

"THERE HAS TO BE SOMETHING WRONG WITH THIS PLACE."

"Cassie, listen, this is a really good deal—"

"*Forget it, Sam.*" That last part came out more forcefully than I'd intended—though not by much. Even though I needed his help, my embarrassment over being in this situation in the first place made accepting that help difficult. Sam meant well, but his insistence on involving himself in every part of my current situation was getting on my very last nerve.

To his credit, Sam—my oldest friend, who'd long ago acclimated to how snippy I sometimes got when I was stressed—said nothing. He simply folded his arms across his chest, waiting for me to be ready to say more.

I only needed a few moments to pull myself together and start feeling badly for snapping at him. "Sorry," I muttered under my breath. "I know you're only trying to help."

"It's all right," he said, sympathetic. "You have a lot going on. But it's okay to believe that things can get better."

I had no reason to believe that things could get better, but now wasn't the time to get into it. I simply sighed and turned my attention back to the Craigslist ad on my laptop.

"Anything that sounds too good to be true usually is."

Sam peered over my shoulder at my screen. "Not always. And you have to admit this apartment sounds great."

It did sound great. He was right about that. But . . .

"It's only two hundred a month, Sam."

"So? That's a great price."

I stared at him. "Yeah, if this were 1978. If someone's only asking for two hundred a month today there are probably dead bodies in the basement."

"You don't know that." Sam dragged a hand through his shaggy, dirty-blond hair. Messing with his hair was Sam's most obvious *I'm-bullshitting-you* tell. He'd had it since at least sixth grade, when he'd tried convincing our teacher I hadn't been the one who'd drawn bright pink flowers all over the wall of the girl's bathroom. He hadn't fooled Mrs. Baker then—I *had* drawn that aggressively neon meadow landscape—and he wasn't fooling me now.

How would he ever make it as a lawyer with such a terrible poker face?

"Maybe this person's just not home a lot and only wants a roommate for safety reasons, not income," Sam suggested. "Maybe they're an idiot and don't know what they *could* be charging."

I was still skeptical. I'd been scouring Craigslist and Facebook since my landlord taped an eviction notice to my front door two weeks ago for nonpayment of rent. There'd been nothing available this close to the Loop for less than a thousand a month. In Lincoln Park, the going rate was closer to fifteen hundred.

Two hundred wasn't just a little below market rate. It wasn't even in the same universe as market rate.

"There are also no pictures with this ad," I pointed out. "That's another red flag. I should ignore this one and keep looking." Because yes, my landlord was taking me to court next week if I didn't move out first, and *yes*, living in an apartment this cheap would really help me get on top of my shit, and maybe even keep me from ending up in this exact situation again in a few months. But I'd lived in the Chicago area for more than ten years. No deal in Lincoln Park *this* good came without a huge catch.

"Cassie." Sam's tone was quiet, patient—and more than a little patronizing. I reminded myself he was only trying to help in his very *Sam* way and bit my tongue. "This apartment is in a great location. You can easily afford it. It's close enough to the El that you'll be able to get to your jobs quickly. And if the windows are as big as this ad says they are, I bet there's tons of natural light."

My eyes widened. I hadn't thought of the lighting in the

apartment when I'd read the ad. But if it did have huge, lake-facing windows, Sam was probably right.

"Maybe I'd be able to create from home again," I mused. I hadn't lived somewhere with good enough lighting to work on my projects in almost two years. I missed it more than I liked to admit.

Sam smiled, looking relieved. "Exactly."

"Okay," I conceded. "I'm at least willing to ask for more information."

Sam reached up and put his hand on my shoulder. His warm, steady touch calmed me, just as it had every time I'd needed it to since we were kids. The knot of anxiety that had taken up what felt like permanent residence in the pit of my stomach these past two weeks began to loosen.

For the first time in ages, it felt like I could breathe again.

"We'll see the apartment and meet the roommate first, of course," he said very quickly. "I can even help you negotiate a month-to-month lease if you want. That way, if it's really awful, you can leave without breaking another lease."

Which would mean I wouldn't have to worry about getting hauled back into court by yet another angry landlord. Honestly, that would be a decent compromise. If this person turned out to be an axe murderer or a libertarian or some other awful thing, a month-to-month lease would let me leave quickly with no strings attached.

"You'd do that for me?" I asked. Not for the first time, I felt badly about how short I'd been with him lately.

"What else am I gonna do with my law degree?"

"For starters, you could use it to make tons of money at your firm instead of using it to help perennial fuckups like me."

"I'm making tons of money at my firm either way," he said,

grinning. "But since you won't let me loan you any of that money—"

"I won't," I agreed. It had been my choice to get an impractical graduate degree and end up hopelessly in student loan debt with few job prospects for my troubles. I wasn't about to make that anyone else's problem.

Sam sighed. "You won't. Right. We've been over that. Repeatedly." He shook his head and added, in a more wistful tone, "I wish you could just move in with us, Cassie. Or with Amelia. That would solve everything."

I bit my lip and pretended to study the Craigslist ad intensely to avoid having to look at him.

In truth, a large part of me was relieved that Sam and his new husband Scott had just bought a tiny lakefront condo that barely accommodated them and their two cats. While living with them would save me the stress and the hassle of what I was going through now, Sam and Scott had just gotten married two months ago. Not only would my living with them hinder their ability to have sex wherever and whenever they felt like it, the way I understood newlyweds tended to, it would also be an awkward reminder of just how long it had been since I'd last been in a relationship.

As well as a constant reminder of what a colossal failure every *other* aspect of my life was.

And, of course, living with Amelia was out of the question. Sam didn't understand that his straitlaced, perfect sister had always looked down on me and thought I was a total loser. But it was the truth.

Honestly, my finding a place to live that was neither Sam and Scott's new sofa nor Amelia's loft in Lakeview was best for all of us.

"I'll be fine," I said, trying to sound like I believed it. My stomach clenched a little at the look of concern that crossed Sam's face. "No, really—I'll be okay. I always am, aren't I?"

Sam smiled and tousled my too-short hair, which was his way of teasing me. Normally I didn't mind, but I'd cut my hair pretty dramatically on a whim a couple weeks ago because I was frustrated and needed an outlet that didn't require an internet connection. It was yet another of my not-great recent decisions. My thick, curly blond hair tended to stick up in odd places if not cut by a professional. In that moment, as Sam continued to mess with my hair, I probably looked like a Muppet who'd recently stuck her finger in a light socket.

"Stop that," I said, laughing as I shrugged away from him. But my mood was better now—which was probably exactly why Sam had done it.

He put his hand on my shoulder. "If you ever change your mind about the loan . . ."

He trailed off without finishing his sentence.

"If I change my mind about a loan, you'll be the first to know," I said. But we both knew I never would.

......................

I WAITED UNTIL I WAS AT MY AFTERNOON GIG AT THE PUB-lic library to reach out to the person with the two-hundred-dollar room for rent.

Of all the part-time, not-art-related gigs I'd managed to string together since getting my MFA, this one was my favorite. Not because I loved all aspects of the work, because I didn't. While it was great being around books, I worked exclusively in the children's section. I alternated between sitting behind the check-out counter, shelving books about dinosaurs and warrior cats and dragons, and answering questions from frantic parents with tan-truming preschoolers in tow.

I'd always gotten along well with older kids. And I liked tiny humans as an abstract concept, understanding—in theory, at least—why a person might intentionally add one to their life. But while Sam and I definitely thought of his spoiled kitties as his children, nobody in my life had an actual *human* child yet. Dealing with little kids twenty hours a week in a public-facing service position was a rough introduction.

Working at the library was still my favorite part-time job, though, because of all the downtime that came with it. I didn't have nearly as much free time during my shifts at Gossamer's, the coffee shop near my soon-to-be-former apartment—which was the *worst* aspect of that particular job.

"Slow afternoon today," my manager Marcie quipped from her chair beside me. Marcie was a pleasant woman in her late fifties and effectively ran the children's section. It was our little inside joke to comment on how slow it was when we worked to-gether in the afternoon, because *every* afternoon was slow here. Between the hours of one and four, most of our patrons were ei-ther napping or still in school.

It was two o'clock. Only one kid had wandered through in the past ninety minutes. Not only was that nothing noteworthy, it was par for the course.

"It *is* slow today," I agreed, grinning at her. With that, I turned to face the circulation desk computer.

Normally, library downtime was for researching potential new employers and applying for jobs. I wasn't picky. I'd apply for just about anything—even if it had nothing to do with art—if it promised better pay and more regular hours than my current cobbled-together situation.

Sometimes, I used the time to think through future art projects. I didn't have good lighting in my current apartment, which made drawing and painting the images that formed the base of my works difficult. And while I couldn't finish my projects at the library, as my paints were too messy and the final steps involved incorporating discarded objects into my work, the circulation desk was big and well-lit enough for me to at least make preliminary sketches with a pencil.

Today, though, I needed to use my downtime to reply to that red flag of a Craigslist ad. I could have replied earlier, but I didn't—partly because I was still skeptical, but mostly because a few weeks ago I'd gotten rid of Wi-Fi to save money.

I pulled up the listing on the computer. It hadn't changed in the time since I last saw it. The oddly formal style was the same. The absurd rent amount was also the same and set off as many alarm bells now as it did when I first saw it.

But my financial situation also hadn't changed. Jobs in my field were still as hard to come by. And asking Sam for help—or my accountant parents, who loved me too much to admit to my face what a disappointment I was—was just as unthinkable as ever.

And my landlord was still planning to evict me next week. Which, to be fair, I couldn't even blame him for. He'd put up with a lot of late rent payments and art-related welding mishaps these past ten months. If I were him I'd probably evict me, too.

Before I could talk myself out of doing it, and with Sam's worried voice ringing in my ears, I opened my email. I scrolled through my inbox—an ad for a two-for-one sale at Shoe Pavilion; a headline from the *Chicago Tribune* about a bizarre string of local blood bank break-ins—and then started typing.

From: Cassie Greenberg [csgreenberg@gmail.com]
To: fjfitzwilliam@gmail.com
Subject: Your apartment listing

Hi,

I saw your ad on Craigslist looking for a roommate. My
lease is up soon and your place sounds perfect. I'm a
32-year-old art teacher and have lived in Chicago for
ten years. I'm a nonsmoker, no pets. You said in your ad
that you aren't home much at night. As for me, I'm
almost never home during the day, so this arrangement
would work out well for both of us, I think.

I'm guessing you've gotten a lot of inquiries about your
apartment given the location, price, and everything else.
But just in case the room is still available, I've included a
list of references. I hope to hear from you soon.

Cassie Greenberg

A pang of guilt shot through me over how much I'd fudged
some of the important details.

For one thing, I'd just told this complete stranger that I was
an art teacher. *Technically*, that was the truth. It's what I'd studied
to be in college, and it isn't that I didn't *want* to teach. But in my
junior year of college I fell in love with applied arts and design
beyond all hope of reason, and then in my senior year I took a
course where we studied Robert Rauschenberg and his method
of combining paintings with sculpture work. And that was it for
me. Immediately after graduation I threw myself into an MFA in
applied arts and design.

I loved every second of it.

Until, of course, I graduated. That's when I learned, in a hurry, that my artistic vision and my skill set were too niche to appeal to most school districts hiring art teachers. University art departments were more open-minded, but getting anything more stable than a temporary adjunct position at a university was like winning the lottery. I sometimes made extra cash at art shows when someone who, like me, saw a kind of ironic beauty in rusted-out Coke cans worked into seaside landscapes and bought one of my pieces. But that didn't happen often. So yes: while technically I was an art teacher, most of my income since getting my MFA had come from low-paying, part-time jobs like this one.

None of this made me sound like an appealing potential tenant. Neither did the fact that my *references* weren't former landlords—none of whom would have good things to say about me—but just Sam, Scott, and my mom. Even if I was a disappointment to my parents, they wouldn't want their only child to become homeless.

After a few moments of angsting about it, I decided it didn't matter if I'd told a few white lies. I closed my eyes and hit *send*. What was the worst that could happen? This person—a perfect stranger—would find out I'd stretched the truth and wouldn't let me move in?

I wasn't sure I wanted the apartment anyway.

I had less than ten minutes to worry about it before I got a reply.

From: Frederick J. Fitzwilliam [fjfitzwilliam@gmail.com]
To: Cassie Greenberg [csgreenberg@gmail.com]
Subject: Your apartment listing

Dear Miss Greenberg,

Thank you for your kind message expressing interest in my extra room. As mentioned in the advertisement the room is appointed in a modern but tasteful style. I believe, and have been told by others, that it is also quite spacious insofar as spare rooms are concerned. To answer your unasked question: the room remains entirely available, should you remain interested in it. Do let me know at your earliest convenience whether you would like to move in and I will have the necessary paperwork drawn up for your signature.

Yours in good health,
Frederick J. Fitzwilliam


I stared at that name at the end of the email.

*Frederick J. Fitzwilliam?*

What kind of name was that?

I read the email again, trying to make sense of it as Marcie pulled out her phone for her daily Facebook scrolling.

So, the person listing the apartment was a guy. Or, at least, someone with a traditionally male name. That didn't faze me. If I moved in with him, Frederick wouldn't be the first guy I'd lived with since moving out of my parents' house.

What did faze me, though, was . . . everything else. The email was so strangely worded and so formal, I had to wonder exactly how old this person was. And then there was the weird assumption that I might be willing to move in sight unseen.

I tried to ignore these misgivings, reminding myself that all I really cared about was that the apartment was in decent shape and that he wasn't an axe murderer.

I needed to see the place, and meet Frederick J. Fitzwilliam in person, before making up my mind.

From: Cassie Greenberg [csgreenberg@gmail.com]
To: Frederick J. Fitzwilliam [fjfitzwilliam@gmail.com]
Subject: Your apartment listing

Hi Frederick,

I'm super glad it's still available. The description sounds
great and I'd like to come see it. I'm free tomorrow
around noon if that works for you. Also, could you send
me a few pictures? There weren't any with the Craigslist
ad, and I'd like to see some before stopping by.
Thanks!—Cassie

Once again, I had to wait only a few minutes before receiving
a reply.

From: Frederick J. Fitzwilliam [fjfitzwilliam@gmail.com]
To: Cassie Greenberg [csgreenberg@gmail.com]
Subject: Your apartment listing

Hello again, Miss Greenberg,

You are welcome to visit the apartment. It makes
perfect sense that you would wish to see it before
making your decision. I am afraid I will be indisposed
tomorrow during the noon hour. Might you be free
sometime after sundown? I am typically at my best
during the evening hours.

Per your request, I have attached photographs of two
rooms that you would likely use with frequency should
you move in. The first is of my spare bedroom as it is
currently decorated. (You may, of course, change the

decor however you wish should you decide to live here.)
The second photograph is of the kitchen. (I thought I
had included both photographs when I placed the
advertisement on Craigslist. Perhaps I did it incorrectly?)

Yours in good health,
Frederick J. Fitzwilliam


After reading through Frederick's email I clicked on the pictures he sent me, and . . .

Whoa.

*Whoa.*

Okay.

I didn't know what this dude's deal was, but he *clearly* did not live in the same socioeconomic sphere as me. It was also possible we didn't live in the same century.

This kitchen wasn't just different from every other kitchen in every other place I'd ever lived.

It looked like it belonged to an entirely different era.

Nothing in it looked like it had been made within the last fifty years. The fridge was oddly shaped, sort of oval at the top and much smaller than most fridges I'd ever seen. It wasn't silver, or black, or cream—the only colors I'd ever associated with fridges—but rather a very unusual shade of powder blue.

It perfectly matched the oven beside it.

I vaguely remembered seeing appliances like these in an old colorized episode of *I Love Lucy* I saw when I was a kid. I got an odd, disoriented feeling when I tried to reconcile the idea that an ancient kitchen like this existed in a modern apartment.

So, I decided to stop trying and moved on to the picture of the bedroom. It was big, just like the Craigslist ad said. Somehow, it looked even more old-fashioned than the kitchen. The dresser was gorgeous, made of a dark wood I couldn't identify, with ornate curlicue carvings along the top and on the handles. It looked like something you might find at an antique show. The large, floral, probably homemade quilt covering the bed did, too.

As for the bed itself, it was an honest-to-god four-poster bed complete with a lacy white canopy hanging above it. The mattress was thick and looked sumptuous and comfortable.

I thought of all the shitty, secondhand furniture in my soon-to-be-former apartment. If I moved in here I could dump it all at a consignment shop.

These pictures, and the emails, suggested that while Frederick might be a lot older than me, he probably wouldn't steal all my stuff the day after I moved in.

I could handle an awkward roommate who was maybe in his seventies as long as he wasn't going to rob or kill me.

Then again, you could only tell so much from tone in an email.

From: Cassie Greenberg [csgreenberg@gmail.com]
To: Frederick J. Fitzwilliam [fjfitzwilliam@gmail.com]
Subject: Your apartment listing

Frederick,

Okay, those pictures are amazing. Your place looks great! I definitely want to see it, but I can't come by in the evening tomorrow until around 8. Is that too late? Let me know, and thanks.—Cassie

His next reply came in less than a minute.

From: Frederick J. Fitzwilliam [fjfitzwilliam@gmail.com]
To: Cassie Greenberg [csgreenberg@gmail.com]
Subject: Your apartment listing

Dear Miss Greenberg,

Eight o'clock tomorrow evening works perfectly with my
schedule. I will make sure to tidy up so that all looks as it
should when you arrive.

Yours in good health,
Frederick J. Fitzwilliam

......................

SAM CAME BY MY APARTMENT THAT EVENING WITH A
bunch of moving boxes and two venti Starbucks coffees.

"Pull up a chair," I deadpanned, gesturing to where my old
secondhand La-Z-Boy used to be. I'd sold it on Facebook for
thirty dollars the day before, which was about what it had been
worth.

Sam smirked and gingerly spread a flattened moving box on
the ground before sitting down on it cross-legged.

"Don't mind if I do," he said.

"Thanks for bringing those over," I said, nodding at the boxes.
Even if I didn't end up moving into Frederick's fully furnished
room, all I planned to bring with me from this place were my
clothes, my art supplies, and my laptop. Just the essentials—but I
still needed boxes to pack it up.

"It was no problem," Sam said. He handed me the coffee
I'd asked him for. He'd said he'd get me whatever I wanted,
but I'd felt guilty about asking for the pricey rainbow-colored

sugar bomb I *actually* wanted and just asked for a plain black coffee.

"I can't wait to live someplace with Wi-Fi again," I mused, taking a sip. I winced at the bitter taste. How could anyone actually enjoy drinking coffee black? It was something I asked myself every time I worked at Gossamer's. "I miss *Drag Race*."

Sam looked affronted. "I've been keeping you posted on the winners, haven't I?"

I waved a dismissive hand. "It's not the same." Reality television had long been a guilty pleasure of mine, and Sam's dry summaries just didn't cut it. "Anyway, you're coming with me tomorrow night, right?"

"Of course," he said. "This was my idea in the first place, right?"

"It *really* was."

"If you're meeting him at eight, I should pick you up around seven forty-five. Will that work?"

"Yeah. I'll be just getting off my shift at the library." The library hosted special activities for kids on Tuesday evenings, meaning it would be all hands on deck until seven-thirty. In all honesty, I loved Tuesday nights at the library. There was usually some kind of arts and crafts–related activity, and I could pretend for a little while that creating was still a significant part of my life.

I'd made a mental note to leave out my *Sesame Street*–themed *Reading Is for Winners!* T-shirt when I started packing. The library liked us to dress up for the kids on Tuesdays.

"Great," Sam said. "If I pick you up then, we'll have plenty of time to get to the apartment. Although . . ."

He trailed off and looked down at his coffee.

I recognized that worried look. "What is it?"

He hesitated. "It's . . . probably nothing. But you should know

I couldn't find a *Frederick J. Fitzwilliam* earlier today when I Googled him."

I stared at him. "What?"

"Yeah." Sam sipped his coffee, looking contemplative. "If my criminal justice clinic taught me anything it's that you should never move in with someone without looking them up first. So I tried searching for him online, figuring that with a name like *Frederick J. Fitzwilliam* I'd find him in two seconds, but . . ."

He shook his head.

That ever-present knot of anxiety in the pit of my stomach cinched itself a little tighter. "Nothing?"

"Nothing," Sam confirmed. "I even checked the Cook County criminal docket. There is nothing anywhere about a *Frederick J. Fitzwilliam*." He paused. "It's like he doesn't exist."

I sat there, stunned. In an age where everything about everyone was knowable with a simple two-minute internet search, how was it possible that Sam hadn't found *anything*?

"Maybe it's a fake name he's giving to people asking about the apartment," Sam suggested. "Craigslist can be creepy. Maybe he wants to stay anonymous."

That made me feel a little better. Because that sounded plausible. I thought back to a time in college when I *wish* I'd thought to give a fake name to someone on Craigslist. I graduated ten years ago, and the Younker College Literary Society still wouldn't leave me alone.

"Yeah," I said. "Though if he wanted to stay anonymous, why'd he bother including an email address in the post? He could have just used the anonymous email account Craigslist automatically generates for people placing ads."

Silence stretched between us as we both pondered what all this could mean, interrupted only by the muffled sound of traffic from the street outside my window.

Eventually, I leaned towards Sam and asked, "If this guy turns out to be the next Jeffrey Dahmer, promise me you'll avenge my death?"

Sam snorted. "I thought you wanted me to go with you. If he's the next Dahmer, we'll both be screwed. Also possibly dead."

I hadn't considered that. "Good point." I thought a moment. "Maybe wait in the car. I'll text you once I'm inside. If I'm not out in thirty minutes, call the police."

"Of course," Sam said, smiling again. Only this time, his smile didn't quite reach his eyes. He was always terrible at hiding his concern from me. "You know, if Scott and I consolidated some of our wedding stuff, I'm sure we could make room for you until you found something more permanent."

I swallowed around the lump in my throat at his renewed offer. "Thanks," I said, meaning it. I had to avert my eyes before adding, "I'll . . . give it some thought."

# TWO

*FJF's To-Do list: October 15*

1. *Dust sitting room furniture.*
2. *Vacuum spare bedroom.*
3. *Purchase decoy foodstuffs for both fridge & pantry in advance of Miss Cassie Greenberg's visit.*
4. *Should Miss Greenberg not wish to let the spare room, ask Reginald how to include photographs in the advertisement to avoid unnecessary future interactions with applicants.*
5. *Renew library books.*
6. *Write mother.*

FREDERICK'S APARTMENT WAS IN A PART OF LINCOLN PARK I rarely visited. It was just a few blocks west of the lake, at one end of a row of fancy brownstones that, if I had to guess, would probably sell for several million dollars each.

I refused to think about that. It was intimidating enough just breathing the same air as the people who lived here. No need to make things worse by dwelling on how I'd never be able to afford living here without winning the lottery or turning to a life of organized crime.

"I'll find parking," Sam said as I exited his car. I looked back over my shoulder at him; he had his worried face on again. "Text me once you get in, okay?"

"Okay," I promised, shivering a little. We'd both calmed down a bit once we realized *Frederick J. Fitzwilliam* might just be a Craigslist alias. But this whole situation was still weird.

I pulled my scarf around my neck a little tighter. October in Chicago was always colder than strictly necessary. The wind really kicked in this close to the lake, too. It cut through my thin T-shirt like scissors through paper.

I probably should have worn my winter coat, even if it would have ended up splattered in paint from tonight's library event.

Tonight's *ridiculously fun* library event, to be precise, which Marcie and I had planned entirely ourselves. If the sheer number of crying children who had to be carried out of the library after it ended was anything to go by, "Paint Your Favorite Disney Princess Night" had been a smashing success. I couldn't help grinning when I thought about it—even though I was underdressed for the weather and shivering, and even though I knew that between my library-issued *Sesame Street* T-shirt, my jeans that were distressed due to age rather than fashion, and my orange Chucks with a hole in one of the toes, I probably looked like I'd gotten dressed inside a dark art-supply closet.

I wished every night at the library was art night, though I knew why that wasn't possible. Art night invariably ended with the children's section in total chaos, with splatters of paint on every surface and various mystery substances ground into the carpet. The janitors—and Marcie, and me—would have to scrub the place down for days.

Somehow, though, none of that mattered. It was impossible to be in a bad mood when I'd just held a paintbrush in my hands for two hours, helped a grinning little boy paint an Ariel the Mermaid with bright red hair, and got paid to do it. Even though I was now off to meet a potential new roommate who may or may not be a serial killer.

I was glad Sam would be waiting out here just in case.

I glanced at my phone to confirm the address and buzzer code Frederick had emailed me. I hurried to the building and quickly punched in the code to get inside, then trudged up the three flights of stairs to the top floor. I rubbed my chilled hands together, relishing the relative warmth of the heated stairwell after spending less than two minutes outside in what passed for autumn in Chicago.

When I got to the top floor—and Frederick's apartment—a bright pink *Welcome!* mat in front of the door greeted me. It featured a golden retriever puppy and a kitten snuggling together in a field of tall grass and was maybe the tackiest thing I'd ever seen outside of a Hobby Lobby.

It was so out of place in this fancy, multizillion-dollar building that I half wondered if the cold weather had done something to my brain and I'd just imagined it.

Then the door to the apartment opened before I even had a chance to knock—and suddenly I wasn't thinking about the cheesy *Welcome!* mat anymore.

"You must be Miss Cassie Greenberg." The man's voice was deep and sonorous. I could *feel* it, somehow, in the pit of my stomach. "I am Mr. Frederick J. Fitzwilliam."

It occurred to me, as I stood blinking stupidly up at the person who might be my new roommate, that I hadn't really considered what the person behind the *Roommate Wanted* ad looked like. It hadn't mattered. I needed a cheap place to stay, and Frederick's apartment was cheap—even if the circumstances surrounding all of it felt a bit odd.

I'd spent a good part of the day wondering whether emailing him had been a good idea, or if he might be a psychopath. But what he looked like? That hadn't really crossed my mind.

But now that I was here, standing less than two feet away from the most gorgeous man I had ever seen . . .

Frederick J. Fitzwilliam's appearance was *all* I could think about.

He looked like he was maybe in his mid-thirties, though he had the sort of long, pale, slightly angular face where it was hard to tell. And his voice wasn't the only thing with high production values. No, he also had this ridiculously thick, dark hair that fell rakishly across his forehead like he'd sprung fully formed out of a period drama where people with English accents kissed in the rain. Or like he was the hero from the last historical romance novel I'd read.

When he gave me a small, expectant smile, a dimple popped in his right cheek.

"I—" I said. Because I still had just enough of my wits about me to remember that when someone introduced themselves, social custom dictated you say *something* in return. "You're . . . huh."

By this point, I was screaming internally at myself to snap out of it. I wasn't someone who usually gawked at people or went automatically into lust mode immediately after meeting someone attractive. Not like this, anyway. I still wasn't certain I even wanted to move into this apartment—but I also didn't want this guy to reject me right off the bat just because I was acting weird and inappropriate.

It didn't matter that Frederick J. Fitzwilliam had the sort of broad, muscular build that suggested he led football teams to victory when he was younger and still worked out regularly now.

It didn't *matter* that he wore a perfectly tailored three-piece suit, the charcoal-gray jacket and starched white shirt clinging to those broad shoulders like they were made specifically for his body, or that his matching gray slacks fit him just as well.

None of this mattered, because this was someone with a room I maybe hoped to rent. Nothing more.

I had to get a grip on myself.

I tried to focus on the more eccentric aspects of his outfit— the frilly blue cravat he wore at his neck; the shiny wing-tipped shoes on his feet—but it didn't help. Even with those unusual accessories he was still the most gorgeous man I'd ever seen.

As I stood there, yelling at myself to stop gaping at him while being helpless to do anything but, Frederick just stared at me with a puzzled expression. I wasn't sure what there was to be puzzled about. He *had* to know how hot he was, right? He must have been used to getting this reaction from people. He probably had to fend horny people off with a stick every time he left his home.

"Miss Greenberg?"

Frederick cocked his head to the side, probably waiting for me to form a complete sentence. When I didn't, he stepped out into the hallway—most likely to get a closer look at the weirdo who'd just shown up at his door.

But his eyes weren't on me anymore. They were on the floor, riveted to the cheesy doormat at my feet.

He scowled at the stupid thing like it had personally wronged him.

"Reginald," he muttered under his breath. He knelt down and grabbed the welcome mat in both hands. I absolutely did *not* stare at his perfect butt as he did it. "Thinks he's so funny, does he?"

Before I could ask who Reginald was or what he was talking about, Frederick turned his attention back to me. I must have looked pretty out of it because his expression softened at once.

"Are you quite all right, Miss Greenberg?" His deep voice conveyed what sounded like genuine concern.

I managed, with difficulty, to tear my eyes away from his perfect face, and stared pointedly down at my shoes. I cringed at the sight of my paint-splattered, beat-up old Chucks. I'd been so flustered I'd forgotten all about the fact that I'd showed up covered in paint and wearing the worst clothes I owned.

"I'm fine," I lied. I stood a little taller. "I'm just . . . yeah. I'm just a little tired."

"Ah." He nodded, understanding. "I see. Well, Miss Greenberg . . . are you still interested in touring the apartment tonight to determine whether it suits your needs? Or would you perhaps prefer to reschedule given your current fatigue and your . . ." He trailed off, his eyes roaming over me slowly, taking in every part of my outfit.

I flushed hot with embarrassment. Okay, yes—clearly I had underdressed for coming here. But he didn't need to make a thing about it, did he?

In a way, though, I was grateful. He might be the most attractive man I had ever seen in my life, but people who were snobby about appearances were seriously one of my biggest pet peeves. His reaction to my clothes helped prod me from my ridiculous lusty fugue state and back to reality.

I shook my head. "No, it's fine." I still needed a place to live, after all. "Let's do the tour. I'm feeling okay."

He looked relieved at that—though I couldn't understand why, given how unimpressed with me he seemed so far.

"Well, then." He gave me a small smile. "Do come in, Miss Greenberg."

I'd seen the pictures he'd sent, so I thought I'd been prepared for what waited for me inside. I saw immediately that the pictures hadn't done the place justice.

I'd expected it to be fancy. And it was.

What I hadn't expected was that it was also . . . *strange.*

The living room—like the pictures of the kitchen and the spare bedroom Frederick had sent me—seemed frozen in time, but not in a way I could put into words and not frozen in any specific period I could name. Most of the furniture and the fixtures on the walls looked expensive, but they were thrown together in such a multi-style, multi-era jumble it made my head ache.

Dozens of shiny brass wall sconces created the sort of dim and atmospheric lighting I'd only ever seen in old movies and haunted houses. And the room wasn't just darkly lit. It was also just . . . dark. The walls were painted a dark chocolate brown that I vaguely remembered from art history classes had been fashionable in the Victorian era. A pair of tall, dark wooden bookshelves that must have weighed a thousand pounds each stood like silent sentinels on either end of the room. Atop each of them sat an ornate brass, malachite candelabra that would have seemed right at home in a sixteenth-century European cathedral. They clashed in style and in every other imaginable way with the two very modern-looking black leather sofas facing each other in the center of the room and the austere, glass-topped coffee table in the living room's center. The latter had a stack of what looked like

Regency romance novels piled high at one end, further adding to the incongruity of the scene.

Besides the pale green of the candelabras, the only other color to be found in the living room was in the large, garish, floral Oriental rug covering most of the floor; the bright red, glowing eyes of a deeply creepy stuffed wolf's head hanging over the mantel; and the deep-red velvet drapes hanging on either side of the floor-to-ceiling windows.

I shivered, and not just because the room was freezing.

In short, the living room was confirmation of something I'd known for years: people with money often had terrible taste.

"So. You like dark rooms, huh?" I asked. It was maybe the most ridiculously obvious thing I could possibly have said—but was also the least offensive thing I could think of. I stared at the carpet as I waited for him to reply, trying to decide if the flowers I stood on were supposed to be peonies.

A long pause. "I . . . prefer dimly lit places, yes."

"I bet you get a lot of light in here during the day, though." I pointed to the windows lining the room's eastern wall. "You must get a fabulous view of the lake."

He shrugged. "Probably."

I looked at him, surprised. "You don't know?"

"Given our proximity to the lake and the size of these windows, I can infer that one can see the lake quite well from here should one wish to do so." He fidgeted with a large golden ring on his pinky finger; it had a blood-red stone as big as my thumbnail in its center. "I keep the curtains drawn, however, while the sun is up."

Before I could ask why he'd waste a view like that by never looking at it, he added, "Should you decide to move in, you may open the curtains whenever you wish to see the lake."

I was just about to tell him that that was exactly what I would do if I moved in when my phone vibrated from inside the front pocket of my jeans.

"Um," I said awkwardly, fishing it out. "Hold on a second."

Crap. It was Sam.

In the shock of realizing that Frederick was hot, I'd forgotten to let him know I wasn't being murdered.

**Cassie? You okay?**

**I'm trying not to freak out.**

**Please text me right away so I don't start worrying that you've been chopped up and put into freezer bags.**

**I'm fine**

**Just got caught up in the apartment tour**

**Sorry**

**Everything's fine**

**Frederick's not a murderer, then?**

**If so he hasn't tried killing me yet**

**But no I don't think he's a murderer**

**I think he might just be REALLY weird**

**I'll text you when I leave**

I sent Sam a pink heart emoji as a peace offering in case he was mad.

"Sorry about that," I said awkwardly, stuffing my phone back into my jeans pocket. "My friend drove me over. He just wanted to check in and make sure everything was okay."

Frederick smiled at that—a crooked, lopsided sort of smile that made me forget that he was too weird and snobby to find attractive.

"That is smart of your friend," he said, nodding appreciatively. "You and I hadn't been properly introduced yet when we agreed to meet. Now, Miss Greenberg—shall we begin the tour?"

But hearing from Sam reminded me that while I did want to get a good look at this place, there was something important I needed answered first.

"Actually, before we do that, can I ask you a question?"

At that, Frederick froze. He took a small step away from me, thrusting his hands deep into the pockets of his gray slacks.

It was another long moment before he answered me.

"Yes, Miss Greenberg." He clenched his jaw, his posture suddenly rigid. He looked like he was gathering courage to face an unpleasant task. "You may ask whatever you like."

I squared my shoulders. "Okay. So, this might be stupid of me to ask, since I'm about to argue against my own best interest here. But my curiosity is literally killing me. Why are you only asking for two hundred per month?"

He took a small step back, blinking at me in what looked like genuine confusion. Whatever he'd been expecting me to ask, it wasn't that.

"I—I beg your pardon?"

"I know what rent in a place like this should be," I continued. "You're only asking for, like—a fraction of it."

A pause. "I am?"

I stared at him. "Yes. Of course you are." I gestured vaguely to our surroundings—to the brass wall sconces and the book-shelves, to the floor-to-ceiling windows and the intricate Oriental rug beneath our feet. "This place is amazing. And the location? *Insane.*"

"I am . . . aware of its attributes," Frederick said, sounding dazed.

"Okay then," I said. "So, what's the deal? The price you're asking will make everyone who sees the ad think there's some-thing wrong with your apartment."

"You think so?"

"I know so," I said. "I almost didn't come because of it."

"Oh no," he groaned. "What would have been a more appro-priate price?"

I couldn't believe this. How could someone wealthy enough to live here be this clueless about the value of what he had?

"I mean . . ." I trailed off, trying to decide whether he was messing with me. The earnest, slightly panicked look in his eyes told me he was not. Which made no sense at all. But on the off chance he really didn't know that two hundred dollars a month was a ridiculous price for this room, I wasn't about to negotiate against my best interest more than I already had by giving him an exact number.

"Definitely more than two hundred a month," I hedged.

He stared at me for a moment and then closed his eyes. "I am going to *kill* Reginald."

That name again. "I'm sorry, but who is Reginald?"

Frederick shook his head slightly. "Oh. I'm . . . never mind." He sighed again and pinched the bridge of his nose. "Reginald is just . . . someone I happen to loathe. He gave me some very poor advice. But there is no need for you to worry about that, Miss Greenberg. Or about him."

I didn't know what to say to that. "Oh."

"Quite." Frederick cleared his throat and said, "In either case, I suppose what's done is done. If you agree to rent the spare room I see no need to punish you for my mistake or your honesty by raising the price. I am happy to leave the monthly rent at two hundred dollars if you move in."

He shrugged. As though discovering he could be getting a lot more money for his room than he was asking for was no big deal.

I couldn't imagine not caring about losing out on that much money.

Just how rich *was* this guy?

Perhaps more importantly: If he didn't care about how much money he might get from renting the room, why did he even want a roommate in the first place?

I didn't have the courage to ask any of this.

"Thanks," I said instead. "Keeping the rent at two hundred would really help me out."

"Good," he said. "Now, since we have apparently reached the *asking questions* phase of the tour, may I ask *you* a question, Miss Greenberg?"

My stomach lurched. Did my gratitude over the cheap rent tip him off that I'd exaggerated my job situation in my email? Did he somehow find out I was about to get evicted?

If that was the sort of conversation we were about to have . . .

Well. Might as well get it over with.

"Ask away," I said, feeling nervous.

"While I sincerely hope that whoever moves into my home will feel that this is also *their* home, two rooms will remain strictly off-limits," he said, with a serious expression. "Should you move in, I would need you to promise to faithfully stay out of those spaces for the duration of our cohabitation. Can you agree to this?"

"Which rooms?"

Frederick held up a single, long finger. "First, you may never enter my bedroom."

"Of course," I said quickly. "That makes sense."

"Due to the nature of my . . . *business,* I am out of the apartment most nights and must sleep during the daytime." He paused, taking in my reaction. "Generally speaking, I rest between the hours of five in the morning and five in the evening, although those precise times will likely fluctuate over the coming months. When I am sleeping, it is imperative that I be allowed to rest undisturbed."

My mind snagged on the *due to the nature of my business* part of what he'd just said. My grasp of what CEOs and other rich business-types actually did for a living was mostly limited to what I'd seen on television—but even still I was pretty sure night shifts weren't a regular thing for business bros.

He must be some sort of doctor, then. Doctors worked nights, right?

Either way, asking me to stay out of his room seemed fair.

"It's your bedroom," I said. "I get it."

That seemed to please him. A smile spread across his face. "I'm glad you agree."

"What's the other room I can't go into?"

"Ah. Right." He pointed towards what looked like a closet at the end of the hallway. "That one."

I frowned. "What's in there?"

"The answer to that question is also off-limits."

Okay—*that* freaked me out a little. Maybe Frederick was a murderer after all. "It's not . . . dead people, is it?"

His eyes went wide. "Dead people?" He looked horrified, putting his hand to his chest in a way that reminded me of an old lady clutching her pearls. "God's thumbs, Miss Greenberg! Why would you think I had *dead* people in my hall closet?"

He seemed to be taking the joke a bit too seriously. "Fine, no dead people. Can you at least tell me if whatever's in there is dangerous?"

"Let's just say I have a rather . . . *embarrassing* hobby." He looked down at his feet, as though his shiny wing-tipped shoes were suddenly the most interesting things in the room. "I may one day divulge that closet's contents with the person sharing my apartment. But if I do, it must be on my terms, at a time and in a manner I see fit." He looked up at me again. "I will not disclose its contents today."

"You collect lace doilies, don't you?" I don't know what possessed me to tease him like this. But the words were out of my mouth before I could stop them. "You have hundreds of them in that closet."

The corner of his mouth twitched a little, like he was trying hard to fight a smile.

"No," he said. "I do not collect lace doilies."

He didn't elaborate. This time I had the good sense to let the matter drop. I shrugged and said, "Either way, it's fine. It's your stuff, and your apartment. So, your rules."

"Should you move in, I do hope you come to think of this as your home as well." He stepped closer to me, dark brown eyes searching mine. His eyelashes were so long and lush, and his gaze was so penetrating, I could feel my knees going weak. He really was unfairly attractive. "Other than those two limitations you will have full, unrestricted use of this apartment."

I swallowed, trying to regulate my breathing. "I . . . I think I can live with that."

"Wonderful." This time, he allowed his smile to stretch across his entire face. "Now with that out of the way—shall we tour the apartment?"

# THREE

*Text messages between Mr. Frederick J. Fitzwilliam
and Mr. Reginald R. Cleaves*

Good evening, Reginald.

> Hey Freddie my boy what's up

Several things are "up."

First, I wanted to inform you that I
have shredded, and disposed of,
that hideous welcome mat I found
in front of my door yesterday.

I assume you are the one
who put it there?

> Awww you didn't like it?

Of course I didn't like it you buffoon.

But I spent so much time picking
out a gift I thought you'd love

I doubt very seriously that
that is the case.

But never mind.

The primary reason I am typing to you
now on my infuriatingly tiny cellular
telephone screen is to inform you that
someone replied to the Craigslist
advertisement you placed for me.

She will be moving in over the weekend.

Hey thats great

There is only one problem.

My new roommate is not at all
what I had been expecting.

In what way

First, she is a woman. Which I knew,
of course, when she replied to my
advertisement and I saw her name.

I have nothing against women, as you
know. I have also come to understand
through my review of the newspapers and
magazines you have brought me that in

the present era it is not unheard of
for unmarried men and women to
live together.

So: while a bit disconcerting, I am not
overly concerned that she is a woman.

My primary concern is that she is a
woman who may not be entirely normal.

                              And you ARE normal?

That is a fair point.

                                    I thought so

I simply worry that this will not work if my
new roommate is someone who thinks it
appropriate to arrive to an appointment
with disheveled hair and ragged, paint-
splattered clothing.

                                 I think itll be fine

Also, she smiles rather a lot,
which I find somewhat

I don't know

Distracting.

                                 Distracting huh?

Distracting as in . . . the woman we met
that one night in Paris, distracting?

You certainly have a lot of
nerve bringing that up.

Sorry

Forget I said anything

Anyway I still think its fine.

No one else has replied to the ad right?

That is correct.

Because of you.

Because of the rent thing?

Yes. Because of the rent thing.

Okay yeah

I made a typo when I filled
out the Craigslist form.

Sorry about that. Thats on me.

I am not so sure you are actually sorry.
Either way, this cannot be put off any
longer. I must have a roommate, and
as soon as possible.

The more time passes, the more
I realize how completely out
of my element I am.

I need help. Badly.

I suppose she will do.

Even if she is odd.

> Well think of it this way. If shes really
> THAT strange, you won't be tempted to
> either eat OR fuck her right?

Why do I still speak to you?

> I mean I made sure you were fed, right?
>
> And set it up so your bills and HOA dues
> were paid on time
>
> I also got u a cell phone

You owed me AT LEAST that
much, given the circumstances.

> You know on second thought it would
> probably be good for you if you DID
> fuck your new roommate
>
> God knows its been long enough

I am blocking your number as soon
as I work out how that is done.

FREDERICK WASN'T THERE TO GREET ME WHEN I MOVED IN. Of course, I hadn't expected him to be. We'd emailed a few times after I said I'd take the room, and he'd explained his nocturnal schedule was a seven-days-a-week thing. He'd be sleeping in his bedroom—not to be disturbed—when I arrived.

So it wasn't a surprise when I rolled my suitcase through the front door and found myself alone in my new, weirdly dark, weirdly decorated living room. It was also freezing in there, like it had been when I'd first visited.

I rubbed at my arms, trying to warm them.

Sam was originally supposed to help me move in, but he wasn't there, either. I suspected his last-minute need to visit an elderly great-aunt I'd never heard of before out in Skokie was his passive-aggressive way of saying he thought my moving in was a mistake.

To my extreme annoyance, he'd done a complete one-eighty on the whole *moving into the two-hundred-dollar apartment* thing once I told him Frederick was hot.

"Living with someone you think is hot never ends well," he'd warned the night before. "You either end up sleeping with them—which is a huge mistake, nine times out of ten—or else you drive yourself nuts because you *want* to sleep with them."

Sam and Scott had come over the night before to help me pack. There wasn't much to do; I'd already dropped most big things off at the consignment shop. But I was feeling a little sad over saying goodbye to yet another apartment, and I was glad for the company.

Even if Sam had mostly used the opportunity to talk me out of moving in with Frederick.

"If they're hot, you either sleep with them or you want to sleep with them, huh?" I stared at him. "You speak from experience?"

"No," Sam had said quickly, looking over his shoulder to see if his husband was hearing this. I was pretty sure he was—Scott kept smiling to himself and shaking his head as he pretended to check his work email at the kitchen table—but he had a much better poker face than Sam. "I'm just telling you what I've heard."

I'd scoffed. "Frederick's hotness will be a complete nonissue. We have totally opposite schedules. I'll barely see him."

"What if his work schedule changes?" Sam had pressed. "What if he suddenly doesn't have some mysterious job that keeps him out all night long? What if next month he starts working from home?"

"Sam—"

"I just don't want you getting hurt again, Cassie." His voice dropped in pitch a little, and his eyes turned soft. My cheeks went hot—knowing he'd been thinking of my long string of stupid decisions when it came to romance. "It'll be hard to plot throwing him off a building for breaking your heart and ruining your credit if he's right there, sleeping in the next room."

"That only happened once," I countered. "Most of my other bad decisions at least had the decency to leave my credit rating alone. And Frederick is so weird I will *never* want to sleep with him, even if he is the hottest human being I have ever personally seen."

Sam still looked skeptical.

"Listen—when I say he's weird, I mean he's *really* weird. I'm pretty sure he collects Precious Moments figurines or something. There's a closet he says is off-limits and he won't tell me what's in it."

Scott—who was clearly listening by that point—had chuckled. "Yeah, that isn't a red flag *at all*."

"I saw no obvious signs of him being a serial killer on my visit," I insisted. "And like you said when you told me to email him in the first place—I'm out of options."

When Sam and Scott left my place that night, I'd almost been glad to see them go. But now I wished Sam were here with me. Now that I was moving in, and was essentially all alone in an unfamiliar apartment, it felt . . . strange. Frederick wanted his apartment to feel like my home, but how could it? The creepy vibe that the too-dark walls and hodgepodge decor gave off was only enhanced by how frigid, and pristine, and completely devoid of any sort of personal effects the room was.

My idea of finally being able to work on my art and watch my garbage television in my new living room seemed ridiculous now. How could I bring either RuPaul or the treasures I found at Chicagoland recycling centers into this spotless room? The apartment felt so cavernous I couldn't help but wonder if there'd be an echo if I shouted. I opened my mouth to give it a try before remembering that Frederick was likely in his bedroom, sleeping. Waking him up by yelling for no good reason probably wouldn't be a good way to begin our new roommate relationship.

I rolled my suitcase down the hallway towards the bedrooms, taking special care to give a wide berth to the hall closet Frederick said was forbidden. As I walked by it, I thought I detected a faint fruity smell coming from it, but that may have just been my imagination. Either way, indulging my curiosity by seeing what was inside would *also* not be a good way to begin our new roommate relationship, since staying out of it was one of Frederick's only rules.

Frederick's bedroom door was closed, of course, but there was an envelope taped to the outside of my door, with *Miss Cassie Greenberg* written on it in flowing cursive.

I took the envelope off the door and saw it had been closed with a blood-red wax seal embossed with the letters *FJF*. I'd never seen an actual wax seal outside of a movie. Did they even exist anymore?

I slid my finger beneath the seal and, breaking it, carefully opened the envelope. Inside it was a single sheet of stiff white stationery, folded into perfect thirds, bearing another highly stylized *FJF* monogram at the top of the page.

Dear Miss Greenberg,

Welcome.

I am sorry I am unavailable to greet you in person. If you have arrived at two in the afternoon as you indicated you would in your last email to me, I am in my bedroom, sleeping. I remind you to please allow me to rest undisturbed.

I have left instructions for you regarding various features of the apartment in places where I trust said instructions will be of most use. I believe I have thought of everything, but if I have missed something crucial, please let me know and I will do my best to address your concerns.

As we have discussed, I suspect we will interact infrequently. When I wish to convey information to you and you are not here, I will leave a note for you on the kitchen table. I ask you to kindly communicate with me in this same way. I strongly prefer more "old-fashioned" methods of communication to email and text messaging. I use the latter as infrequently as possible.

I look forward to greeting you properly in a few hours if you are still in the apartment when I rise at sundown.

Yours in good health,
Frederick J. Fitzwilliam

Frederick's handwriting was easily the prettiest I had ever seen, his cursive gracefully slanting across the page like the lettering in a formal wedding invitation. The last time I'd gotten a handwritten letter was in the sixth grade, when my class did a pen pal exchange with a sixth grade classroom in France. Somehow, it didn't surprise me that my new roommate wrote letters often enough to justify having monogrammed stationery.

Smiling a little, I stepped into my new bedroom.

There was a second envelope lying on the mattress, beside an intricately carved wooden bowl full of olive-shaped bright orange objects. Were they fruit? They smelled strongly of citrus, but they were unlike any fruit I'd ever seen before.

Bewildered, I slowly opened the second envelope—which had also been closed with an old-fashioned seal—and pulled out the crisply folded, fancy sheet of paper inside.

*Dear Miss Greenberg,*

*I am told it is customary to give housewarming gifts when a person moves into a new home. I don't know if you even __like__ fruit, but I had these kumquats on hand and thought I would gift them to you.*

*I hope you enjoy them.*

*With kind regards,*
*Frederick*

I set down the letter, amazed.

He'd gotten me a move-in gift.

I'd had over a dozen living arrangements since high school. Before now, the closest thing I'd ever gotten to a move-in gift was the communal password to a roommate's ex-boyfriend's Hulu account.

I glanced at the bowl again, picking up one of the tiny orange fruits and sniffing it. Up close the citrus smell was strong and unmistakable.

I had never seen fruit like this before and had no idea what a kumquat even was. I loved citrus fruit, though. Somehow, I had a feeling these were organic, too.

I reached for my phone to tell Sam about this. He wasn't going to believe that my weird new roommate got me a bowl of exotic fruit as a move-in gift. But then, I thought better of it. If Sam was already concerned about me moving in with a hot roommate, he'd be even more concerned if he knew that said hot roommate bought me a gift—as random and fruity as it might be.

No. Even though I always told Sam everything, I needed to keep this detail to myself.

Curious, I bit into the small fruit in my hand. Sunlight burst on my tongue.

*Delicious*, I thought, popping the rest of it into my mouth.

.....................

IT WAS AFTER FIVE BY THE TIME I GOT ALL MY STUFF MOVED over from my old apartment. Everything I owned—my art supplies, my clothes, the half-broken rainbow-colored guitar I'd dragged with me on every move since college even though I barely knew how to play—fit easily inside my new bedroom closet.

When I shut the closet door, you couldn't even tell anyone had just moved in.

I leaned back against the wall and surveyed the room. I still couldn't believe this space was mine. It all felt surreal—the four-poster bed that took up a third of the room; the antique dresser and desk set; the mostly bare walls.

I thought back to Frederick saying I could redecorate. Normally I liked to cover my walls with things I'd made. But it was hard to picture most of my pieces in this room. Especially my most recent project, which I called *The Eternal Sunshine of Late-Stage Capitalism*, made mostly out of a rusted-out carburetor and rainbow-colored confetti.

But the decor in the room sucked. Yes, the furniture was fancy and old, but it was as much a mishmash of style and era as the living room was. A single framed oil painting of a fox-hunting party was all that hung on the walls. It was huge, hung on the wall directly opposite of my bed, and was maybe the ugliest thing I'd ever seen. It featured a dozen long-dead men riding horses in a field, dressed in wigs and red coats. Beagles ran alongside them.

I'd studied in London during my junior year of college, and I remembered learning that this style of painting had been very popular in English inns in the eighteenth century. It arguably matched the decor in the room a lot better than my own projects would. But it was also hideous. I didn't think I'd be able to sleep there knowing what fate awaited those poor historical foxes.

After a few moments' consideration I decided the seaside landscape project I did the previous summer after my trip up to Saugatuck, on the eastern coast of Lake Michigan, would look great in that spot.

While landscapes weren't my usual thing, I thought I did a decent job with that series. I'd been in a rare mood for watercolors on that trip, and I thought the warm, sandy tones I'd used would go well with the color scheme of the room. As would the seashells and pieces of beach trash I'd glued to the canvas once the paint had dried.

I decided to write Frederick a note before getting any of my pieces from Sam's storage unit, just to be on the safe side.

Hi Frederick,

I'm all moved in! Tomorrow I'm going to hang up some of my art in my bedroom if that's okay with you?? The walls in my bedroom are kind of bare, and you said I could redecorate if I wanted to. I have a lot of pieces I'm proud of that I'd like to display in there, but this IS your apartment, so I wanted to be sure it was okay before I brought stuff over from Sam's. Especially because my art is a lot different in style from the way the rest of the place is decorated.

Also, thank you for the fruit! I'd never had a kumquat before. They were delicious.

Cassie

My handwriting was nowhere near as nice as Frederick's, and I didn't have an envelope to put my note in. But there was nothing to be done for it. I set it down in the center of the kitchen table, figuring that if he still wasn't awake by the time I had to leave for my shift at Gossamer's, he'd see it there.

I was exhausted from moving and regretted agreeing to take a shift at the coffee shop that night. All I wanted was to relax in my new bedroom and listen to music. But I needed the money and wasn't really in a position to say no to shifts, no matter how tired I was.

I still had an hour before I needed to leave for work. Plenty of time to eat something. I'd had the foresight to save some of my nonperishables for the move, which was a very good thing. I'd been so busy with moving I'd forgotten lunch—something I rarely did. The fruit was tasty, but it wasn't a meal.

And now I was starving.

I went into the kitchen and for the first time noticed just how *clean* it was. The picture Frederick had sent me hadn't really captured that. The white tile floor didn't have a speck of dirt on it. Neither did the old-fashioned stove or the pale pink countertops.

I'd assumed Frederick had people clean for him. But this was more than clean.

This kitchen looked like it had never been used.

Would my dinner be the first meal ever prepared in there? Impossible. And yet somehow, I couldn't shake the feeling that it was true. If so, it was pretty pathetic that my spaghetti noodles with a little salt added for flavor would be the one to break the seal.

I knelt down and opened one of the kitchen cupboards at random, looking for a saucepan. It was completely empty, save for bare shelves, the liner that had been placed on them, and a layer of dust.

Frowning, I opened the cupboard next in line. This one was packed with a bizarre assortment of food I'd have to be on the verge of starving to eat—jars of cocktail onions and gefilte fish, boxes of Hamburger Helper and cans of asparagus—but nothing to cook it in.

"Huh," I muttered. Where were Frederick's pots and pans? Did he just get takeout every day?

"Miss Greenberg."

At the sound of Frederick's voice, I jumped and smacked the top of my head on the underside of an open drawer.

"*Fuck*," I muttered, rubbing my head. It was already throbbing. I was pretty sure I'd have an ugly bump there in the morning.

I stood up and . . . there he was. My new roommate, standing
right in front of me. He looked like he'd just stepped out from a
magazine photo shoot, his hair artfully tousled and falling perfectly over his forehead. He was standing much closer to me than
he had when I'd toured his apartment, and he seemed to notice
that, too, his eyes widening and nostrils flaring a little as though
he were breathing me in. He was dressed even more formally
than he'd been the night I'd met him, adding a red silk ascot and
black top hat to the charcoal-gray three-piece suit that fit like the
gods had made it specifically for him.

It was an odd look, to be sure. But—god help me—it worked.
My mouth watered for reasons having nothing to do with hunger.

If he noticed how overwhelmed I was by his appearance, he
showed no sign of it. He simply frowned, brow furrowed in concern.
He stepped a little closer. He smelled like fabric softener, the citrus
fruit he'd put in my bedroom, and something deep and mysterious
I had no name for. "Are you quite all right, Miss Greenberg?"

I nodded, flustered and embarrassed. "Yeah." I rubbed at the
spot where my head had met the counter. A bump was already
starting to form. "Where are your pots and pans, though?"

"Pots and pans?" He stared at me, puzzled. As though the
words were in a language he didn't understand. Eventually, he
shook his head. "I'm sorry, but . . . I don't follow."

Now it was my turn to be confused. What about my question
was hard to understand?

"I was going to cook myself some spaghetti before I went to
work," I explained. "I didn't get a chance to eat lunch today, and
I'm starving. They have sandwiches and things at Gossamer's, but
the food there is pretty gross and super marked up, and we only
get a fifty percent employee discount. Which, if you ask me, is
basically wage theft. I already bought this spaghetti, so . . ."

Frederick's eyes went very wide. He smacked his forehead.

"Oh!" he exclaimed. "You want to *cook* something!"

He said the words as if he'd just had a profound realization. I stared at him, trying to make sense of his bizarre reaction. "Yes. I want to make my dinner. So—where are your pots and pans?"

He rubbed at the back of his neck.

"They're . . . um." He paused, glancing at me, before turning his attention back to the distressingly white tile kitchen floor. And then, his eyes lit up, and he met my gaze again. "Oh! I am having my pots and pans *repaired*."

Was that even something you could *do* with pots and pans? "You're having them repaired? Really?"

Maybe his had extra features that required regular maintenance. In fairness I didn't cook much myself and hardly kept up with the latest trends in cookware.

"Yes." Frederick grinned at me, looking extremely pleased with himself. Goddamnit if his megawatt smile didn't just light up his entirely too good-looking face. "My pots and pans are at the shop. Being repaired."

"All of them?"

"Oh. Yes," he said, nodding vigorously. "All of them."

"So . . ." I trailed off and looked around the kitchen in confusion. "What are you cooking with until they get back?"

"I . . . don't cook often," he admitted, quietly.

"Ah." I could have kicked myself for dropping off my crappy pots and pans at the consignment shop. Eating out three meals a day might be an option for someone like Frederick, but it wasn't an option for me. "I guess I'll run by Target and pick up a few after work tonight."

"No, Miss Greenberg," Frederick said. "I told you the apartment would be fully furnished. I gather that your expectations were that the kitchen would have everything you needed to cook your meals."

"I mean . . . yeah. Sort of."

"Then I will purchase cooking implements when I am out this evening." He smiled at me, a little sheepishly. "Please forgive the oversight. It will not happen again."

I opened my mouth to thank him. But before I could get out the words, Frederick sprang away from me and bolted from the apartment, ostensibly to get me something to cook my meals.

# FOUR

*Text messages between Mr. Frederick J. Fitzwilliam
and Mr. Reginald R. Cleaves*

Can I bother you for a favor, Reginald?

> I thought you weren't
> speaking to me anymore

Soon you will be rid of me forever.

But I need help one last time,
and fairly urgently.

> What is it

Where does one purchase cooking
equipment in the twenty-first century?

And can you tell me how to get there?

**Oh SHIT**

**We forgot to get pots and pans didn't we**

**I also need to borrow your little plastic
money card thing one last time.**

I SUSPECTED THE OWNERS OF GOSSAMER'S HAD ORIGINALLY wanted the place to be an artsy hipster coffee shop, with indie bands performing on the weekends and local art on the walls. It was in an old building Chicago tour guides would have called *architecturally significant*, with pretty, stained-glass windows facing the street and Frank Lloyd Wright–inspired clean lines. The furniture was thrift-shop funky, and all the coffee drinks had names starting with *We Are* and ending with an inspiring adjective.

None of us who worked there understood why a coffee shop that mostly served finance bros bothered with hipster naming conventions for their entirely generic drink offerings. Because despite what I suspect were the owners' original plans, Gossamer's neighborhood was much more suit-and-tie than hipster. Its location—right by a Brown Line stop—meant most of our customers were commuters on their way to or from their jobs in the Loop, with the occasional college student thrown in for variety.

Of course, I'd rather have worked at an *actual* hipster coffee shop. But a job was a job. And this one didn't pay half bad.

Even if the food sucked and the drinks had silly names.

The dinner options were extra limited when I got there for my evening shift. Usually, by six o'clock most of Gossamer's pre-made food had long since been sold. The only sandwiches left were a sad, soggy peanut butter and jelly and a hummus and red pepper on wheat bread. Whoever supplied Gossamer's pre-made food really needed to learn how to make friends with flavor. And texture.

My shift didn't start for fifteen minutes, so I had just enough time to scarf something down. I grabbed the hummus and pepper sandwich—the less tragic of the two options—and made my way to one of the tables near the back.

There was only one customer there—a guy who looked about thirty-five, with dirty-blond hair and a black fedora tilted so far forward it covered half his face. He had a mug of something hot and steaming in front of him.

I could feel his eyes on me as I crossed over to the table in the corner where I usually ate before my shifts.

He cleared his throat.

"Hm," he said, to no one. "Let me see." He was openly staring now, leaning slightly towards me, a weird, calculating expression on his face. His tone, his expression, even his posture—everything about him suggested he was sizing me up. Evaluating me. Not in a sexual or predatory way, exactly. More like he was an interviewer trying to decide whether I was right for a job.

It was still creepy as hell.

I glanced at the front door, hoping my manager Katie was on her way.

After another few moments the guy nodded as if he'd come to a decision. "I don't know what he was so worried about. You should do fine."

The job interview apparently over, he turned his full attention back to his phone.

Gossamer's sometimes got perverts at night. Just part of working at a coffee shop. My typical approach was not to engage with them and just let my manager handle it if things got too weird. But at that moment I was exhausted from my move and too unnerved by this bizarre interaction to wait for Katie.

Against my better judgment, I engaged.

"What did you just say?"

"I *said* you should do fine," he replied without looking up from his phone, sounding annoyed at the interruption.

"What do you mean, *I should do fine?*"

"Just exactly that." He glanced at me, smirking. He pushed back from his chair and stood up. I noticed, for the first time, that he was wearing a floor-length navy-blue trench coat that clashed horribly with his black fedora. Underneath it was a bright red T-shirt that said *Of course I'm right. I'm Todd!*

Probably not a pervert, then. Just a garden variety weirdo. We got those sometimes, too.

"I'll be going now," he said, importantly but unnecessarily. "I must meet a friend in need at Crate & Barrel."

When I looked up again he was gone. The only sign he'd even been there was the mug of still-steaming *We Are Legion* he'd left behind. The most expensive cappuccino drink we made. It was completely untouched.

Of course it was.

God. Customers who ordered expensive coffee they didn't even drink were so annoying and wasteful. I brought "Todd's" mug to the blue plastic tub where we bussed the dishes, scowling and irritated.

There weren't many of us scheduled to work that night. Loading the dishwasher would probably end up being my job. But I could do that later. I still had a few minutes before my shift started, and my hummus and red pepper sandwich wasn't going to eat itself.

......................

THANKFULLY, KATIE SHOWED UP A FEW MINUTES AFTER "Todd" left, and then Jocelyn—another barista—showed up at seven-thirty. With the three of us working it ended up being a slow night. A few more customers trickled in, mostly students looking for a relatively quiet spot to study and socialize over homework and lattes. Thankfully, there were no more leering oddballs in trench coats and fedoras.

Shortly after Jocelyn showed up, I was wiping down a table that had just been vacated when my phone buzzed in my pocket with a new text.

I pulled it out and glanced down at the screen.

**Hello Cassie. This is Frederick.**

**I have a question for you.**

I looked over my shoulder to where Katie was waiting on a customer and Jocelyn was making a drink behind the counter. They seemed to have things well enough in hand that I could reply to him now.

**Sure! I'm at work but I have a minute.**

**What's up?**

**Do you eat sauce?**

I stared at my phone. **Sauce?**

**Yes. Do you enjoy eating it?**

**Why**

**I am presently at a store that sells cooking implements. An entire section of the store is dedicated to "saucepans."**

Other customers seem quite enamored
with them but before I purchase one for
the apartment I wanted to confirm that
sauce is something you eat.

A bark of unexpected laughter escaped me before I could
stop it.

Who would have thought Frederick had such a dry sense of
humor?

you're hilarious

I am?

Yes, I just lol'd in public ;)

I do not know what
"lol'd" means.

OMG, I'm going to get in trouble
here at work if I keep laughing.

Oh. I apologize.

I didn't intend to get you in
trouble with your employer.

It's fine.

My manager is cool.

Though I should probably get to work.

> Of course. I will see you
> at home eventually.
>
> With saucepans.

By this point I was smiling so broadly my cheeks hurt.
Maybe this new living situation would work out after all.

.....................

BY THE TIME I GOT BACK TO FREDERICK'S BROWNSTONE IT
was nearly midnight.

I was exhausted. I usually was after a shift spent making
drinks and cleaning tables, but it was made worse by having spent
the first part of the day lugging heavy boxes around and moving
into Frederick's apartment. I felt all but dead on my feet as I
trudged up the stairs to the third floor.

As I unlocked the front door to the apartment and let myself
in, I decided that first, I would take a shower to wash off the
grime from all the running around I did that day. Then I would
collapse into bed. I didn't have anywhere to be in the morning—
Gossamer's didn't need me to come in, and neither did the
library—so the next day I would sleep in as long as I could.

I was all set to embark on the first part of my plan when the
enormous number of boxes stacked in neat piles on the kitchen
counters caught my eye. Those hadn't been there when I'd left
for work that evening.

Curious, I made my way into the kitchen—and stopped short
when I realized what all these boxes were.

Frederick had made good on his promise to find me cookware.

And not just any cookware.

He'd gotten five Le Creuset saucepans, six Le Creuset frying pans of varying sizes, two of the largest woks I had *ever* seen, a waffle maker, a Crockpot, and a toaster oven. When I turned, thunderstruck, to see the boxes stacked on the kitchen table, I realized he'd also purchased ten place settings' worth of silverware from Crate & Barrel.

Stunned, I picked up the note with my name on it that lay beside the place settings. As with Frederick's previous notes to me, he'd written my name on the outside of the envelope in cursive so fancy it was nearly calligraphy.

*Dear Miss Greenberg,*

*Please let me know if these cooking implements will suffice. You never answered my questions vis-à-vis your feelings on sauce, so if the saucepans are not of use I can return them to the establishment where I purchased them.*

*Regarding your questions concerning redecorating your bedroom, as I told you when you moved in you are welcome to redecorate your bedroom however you like. I ask only that you not destroy anything currently in the room. Many items in my home are heirlooms that have been in my family for a great many years. My mother in particular would become cross should harm come to them.*

*When you said you were an art teacher I admit it had not occurred to me that you also created art of your own. In hindsight, that was foolish of me. Do let me know when you have redecorated. I would very much like to see some of your work.*

*Yours in good health,*
*Frederick J. Fitzwilliam*

I set down the note, smiling despite my exhaustion.

*Please let me know if these cooking implements will suffice.* He had to be joking, right? These were the nicest pots and pans I'd ever seen outside of the high-end stores on the Magnificent Mile.

As for the rest of Frederick's note, I couldn't help but wonder what he'd think when he saw the ancient fox hunt painting currently hanging in my bedroom replaced with a canvas full of Lake Michigan's finest beach trash. Based on his other decorative choices I doubted he'd like my work at all.

But the fact that he was at least *curious* about my art made me feel warm inside, for reasons I was too tired to analyze.

In fact, I was so tired I felt about ready to collapse. But before I showered and went to bed I wanted to write a reply.

*Frederick,*

*The pots and pans you got are AMAZING. You totally didn't need to get anything this fancy just for me. Especially since my cooking repertoire is fairly limited. The next time we're both in the apartment I'd be happy to cook you something to thank you (as long as it's scrambled eggs, pasta, or beans).*

*Cassie*

I made my way into the bathroom and stripped down. Frederick's bathroom was massive—at least twice the size of the bedroom in my old apartment. I wasn't sure I'd ever get used to it. The floor was white tiled marble, which was achingly cold beneath my feet. I supposed I shouldn't have been surprised by that, given how cold Frederick kept the rest of the apartment. I'd have to talk to him about that at some point; wearing sweaters whenever I was home wasn't something I really wanted to do.

I opened the door to the glass-walled shower and hurried inside, turning up the water temperature as high as it would go and letting the hot steam warm me.

Years of high student loan payments and minimum wage jobs taught me to fear utility bills and to keep my showers efficient and quick. But Frederick paid the utilities here. Just for once, I decided to treat my sore and aching muscles and linger for a while.

I sighed, luxuriating in the feel of the steady spray and perfect water pressure hot against my back. I let my mind wander as the water sluiced over me, thinking through how I might spend the next day. With all the chaos of my eviction notice and moving, I hadn't been to the studio where I did most of my work in weeks. After sleeping in as long as I could, maybe I would head out to Pilsen and poke around on something new the rest of the day.

After a while—ten minutes? an hour?—I glanced down at my fingers. They were wrinkled as prunes from the water. How long had I been in there?

I reluctantly turned off the hot water and opened the shower door. The air felt even colder than it had earlier after the hot shower I'd just taken, causing a riot of gooseflesh to erupt on the backs of my arms. I grabbed my towel off the back of the door where it hung from a silver chrome hook and wrapped it tightly around my body, tucking it under my arms.

My shower had steamed up the mirror. I quickly rubbed the back of my hand over it so I could see my reflection.

I frowned at what I saw.

My hair was growing back from the impulsive scissors incident from a few weeks ago, but it was still shorter than I usually

kept it. And weirdly uneven. Once it dried, it was going to stick
up in the back no matter how much product I put in it.

Once I got my feet under me a little more, the first thing I was
going to do was make an honest-to-god visit to an actual salon to
fix what I'd done to myself. In the meantime, I should probably
do what I could to make myself look presentable.

I thought of the fabric shears in my bedroom. They were
probably too dull to do a *good* job on my hair. But they'd be better than nothing.

Tucking my towel a little more tightly around my body, I
opened the bathroom door and prepared to make a beeline
straight for my bedroom—

—and barreled directly into Frederick, my face smashing
right into his chest.

His *bare* chest.

I must have been overheated from the shower, or from
embarrassment—or both—because his flesh felt almost unnaturally
cool. He stood there as unmoving as a statue, a pair of small white
linen shorts slung distractingly low on his hips, as I yelped and sprang
away from him. His right hand was raised in a fist, as though he'd just
been about to knock on the bathroom door when we collided.

His eyes were wide as saucers, his face as pale as moonlight.

We babbled out our apologies at the same time.

"*Miss Greenberg!* Oh, I beg your pardon, I—"

"*Shit!* I'm so sorry! I didn't—!"

In hindsight, it should have occurred to me that living with
another person meant walking around in nothing but a towel
wasn't something I could do anymore. But he'd made such a big
deal about usually being out all night. How was I supposed to
know that at the exact moment I'd decided to leave the bathroom
he'd be standing right outside the bathroom door, *shirtless*?

As I stood only a few inches away from him in nothing but a towel, my wet hair dripped steadily onto my bare shoulders. His chest was at a level with my eyes, and . . .

I tried not to gape. I *really* did. Gaping at my new, barely dressed roommate when I was mostly naked myself was not only gross but also wildly inappropriate. But I couldn't help myself. This man had been hiding an actual, honest-to-god six-pack beneath his perfect-fitting clothes. His broad chest tapered down to a narrow waist, the way he wore his shorts making him look like he was a goddamn underwear model instead of a doctor or CEO or whatever the hell he was.

Frederick wasn't just attractive, I realized.

He was a *Greek god*.

The seconds ticked by as we stood there—me ogling him, him staring wide-eyed at a spot of nothing just beyond my left shoulder. I tried to think about anything but how close we were standing, how little we were wearing, and the way my heartbeat was suddenly racing. And then, because I'd never had much of a self-preservation instinct, I had a sudden, nearly irresistible urge to trace the solid lines of his chest with my fingertips. To see if those abs of his were as rock hard as they looked.

What would he do if I did?

Would he kick me out and find a roommate who actually knew how to behave appropriately in awkward situations? One who could also maybe pay him rent closer to market rate? Or would he pull my towel away and toss it to the side before he took my body in those giant hands of his, and—

I clenched my hands into tight fists and forced them down by my sides before I had a chance to do anything stupid. The prickling heat of a furious blush rose up through my body, warming my cheeks and making my hands sweat.

Frederick wasn't blushing, though he still looked at least as embarrassed as I felt. To his credit, he kept his eyes fixed firmly on the wall behind me. He honestly looked like he might *die* if he let his gaze shift towards me by so much as an inch.

Clearly, he wasn't even half the perv I was.

He was a gentleman.

A totally misplaced rush of disappointment went through me at the realization.

I cleared my throat to try and keep my thoughts on the matter at hand. "I didn't think you'd be . . . I mean, you said you're usually out at night, and . . ."

"I apologize, Miss Greenberg." His voice sounded strained. He still wouldn't look at me. "The shower was running for so long I assumed you had left the apartment without turning it off. So I came." He paused, eyes going even wider when he realized what he'd just said. "To the bathroom, that is. To turn it off. The water, I mean."

He dipped his head towards me in an awkward bow. At this point my face must have been so red it could be seen from space. "Please forgive me, Miss Greenberg. It will never happen again."

And then he stepped around me, making sure not to brush up against any part of my body as he passed.

I heard the click of the bathroom door behind me, and then what sounded a lot like the contents of the medicine cabinet crashing to the tiled bathroom floor.

"Are you okay?" I called out, alarmed. Had he been so mortified by what just happened he fell down?

"Yes! Perfectly fine!" Frederick said, sounding strangled, before letting out what sounded like a string of low, muttered curses.

I was so embarrassed I hardly remembered walking into my bedroom. But the second I was inside my bedroom I slammed the door shut and then flung myself face-down onto my bed, all thoughts of sleep forgotten. My heart was hammering so hard it felt like my ribs might break. I tried to tell myself that it was simply because what just happened was one of the most awkward moments of my life. But deep down I knew that was only part of it.

I didn't want to think about how incredible Frederick looked without a shirt. Nothing good could come from that line of thinking. With everything else going on in my life, having lurid fantasies about a handsome man who was miles out of my league and my roommate to boot was the last thing I needed to be doing with my time.

With difficulty, I forced myself to think about my plans to get my canvases out of Sam's storage unit the next day.

My hair was still a disaster. That needed my attention, too.

I grabbed the fabric shears from the top of my desk. They were even duller than I remembered. But if I messed up my hair even more, at least it would stop me from thinking about what just happened with my roommate.

I started cutting, and . . . well, the end result was marginally better. If you squinted. At least the ends were even.

I turned off the lights and climbed into bed, cringing at how reliably good I was at messing up my life, even when nothing else went according to plan.

# FIVE

Diary entry of Mr. Frederick J. Fitzwilliam,
dated October 20

Dear Diary,

Oh, gods.

Is it possible for a person like me to die from shame?

I sit at my desk at 2 in the morning, desperately trying to remind myself that Miss Greenberg is a lady. A lady whose beauty far surpasses what I noticed when we first met. A lady with lovely curves, delightful freckles dusting the bridge of her nose, and a mouth that will now haunt my dreams—but a lady nonetheless.

It would appear I must also remind a certain traitorous part of my anatomy—one that has not responded thusly to a woman in over one hundred years—of this fact as well.

My thoughts go down a dangerous path and I do not know how to proceed. Before seeing Miss Greenberg nearly unclothed this evening I wanted nothing more from her than the opportunity to learn about the modern world by observing her from a respectable distance. A day ago, the idea that I might want anything else from her had never crossed my mind.

But now . . .

God's thumbs, but I am the worst, filthiest sort of reprobate.

I do not know if Miss Greenberg has living parents. I must find out if she does—and if so, I must apologize to them for putting their daughter into such a compromising position. I must apologize to Miss Greenberg as well, of course. Preferably with a gift that adequately expresses my contrition. I will consult Reginald to see if he has ideas on what might be suitable. (He has, after all, long since been in the habit of needing to apologize to women.)

In the meantime, I shall go down to the lake and run out my frustrations. It's been entirely too long since I have gone for a nighttime run. Hopefully, the rush of cool night air will clear my head. If that doesn't do it, hopefully one of the library books Reginald has leant me will do the trick.

In entirely unrelated news, tonight I learned there exists a truly staggering array of cookware options. The twenty-first century may be what finally kills me after all these years—if living with Miss Greenberg doesn't do it first.

FJF

I SLEPT LATER THAN USUAL THE NEXT MORNING, DOING everything I could to delay leaving my bedroom and risk having to see Frederick again so soon after what happened the night before.

Fortunately, there was no sign of him once I did finally poke my head out of my room, my giant art bag slung over one shoulder. Of course, he *shouldn't* have been outside his room right then given that it was eleven in the morning. But I breathed a sigh of relief all the same.

The inevitable could be put off a little longer.

Frederick's bedroom door was closed. But it was always closed—even when I'd bumped into him the night before—so that didn't tell me if he was asleep in there or not. I kept my tread as light as possible, just in case, as I made my way to the front door.

Moving quietly was awkward and stressful; my gait wasn't exactly what one would call graceful, even when I wasn't carrying an art bag that weighed a ton. Fortunately, Frederick's bedroom door stayed shut.

If he was in there, and had heard me, he was trying to avoid me as much as I was hoping to avoid him.

Which was fine. Completely fine. Preferable, in fact, to the alternative.

I didn't think I had ever been happier in my life to walk into my art studio when I got there an hour later.

Calling it *my* art studio wasn't accurate, of course. The space was called Living Life in Color and was owned by Joanne Ferrero, an elderly eccentric who decades ago had been a reasonably big deal on the Chicago art scene. It was located on the first floor of a small building in Pilsen and was shared by about two dozen local painters, metalworkers, and potters who approached their craft with varying degrees of seriousness. Some of them, like me, hoped to make a career out of art one day and spent as much time there as their schedules would allow. Others—like Scott, who was sketching something at the large communal table that took up the bulk of the studio space when I arrived—had regular day jobs and simply rented space there to indulge a creative hobby and blow off some occasional steam.

"Hey, Scott," I said, happy to see him. Because it was mid-morning on a Wednesday there was hardly anyone in the studio, and there was plenty of space at the table. That suited me just fine; I liked being able to spread out all my supplies when I worked.

I pulled up a chair to the table and started rummaging around in my bag for my pencils.

"Hey." He stopped what he was working on—a charcoal sketch of a bouquet of roses, Sam's favorite flower—and turned to face me. "I'm glad you're here. Sam and I were going to reach out to you about an opportunity we just found out about."

"Oh?" I walked over to the shelf marked *C. Greenberg* where I stored a lot of my in-progress canvases. With my eviction notice and then my move, I hadn't been to the studio in almost two weeks. Fortunately, my current work in progress—a watercolor field of sunflowers done in bright yellows and greens, over which I planned to superimpose as many fast-food wrappers as I could get to fit on the canvas—seemed none the worse for wear for my absence.

"Yeah," Scott said. "You know our friend whose family owns that art gallery in River North?"

I bit my lip, drawing a blank. Who was he talking about? He and Sam had lots of friends, but most of them were either Scott's colleagues from his university's English department or other lawyers like Sam. I'd remember someone with an art gallery, wouldn't I?

I sat back down at the table, and then it hit me.

"You mean David? Your wedding coordinator?"

I'd almost forgotten that after their bachelor party, Scott and Sam had struck up an unlikely friendship with the guy they'd contracted to plan their wedding. I vaguely remembered David telling us he came from serious family money, and that among the other things they owned was a wildly unprofitable art gallery near the Loop.

I was pretty sure this conversation had happened while everyone involved—including myself—was in the process of getting extremely drunk on celebratory champagne. Which is probably why I'd forgotten all about it until that moment.

"That's David," Scott agreed.

"Yes, okay, this is ringing a vague bell. What about him?" Was I misremembering that this art gallery was mostly just a tax write-off for David's rich family? Could it have taken off enough in the six months since I'd last seen David for it to be able to hire someone? That seemed hard to believe.

But why else would Scott be bringing this up?

"At dinner last night, David told us that his family's gallery is planning a juried art show with another, bigger gallery in River North." He paused, fighting a smile. "With a gallery that's actually *successful*, I should say."

My eyes went wide. I hadn't had a piece accepted into a juried show in years. Chicago only had so many juried shows per year, and I wasn't bringing in enough money with my art to submit my pieces more widely. If I could get a piece into this show, and possibly even win a prize, it could be just the shot in the arm my non-career needed.

"Do you know anything about what mediums they're looking for?" The last time I'd spoken with David we'd discussed whether *Eye of the Tiger* was a tasteful choice for Sam and Scott's first dance. We hadn't chatted about his taste in art. Scott pushed the sketch he was working on to the side and pulled his tablet from his bag.

"Let's look it up."

I watched as he typed *River North art exhibition* into the search bar, reminding myself there was no point in getting excited, or thinking that maybe my luck was finally starting to improve, until I saw what this show was about. Despite my best efforts at staying calm, though, my palms were already sweating by the time Scott found what he was looking for and turned his tablet around so I could see it.

"Oh," I said, pleasantly surprised when I saw the theme listed at the top of the call for submissions. "They're asking for pieces inspired by contemporary society."

"That's great," Scott said. "It doesn't get more contemporary than what you do."

I hummed in agreement, scrolling down the page. It only got better the more I read.

"It looks like all mediums are welcome," I said, my smile growing. "Including multimedia works." My pieces, which combined traditional oil and watercolor paintings with found objects, were the very definition of multimedia.

Scott tapped the bottom of the screen, where the prizes were listed. "Did you notice that the grand prize is a cash award of one thousand dollars?"

My throat went dry. There would also be a few smaller awards given out for excellence in different categories, and I'd be delighted to win any of them because the most important thing about winning a prize at a juried art show is the recognition that comes with it, but . . .

Well, a thousand dollars would *really* come in handy.

"The fine print here says only twenty applicants will be selected," I said, feeling the familiar beginnings of doubt creeping in. This had the makings of an incredibly competitive selection process. Getting into it in the first place would probably be a tall order.

"You never know if you don't try," Scott said, not unkindly. "You should go for it, Cassie."

I handed Scott back his tablet and took a deep breath. "I should," I agreed. Maybe nothing would come of it, just like nothing had come from most of my attempts to get recognition for my art these past few years.

Then again, maybe my luck was finally starting to turn around.

....................

FREDERICK WASN'T HOME WHEN I GOT BACK FROM THE studio that evening.

I didn't see him the next day—or evening—either.

Running into him again at some point was inevitable, of course. We lived together. But hopefully the longer we put that off, the less awkward the inevitable would be. In the meantime, our conversations, such as they were, were limited to notes we left for each other on the kitchen table. They mostly concerned the logistics of our living arrangement and, honestly? It was easier that way. Frederick made no reference in any of his notes to having seen me almost naked the other night. Neither did I. It was like we'd reached some unspoken agreement to pretend nothing awkward, or hot, or awkwardly hot had ever happened between us.

It was probably for the best. Sam would think so, anyway.

Even if my mind kept replaying that moment when Frederick and I bumped into each other after my shower when I should have been focusing on other things.

Dear Miss Greenberg,

I do not wish to be a nag, but please do remember to collect your discarded socks from the living room floor before retiring to bed. I just slipped on a sock I know isn't mine on my way to the door and very nearly injured myself.

(Also, I must ask—are fuzzy blue knee socks with green puppets on them the current style?)

With kind regards,
Frederick J. Fitzwilliam

Frederick,

Ack! So sorry about the socks! I'll do better, I promise.

And no, HA, fuzzy Kermit the Frog socks are not "the current style." OBVIOUSLY, hahahaha. You're hilarious. Those were a joke from my friend Sam.

Also, before I forget could you please remember to give me your WiFi network name and password? Sorry to keep harping on this, but I've been using my phone as a hotspot since moving in, and it eats through my data.

Cassie

*Dear Miss Greenberg,*

*I had not intended to be funny in my note to you, though I am pleased to have made you laugh regardless.*

*On an unrelated note, the woman who lives on the second floor just informed me Thursday is "trash day." I was unaware of this, as I am not in the regular habit of throwing things away.*

*Now that there are two of us here we might want to participate in this weekly ritual. I assume you throw things away? If so, would you be so kind as to procure a rubbish bin? I do not own one, nor do I know what one costs or how one would go about obtaining one. I will deduct whatever you spend in purchasing one from your monthly rent.*

*With kind regards,*
*Frederick J. Fitzwilliam*

*ps: Regarding your questions concerning WiFi and network names and passwords I do not believe I have any of those things, but I will confer with Reginald and let you know.*

I stared at that note for a while before replying to it.

How could a grown adult not have a trash can? And not know where to get one?

And he didn't know if he had Wi-Fi? That had to be another of his peculiarly dry jokes. I'd follow up with him about that the next time I saw him.

*Frederick—I don't throw much away either. I don't like getting rid of anything that might have a use later, especially since upcycling is a big part of my art. But on principle I feel like two grown-ups should own at least one single trash can between them. Right? I'll get one at Target after work.*

*Cassie*

*ps: Why do you keep calling me Miss Greenberg? There's no need for us to be so formal with each other, is there? Just call me Cassie. :)*

Before I could talk myself out of it, I added a quick smiling sketch of myself, holding a garbage can in my arms, before leaving the note on the kitchen table. I hadn't drawn little cartoon figures in a while, and I told myself it was good practice to drown out the voice in my head yelling at me for flirting with him.

Frederick's reply was waiting for me on the table when I got home from work with our brand-new kitchen trash can.

*Dear ~~Miss Greenberg~~ Cassie,*

*The picture you drew for me on your latest note is lovely. Is that meant to be you? You clearly have a great deal of talent.*

*Thank you for handling the rubbish bin situation.*

*Per your request, going forward I will do my best to refer to you by your first name rather than "Miss Greenberg." However, calling you "Cassie" goes against both my upbringing and my instincts. As such, please be patient with me if I occasionally forget and revert to more formal manners of address.*

*FJF*

I quickly tamped down the strange rush of pleasure that shot through me at his compliment on my art, reminding myself that I'd spent less than ten minutes on that doodle and he was clearly only trying to be nice. I chose instead to focus on how weird he was being about calling me by my first name.

> Frederick,
>
> It goes against your upbringing and your instincts to call me Cassie instead of "Miss Greenberg"? Really? Who raised you, Jane Austen?
>
> Cassie

At the end of that note I drew a hasty caricature of someone in old-fashioned garb, just to be a jackass.

His reply was waiting for me on the kitchen table the following morning.

> Dear Cassie,
>
> Not . . . exactly Jane Austen, no.
>   Also, is that meant to be a picture of me?
>
> FJF

> Frederick,
>
> Not exactly Jane Austen, eh? Intriguing. Well in either case, thank you for trying to call me by my first name.
>   And yes, that's supposed to be a picture of you. Don't you see the resemblance?? Tall, stick-figure arms and legs,

surly expression, clothes straight from the set of <u>Downton Abbey?</u>

Cassie

Dear ~~Miss Greenberg~~ Cassie,

Oh, yes. I suppose I do see SOME resemblance. Though I do think my actual hair looks much better than it does on the bald little man you've drawn here. Don't you?

    (What is <u>Downton Abbey?</u>)

FJF

Frederick,

<u>Downton Abbey</u> is an English TV show. I think it's set about a hundred years ago? Something like that. Anyway, it's not really my thing, but my mom and all her friends love it. Also, you dress just like Cousin Matthew, one of the characters.

    Oh, and by the way—you got a few packages this morning. I stacked them on the table for you—right beside your Regency romance novels. (You've been getting a lot of packages lately, actually. I know they're not addressed to me, so I'm not examining them too closely, but I have to admit—I am INTRIGUED. They're so weird???)

    (Also, Regency romance novels, huh? I haven't read many of them myself, my guilty pleasures trend more towards trash television, but—I definitely approve.)

Cassie

*Dear Cassie,*

*Cousin Matthew, you say? Interesting. (Is he bald, too?)*

*Thank you for handling the packages for me. You are correct; they are strange. Hopefully there will not be any more of them.*

*I am glad you approve of my reading selections. I do not care much for the focus on romance, but I find reading stories set in the early nineteenth century comforting. I guess you could say they remind me of home.*

*FJF*

I reread his most recent note, as amused by his defense of his Regency romances as I was disappointed in his lack of a more concrete explanation for the packages he'd been getting.

Because those packages . . .

Well.

They were truly something else.

He'd gotten six of them since I'd moved in. They all had the same return address—the sender was an *E.J.*, from New York—written in an ornate, flowery cursive that reminded me a lot of Frederick's pretty handwriting but for the fact that it was always written in blood-red ink.

The packages came in different sizes and shapes, each wrapped in a hideous floral wrapping paper that reminded me of the decor in my grandmother's Florida condo. Some of the packages emitted strange smells. One of them appeared to have smoke coming out of it. I swore I could hear actual hissing coming from another.

Those had to be optical illusions, I decided. There was no way the mail would deliver anything that was *actually* on fire. Or living snakes.

Even though those packages were addressed to Frederick, not me—and even though their contents were patently none of my business—since he hadn't given me clarification in his notes I decided I'd ask him about them the next time we were in the same room together.

Whenever that might be.

.....................

"YOU'VE HAD A GOOD RUN," I MURMURED APOLOGETICALLY to the painting of the hunting party in my bedroom.

I felt a little bad that I was taking it down and replacing it with my own art. It wasn't the painting's fault it was hideous; someone, somewhere, had put a lot of effort into making it. It also looked seriously old, making me wonder if it was what Frederick had meant when he'd referred to family heirlooms.

Either way, this was my bedroom now, and that painting was nightmare fuel.

I gingerly lifted it from the wall. It must have hung there for years, because the paint on the wall behind it was half a shade darker than the matte cream covering the rest of the bedroom.

I picked up the first of the three small canvases I was about to hang in Ye Olde Hunting Party's place, smiling as I remembered how fun the week I'd made them had been. We'd been on vacation in Saugatuck, and Sam had teased me for spending so much of our beach vacation combing the beach for trash—but then, he'd never understand how it made me feel to take what other people threw away and turn it into art that would outlast us all.

I didn't have a big important lawyer job like he did—but through my art, I made a statement. And left my own mark on the world.

I grabbed my hammer, then dragged the antique desk chair that had to be at least as old as the city of Chicago to the spot where I planned to hang my series. I climbed on it and started banging a nail into the wall.

After a few loud whacks with the hammer, I froze, realizing what I was doing.

It was five o'clock.

I was still a little fuzzy on Frederick's exact schedule. Would he still be asleep?

If he was, hammering into the wall would probably wake him up.

If it did, he would likely leave his room and come lecture me about waking him.

I still didn't think I was ready to see him again.

I gingerly set the hammer down on the floor, hoping against hope that Frederick hadn't heard it.

But a few minutes later his bedroom door creaked open.

*Fuck.*

"Good evening, Miss Greenberg."

Frederick's voice was deeper than usual, and thick with sleep. I turned slowly to face him, bracing myself for a lecture on the importance of keeping quiet when one's roommate was trying to rest.

His voice and disheveled hair implied he'd just woken up, but he was fully dressed in a three-piece, pinstriped brown suit and a pageboy hat. He looked like an English professor from the set of a period film, off to give a lecture on the symbolism found within *Jane Eyre* or something—not like someone who'd just rolled out of bed.

Not that I'd ever had an English professor who looked like *that*.

He didn't launch into a lecture about *Jane Eyre*, though. He also wasn't staring at me the way I was staring at him. He was frowning at my Lake Michigan shoreline canvases where they sat propped against my bedroom wall, as though confused about what he was looking at. His arms were folded tightly across his broad chest as he scowled, which absolutely did *not* make me think about what his bare chest had looked like the other night. Or the way it ostensibly looked right that very second beneath his too-formal clothing.

"I'm sorry I woke you up," I offered, to steer my thoughts towards safer ground.

He waved a hand. "It's fine. But . . . what are those?" He nodded in the direction of my landscapes.

"You mean my landscapes?"

"Is . . . is that what those are?" His eyebrows rose. He stepped into the room, as though to take a closer look. "You *made* these?"

He sounded and looked at least as confused as my grandfather did whenever he saw one of my pieces—but he didn't seem horrified. He also didn't look or sound particularly complimentary or blown away by my creations, though. Which was valid. I'd long since made peace with the fact that my art wasn't everyone's cup of tea.

But this series was probably the most broadly accessible work I'd done in years. For starters, it was obvious these were lakeside images. If I was being honest, after the compliments he'd paid me on my silly little sketches on our notes to each other, part of me had hoped he'd immediately understand—and appreciate— what I was trying to do with these canvases.

"I made them, yes," I confirmed. I tried to sound confident, though my voice was shaking a little.

"And you mean to hang them up?" Frederick eyed the nail I'd just hammered into the wall. "In here?"

"Yeah."

"Why?" he asked, striding towards my canvases. He looked down at them, hands stuffed deep into the pockets of his trousers. He seemed utterly bewildered. "I grant you that the painting hanging here previously was dated, but—"

"It was hideous."

He glanced at me, the right corner of his mouth ticking up in amusement. "That is fair. It was my mother's, not mine. But Cassie . . ."

He stood up, shaking his head.

"Yeah?"

"It's *trash*," he said, emphasizing the final word.

My hackles rose. I'd heard this sort of criticism before and was an expert at just brushing it off. But after the excitement of learning about the art exhibition a few hours ago, I wasn't in the mood.

"My art is *not* trash," I said, defiantly.

Frederick looked at the canvas again, really peering at it this time—as though trying to decide whether he'd been right in his initial assessment.

He shook his head again. "But . . . but it *is* trash."

A beat passed before I realized he meant that literally.

"Oh." I cringed inwardly. "I mean—yes, okay. It's *made* of trash."

He raised an amused eyebrow. "I believe that's what I just said."

It wasn't *exactly* what he'd just said, but I let it drop. "Yes," I said, feeling my face grow warm with embarrassment over the misunderstanding. "You did."

"I admit I don't understand." He shook his head. "Based on the parts of this . . . this scene that are not covered in refuse, and the drawings you have done for me, I know you are an artist with talent. Maybe I have old-fashioned views, but I simply don't understand why you would spend your time creating something like this." He shrugged his shoulders. "The sort of art I am used to seeing is more . . ."

I raised an eyebrow. "More what?"

He bit his lip, as though searching for the right words. "Pleasant to look at, I suppose." He shrugged again. "Scenes from nature. Little girls wearing frilly white dresses and playing beside riverbanks. Bowls of fruit."

"This piece shows a beach and a lake," I pointed out. "It's a scene from nature."

"But it's covered in refuse."

I nodded. "My art combines objects I find with images I paint. Sometimes what I find and incorporate is literal trash. But I also feel that my art is more than just trash. It's *meaningful*. These pieces aren't just flat, lifeless images on canvas. They *say* something."

"Oh." He came even closer to the landscapes, kneeling so he could peer at them up close. "And what does your art . . . say?"

His nose was just a few inches from an old McDonald's Quarter Pounder wrapper I'd laminated to the canvas so it looked like it was rising out of Lake Michigan. I'd meant for it to represent capitalism's crushing stranglehold on the natural world. Also, it just sort of looked cool.

But I decided to give him a broader explanation.

"I want to create something memorable with my art. Something lasting. I want to give people who see my works an experience that won't fade away. Something that will stay with them long after they see it."

He frowned skeptically. "And you accomplish that by displaying ephemera others throw away?"

I was about to counter by telling him that even the prettiest painting in the fanciest museum faded from memory once the patrons went home. That by using things other people throw away, I took the ephemeral and make it permanent in a way no pretty watercolor ever could.

But then, all at once, I noticed how close we were standing. During our conversation he must have crept closer by increments until now there were just a scant few inches of space separating us. My mind flashed back to the other night—my wet hair dripping onto my bare shoulders, his dark brown eyes wide with surprise as he looked everywhere but at me.

He was looking at me now, though. And his eyes were everywhere. They trailed slowly down the slope of my neck, lingering at the small, jagged scar beneath my ear I got as a small child before moving on to the gentle curve of my shoulders. I wasn't wearing anything particularly nice, just a thin T-shirt and an old pair of jeans—but his gaze was heated all the same. It made me feel dizzy and warm in a way I didn't have words for.

I wanted to move closer to him, so I did, not bothering to stop and wonder if that was a good idea. But then a moment later he straightened, as if returning to himself, and then quickly stepped back and away from me. He stuffed his hands deep into the pockets of his trousers once again, staring down at his shiny wing-tipped shoes as though they were the most fascinating things in the world.

The moment was over. But somehow, it felt like something between us had changed. There was a sweet, electric anticipation in the air that hadn't been there before. I wasn't sure I had words for what it was. All I knew was that I wanted to feel it again. I wanted to feel *him*. The hard planes of his broad chest beneath my hands. His lips, his breath, hot and sweet against my neck.

I shook my head to try and clear it. This was a man I hardly knew, I reminded myself. This was my *roommate*.

It didn't work.

"I . . . can try and explain my art to you," I offered, just for something to say. In my head, Sam's voice shouted, *Bad idea, bad idea*, like a warning klaxon. I ignored it. Quite frankly, in that moment I didn't care if it was a bad idea. My heart was racing, blood pumping hot inside my veins. "If you want."

He hesitated, still not looking at me. He shook his head.

"That is probably not a good idea," he said, echoing the voice in my head. "I suspect I am a rather hopeless case when it comes to modern art."

I could sense that he was trying to put some distance between us after . . . well, after whatever it was that had just happened. I didn't want him to.

"I've never met anyone who's a hopeless case."

His eyes fluttered closed.

"You have never met anyone like me, Miss Greenberg," he said, sounding almost sad about it, before turning and walking out of my bedroom.

It was another few minutes before I was able to collect myself enough to think straight. When I did, I sank to my bed, burying my face in my hands.

Sam's words of warning from the other day suddenly came back to me: *Living with someone you think is hot never ends well. You either end up sleeping with them—which is a huge mistake, nine times out of ten—or else you drive yourself nuts because you want to sleep with them.*

I groaned.

Well, it looked like Sam had been right.

What the hell was I going to *do*?

# SIX

Letter from Mr. Frederick J. Fitzwilliam to
Mrs. Edwina Fitzwilliam, dated October 26

My Dearest Mrs. Fitzwilliam,

I hope this letter finds you well and in good spirits.

A lot has changed in the fortnight since I last wrote. I
now live with a young woman by the name of Miss Cassie
Greenberg. I am learning a tremendous amount about art,
twenty-first-century popular culture, profanity, and attire
simply by observing her and being in her very occasional
presence. Every day I feel more myself again, and more at
ease in this strange modern world.

And so again I ask: please stop worrying so much over
me. There is no need for you to write so often, nor for you
to repeatedly inquire after my health with Reginald. (Yes,
he has told me everything.) I am as sound in mind, body,
and spirit as I have ever been.

Furthermore, I must insist you end the arrangement

you have made with Miss Jameson on my behalf. I hardly
know this woman, and, as you well know, Paris was over
a century ago. I would end the arrangement myself, but I
think that would not only be unwise, but also unfair to
both me and Miss Jameson. Please also ask Miss
Jameson to stop sending me gifts. She has ignored my
entreaties even though I have sent each gift back to her,
unopened as they arrive.

I will write more soon. Give my regards to everyone on
the estate. I hope the weather in New York has been very
fine.

love,
Frederick

......................

Hey Frederick,

Would it be okay if I turned the temperature in the
apartment up a few degrees? I haven't wanted to say
anything about it since you pay for utilities, but it's a little
colder in here than I'm used to. Even three blankets isn't
cutting it at nighttime.

Cassie

Dear Cassie,

Please accept my apology. Cold temperatures do not
bother me the way they do other people, and I should have
anticipated you would prefer a warmer place to live. Let

me know the temperature I should set the thermostat to
for you to be more comfortable and I will take care of it.

I wish you had said something about this to me
earlier. I hate the idea that you've been uncomfortable since
moving in.

FJF

ps: That picture you drew of yourself wearing a parka and
mittens is adorable, though it does make me feel like even
more of a heel for keeping you in the cold for so long.

Frederick,

Thank you!!!!! I didn't like the idea of you having higher utility
bills because of me, though (which is why I didn't say something
earlier). Can I pay the difference?

(Also, I'm glad you like the picture. Adorable, though?! I
spent like 5 minutes on it. The mittens are totally lopsided.)

Cassie

Cassie,

Do not worry about the difference in the utility bill. I will
cover it.

And if you drew something that precious in only five
minutes I daresay you are very talented indeed. I find the
lopsided mittens especially charming.

FJF

I WAS HALFWAY DOWN THE BLOCK TOWARDS THE EL, ON MY way to my library shift, when I realized I'd forgotten my sketchpad.

I glanced at my phone. It was *Night at the Museum* night at the library, and the children would start showing up in forty-five minutes. I couldn't draw at work with a library full of kids armed with paintbrushes, but at that hour there were usually some open seats on the train so I could sketch en route. I was in the beginning stages of thinking through what my piece would be for the art exhibition. My conversation with Frederick the other night about my art had provided a little inkling of a submission idea: I'd create a traditionally painted pastoral scene—a field of daisies, possibly a pond—and then subvert it with something decidedly *un*pastoral, like plastic wrap or soda straws worked into the canvas.

It was still early days, and I had more thinking to do before I was ready to put paint to canvas. But I'd been taking my sketchpad with me everywhere I went in case inspiration and a few minutes' free time happened to coincide.

It was just after six. I had just enough time to run back home, get my sketchpad, and then get to the library in time for art night. It would be tight, and Marcie would likely be a little irritated with me—but I'd make it.

I took the stairs up to our apartment two at a time, not worrying about how much noise I made. I didn't know if Frederick was home, but at this hour he'd either be already awake or out. Either way, I didn't have to worry about waking him up.

My sketchpad was where I'd left it on the kitchen table, beside the note I'd left for Frederick earlier that morning:

*Hey Frederick—I won't be home much the next few days. I have a late shift tonight and I'm having dinner at Sam's*

tomorrow. So could you take out the trash this week?
Thanks! I promise I'll do it next week.

Cassie

At the bottom of the note, I'd sketched a little smiling cartoon guy holding a trash can above his head. Frederick claimed to like my little drawings, and his compliments—always worded in such formal language, but seemingly genuine all the same—always made my stomach do a funny little swoop.

As I picked up my sketchpad from the kitchen table I noticed he'd written a short reply:

Dear Cassie,

Yes, I can take out the trash can. It is no trouble whatsoever, and you do not need to worry about "making it up to me."

Additionally, that drawing is very nice ~~(all of your drawings are very nice, everything about you is very nice)~~ but is that supposed to be me? I am certain I never smile quite like _that_.

Yours,<br>FJF

He'd added his own drawing of a stick figure to the note, with an exaggerated frown nearly as big as its head. I couldn't help but laugh.

The drawing was so silly.

And Frederick was about the furthest thing from _silly_ a person could be.

Or so I'd thought, anyway.

Also—the *Yours, FJF*?

*Yours.*

That was new.

I refused to let myself think about what it could mean. All the same, I couldn't stop the smile from spreading across my face as I picked up my sketchpad.

I was still smiling as I opened the fridge to grab an apple before leaving for the library.

But when I saw what was inside, my face froze.

My entire body froze.

Time stopped.

After what might have been multiple minutes of my staring numbly at the contents of the refrigerator, I began to shriek.

My sketchpad slipped from my hands and fell to the ground, forgotten. I continued staring into the fridge, my mind reeling as I tried to make sense of what I was seeing.

There had to be at least thirty bags of blood in there, arranged in orderly rows alongside a bowl of kumquats, my half-finished gallon of orange juice, and a box of Velveeta. Each bag was labeled by blood type and date, and bore the kind of barcode sticker I vaguely remembered being put on blood donation bags when I'd donated in the past.

The sharp, metallic tang of blood was thick, filling the air and nearly making me gag.

Unlike what I'd seen at blood centers, not all these bags were sealed. Some were nearly empty, with a pair of small puncture wounds at the top. Blood dribbled from one of them, leaving a small, sticky, red and drying puddle on the middle shelf.

None of it had been there that morning.

Why was it there *now*?

I was still standing in front of the open fridge, gaping at its contents, growing dizzy at the smell of blood and at the shock of what I'd found but too stunned to move away, when the front door to the apartment opened. I distantly heard the heavy tread of Frederick's footsteps as he stepped inside.

"Frederick," I called out, my voice thick. "What . . . *what* is all this doing here?"

Something very heavy dropped to the floor. And then came Frederick's strangled gasp.

"Oh, *fuck*."

I looked at him, my hand still tight around the handle of the refrigerator door. Frederick's eyes were saucer-wide, his hands clutching at his hair in both hands. There was a large package wrapped in bright pink wrapping paper and tied with a pale pink ribbon at his feet. "Please—I can explain. Don't . . . don't get hysterical."

I gaped at him. "I *wasn't* getting hysterical before you said *that*."

He buried his face in his hands. "You . . . weren't supposed to see that. You said you'd be gone tonight. I—"

"Frederick?"

"This was not how *any of this* was supposed to *go*."

I waited for him to continue, to explain why I'd just found bags of blood in the same place I kept my breakfast. When he just continued standing there, gaping at me open-mouthed like a fish out of water, I closed my eyes and let the fridge door swing closed.

I counted slowly to ten, breathing deeply through my nose to try and calm down. "Frederick—" I began.

"Did you get any O-negative this time, Freddie? I'm famished." A loud male voice came in from the hallway, his words so hard to process they made the rest of whatever I'd been about to say die in my throat. A moment later, a vaguely familiar-looking guy with dirty-blond hair strode into the apartment like he owned the place, his hands stuffed deep into the pockets of his jeans. His black T-shirt said *This Is What a Clarinet Player Looks Like,* and stretched a little too tightly across his chest.

All at once I realized where I'd seen him before.

He was the weird guy in the trench coat and fedora who appraised me at Gossamer's the other night.

I was stuck on what he'd just said.

*Did you get any O-negative this time, Freddie? I'm famished.*

I tried to make sense of what I was hearing, but my brain felt sluggish—like it was processing things at half its normal rate of speed.

I had no idea *who* weird coffee shop guy was or why he was there. He, however, recognized me right away.

"Hey, Cassie Greenberg." He sounded surprised to see me but not unhappy about it. He grinned, showing off perfectly straight, gleaming white teeth. He reached out his hand towards me. After an awkward beat I realized he wanted me to shake it. Slowly, as though moving through a dream, I clasped his hand in mine.

It was like holding onto a block of ice.

"I'm Reggie," he said, still smiling. "We met the other night at the café." He paused. "Well. *Sort of* met, anyway."

*Reggie.*

Was this the *Reginald* Frederick had mentioned a few times in passing? He gave my hand a few quick pumps before I pulled out of his grip.

I looked between him and Frederick—who, for his part, looked like he wanted the ground to open up and swallow him whole—trying to understand what was going on.

"I told Freddie he needed to come clean with you." Reggie

elbowed Frederick in the ribs good-naturedly. "But I gather from the look on your face that he didn't listen to me."

He jabbed Frederick in the ribs again—more forcefully this time. But Frederick was clearly ignoring him. His eyes bore into mine, beseeching me wordlessly to understand . . . something.

"Miss Greenberg," he began, sounding desperate. "Cassie," he amended.

"What do you need to come clean with me about, Frederick?" Instinct told me I couldn't trust Reggie—*Reginald*—as far as I could throw him. But Frederick's desperation confirmed that he was right about at least one thing: there was a *lot* Frederick wasn't telling me.

"Speak up, Freddie!" Reggie encouraged. He clapped Frederick on the back.

"Leave," Frederick muttered, his tone murderous. "Now."

"In a minute," Reggie said, in a light singsong. "It's been a while since I've seen a good show." He stepped fully into the living room, moving around both Frederick and the large, wrapped package at his feet, and then strode directly to the kitchen, where I still stood rooted to the spot beside the fridge of doom.

"I think I'll have a snack before I go," he whispered in my ear, conspiratorially. He opened the fridge with a flourish, then reached inside and scooped up several plastic bags of blood.

My eyes went wide.

With a wink at me, Reggie bit into one of the bags with what looked, to me, a hell of a lot like fangs.

As I watched him drink the bag down, then toss it into the trash—empty in seconds, drained entirely dry—and bite into a second, I felt the room start to spin. I'd never been a particularly squeamish person; but then, nothing in any of my life experiences had prepared me for what I was seeing now.

"Reginald," Frederick growled warningly. "Get out. *Now.*"

He pouted. "But I just got here! We were going to have a little party before your roommate got here."

"*Reginald.*"

"*Freddie.*" Reginald rolled his eyes. "Stop being silly. You're just as hungry as I am. Don't you want a snack, too?"

Without waiting for an answer, Reggie grabbed another bag from the fridge and tossed it to Frederick—who caught it, easily.

The sight of Frederick—my roommate who stayed out all night for cryptic reasons and slept all day, who dressed in vintage suits and spoke like someone from a different era—holding a bag of blood . . .

The last piece of the puzzle slid into place.

I knew exactly what he hadn't been telling me.

"Frederick . . ." I began, the floor beneath my feet going decidedly wobbly.

How was any of this *real*?

Frederick cleared his throat. "It occurs to me that it is long past time I told you several . . . very specific things about myself." He was glaring at Reginald, but it was clear he was talking to me. He had the decency to sound sheepish. Which . . . well. Good. I was pretty sure he'd been lying to my face about a lot of very important things since I'd met him.

Feeling bad about it was certainly a step in the right direction.

"Go on," I prompted.

"I'm . . . not what you think I am."

I snorted. "I figured." My words came out frostier than I'd meant them to. But come on. Did he think I was an idiot? "What *are* you, though?"

I knew, though. A person would have to be pretty dim to stumble upon their roommate's blood stash, *and* watch his friend help himself to some of it like it was something he did every day, and not immediately realize some pretty uncomfortable truths.

I still needed to hear him say it, though. After a lifetime of thinking people like Frederick only existed in young adult novels and old horror movies, it was the only way I'd believe what I'd seen with my own two eyes.

Frederick sighed, running a hand over his perfect face. He bit his lip, hesitating—and, no, my eyes were *not* helplessly drawn to the way his white teeth pressed into the soft, plump flesh of his bottom lip. I was done fantasizing about my unfairly hot roommate. That phase of my life was one hundred percent *over*.

"I am a vampire, Cassie."

His voice was very quiet, but his words blew through me with the force of a hurricane. I'd already guessed the truth, but I still stumbled under the weight of his confession.

All it once, it felt like all the oxygen had been sucked from the room.

I had to get out of there.

Now.

Sam and Scott would take me in. Getting them to believe my roommate was a vampire might be difficult, but—

No. Getting them to believe my roommate was a vampire would be impossible. Sam was a lawyer, and Scott was an academic. They didn't have enough imagination between them to change a light bulb. And I'd always been the eccentric friend. The one who could throw killer bachelor parties and collected existential crises like Pokémon, but who was perennially messing up in most important areas of her life.

They'd probably think I was delusional if I told the truth.

But it didn't matter. They'd see I was desperate when I showed up late at night and unannounced. They'd take me in.

I had to laugh over how stupid I'd been. I'd started having feelings for Frederick. Meanwhile, he'd been waiting for the perfect opportunity to bite my neck!

"Cassie," Frederick said, looking panicked. "I can explain."

"I think you just did."

"I did not. I gave you some information that I should have shared with you at the outset, but—"

I huffed a breath. "I'll say."

He looked chastened, gaze dropping to the floor. "I would still like a chance to explain myself fully. If you will allow it."

But I was already inching my way towards the front door. "What is there to explain? You're a vampire. You've been biding your time, waiting for your chance to pounce on me, sink your teeth into my neck, and drink my blood."

"No," Frederick said, emphatically. He shook his head. "It has never been my intention to harm you."

"Why should I believe you?"

He paused, considering my question. "I realize that I have not given you much reason to trust me. But really, Cassie. If I were going to feed from you, wouldn't I have done so before now?"

I stared at him. "That's supposed to be reassuring?"

He winced. "It . . . sounded better in my head," he admitted. "But please believe me when I say that for all intents and purposes I have not fed on a living human in over two hundred years."

*In over two hundred years.*

The room went all spinny again as the full extent of what he was telling me sunk in.

Frederick wasn't just a vampire.

He was also seriously, *seriously* old.

"I can't do this," I mumbled. I had to get away. "I'm leaving."

"Cassie—"

"I'm *leaving*," I said, stumbling out of the kitchen. "Throw out all my stuff if you want. I don't care."

"Cassie." Frederick's voice sounded pained. "Please, let me explain. I need your help."

But I was already throwing open the front door of the apartment and dashing down the stairs, my heartbeat pounding in my ears.

# SEVEN

*Text messages between Mr. Frederick J. Fitzwilliam
and Mr. Reginald R. Cleaves*

Hey Freddie

You okay?

No. I am the opposite of okay.

The woman who I had hoped would teach
me how to live in the modern world has
fled from me because of you.

What were you thinking, behaving that
way in front of my roommate?

She deserved to know
the truth about you.

I was still working my way up to telling her.

She's human

Not telling her ur a vampire right
off the bat was a dick move

                I do not know what "a dick move" is.

Im insulting u

                Well I suppose, in this case,
                I rather deserve it.

Why hadnt u told her

                It's complicated.

Complicated?

                Yes.

lol

                Cassie says "lol" in some of our
                notes to each other, but I do
                not know what it means.

Wait

You and Cassie leave notes for each other?

Also since when do you call her
Cassie instead of Miss Greenberg?

I call her Cassie because she asked me to.
And yes, we leave notes for each other.

We are roommates, after all.

Or we were roommates, rather.

Do you text each other too?

Sometimes.

But you HATE texting

That is true.

You never text me back
unless ur having a crisis

Yes. But you are an asshole.

How often do you and Cassie text?

I do not keep track of such things.

Our typical method of communication
is to leave notes for each other on
the kitchen table. That way I do not
need to use this infernal device to
communicate with her.

Sometimes she draws me
pictures on the notes.

They are lovely.

She's quite a talented artist.

In fact, she's quite good at a lot of things.

I dont believe this

What don't you believe?

You're into her

You REPROBATE! How dare you?!

What?????

Oh. No, lol

"You're into her" is just a modern
figure of speech, bud

It just means you have romantic
feelings for her.

Oh.

I see.

You're still wrong, though.

Right, lol

Listen. How long have I
known you?

I shudder to think.

Have you EVER talked with a woman
more than once a month before

No. But I've also never lived with
a woman before, either.

When you think about Cassie not
living with you anymore how
does that make you feel

When I think about Cassie never
returning to me it makes me sad.

Waking up in the evening isn't exciting
anymore now that I know I won't
be seeing her face.

So you're into her, is what I'm hearing

Absolutely not. I am NOT "into her."

I just like her drawings.

And her everything.

Oh this is gonna be good

SAM LIVED IN A PART OF TOWN THAT WAS POPULAR AMONG
young professionals who had tiny little purebred dogs and worked
sixty hours a week at their jobs in the Loop.

Visiting Sam and Scott in their second-floor brownstone apartment usually reminded me of what a colossal failure I was in most areas of my life. And staying with them after fleeing Frederick's apartment was supremely awkward.

For one thing, sharing one small bathroom with two guys—even guys as neat and tidy as Sam and Scott—was not ideal. I didn't have quite enough time to myself in there in the mornings, and because they were a lot hairier than I was, the bathtub drain was twenty-five percent grosser than strictly necessary. For another, their cats Sophie and Moony, while adorable, liked to walk on me in the night as I tried to sleep on the living room couch.

For yet another, Sam and Scott were newlyweds in every sense of the word. Their walls were regrettably thin. Sam was *loud*. Bunking in the living room gave me a front-row seat to their nightly sex-having, a punishment no one deserved. Least of all me, Sam's best friend since the sixth grade.

As bad as living with a vampire who hid being a vampire from me had been, living with newlyweds—even for just two days—might have been worse.

"Good morning," Sam said, yawning, as he left his bedroom. He was sporting a huge purple hickey on his neck. I was pretty sure I'd heard every second of the hickey-giving process the previous night. God, I wished I hadn't.

"Morning." I pushed back the quilt I'd slept under and rubbed my eyes. I was exhausted. Between all the sex happening in the next room, Moony's penchant for getting soft white fur on my pillow, and Sam's lumpy couch, sleep had been elusive the past two nights. But I didn't want Sam to know that. The accommodations might be lacking in several very key respects, but he and Scott were still doing me a huge favor.

And neither of them had asked any probing questions about

why I was there when I'd shown up two nights ago. I was grateful for that.

Sam pulled out the box of oatmeal from the pantry and asked, his back still to me, "What are your plans for the day?"

I didn't know if that was a passive-aggressive comment on my still sleeping on his couch two days after showing up with none of my stuff and no explanations. It felt like one, though. In an hour he'd be leaving in his slacks and button-down shirt, ready for another day as a law firm associate—and I'd still be semi-homeless and as unsure of my next move as ever.

I looked away, fidgeting with the fringe of the quilt still covering my legs.

"I'm going to the recycling center today."

That was part of the truth, anyway. Sam didn't need to hear the rest of it—which was that before heading to the recycling center I planned to watch a few episodes of *Buffy the Vampire Slayer*. For research—or so I told myself. The show had to be wildly inaccurate when it came to vampiric details, but after two days of processing what had happened with Frederick the other night, my panic over the situation was fading. And my curiosity was growing.

What was it like to be an immortal who drank human blood? Did Frederick's heart beat? What were the rules governing how he lived and ate . . . and died? It wasn't much, but without getting back in touch with Frederick himself, *Buffy* was about all I had for guidance. It had to be a more accurate representation of vampires than *Twilight* or those old Anne Rice novels, right? Plus, it was an enjoyable show.

The fact that *Buffy* also showed romantic human–vampire relationships had absolutely nothing to do with my interest, of course. Neither did the fact that I hadn't been able to get Frederick's pleading eyes, or his assurances that he would never hurt me, out of my head since the morning I first woke up on Sam's sofa.

"The recycling center, huh?" Sam's back was still to me as he rummaged through the cupboards for a saucepan.

"Yeah," I said. "I need to get cracking on my art show submission." Since running out of Frederick's apartment, my idea of a pastoral scene that incorporated bits of disposable plastic was beginning to take shape in my mind. But I still needed to think through some of the finer details. What colors would work best for the decaying manor house I'd be painting? Should the field in front of the house abut a lake or a stream?

Would soda straws or candy bar wrappers work best for the subversive part of my project—or should I use a combination of both?

I hoped I'd come to some conclusions at the recycling center that afternoon. I always did my best thinking at the dump.

Sam's smile was warm and encouraging. "I'm so happy you're putting yourself out there like this, Cassie."

"Me, too." It was the truth. "There's no way to know if the art exhibition will accept my piece, but it feels good to be working towards something big again."

Sam made his way into the living room as he ate his oatmeal. "By the way," he said, faking nonchalance, "someone slid a letter addressed to you under our door last night."

I looked up at him, surprised. "Really?"

"It's so fancy that at first I thought it might have been a summons to visit the King of England." He raised an eyebrow at me. "But then I remembered those aren't usually slid under the door in the middle of the night."

Sam held up an envelope I hadn't seen him bring into the living room and tossed it onto the coffee table between us.

My breath caught.

It was Frederick's stationery—a square, off-white envelope identical to those he used for all his notes to me. Even if he'd used regular notebook paper, though, I would have immediately known this was from him. He'd written *Miss Cassie Greenberg* on the front in the same fancy handwriting, and with the same blue ink, he used for all our correspondence.

His familiar blood-red wax seal held the envelope closed.

*FJF*

Before meeting Frederick I hadn't known wax seals still existed. Everything about that man was an anachronism, I realized. Out of place. From a different time altogether.

Just how many clues about who and what he truly was had I missed?

Sam pretended to turn his attention back to his oatmeal, but I could feel his eyes on me as I slid my finger beneath the seal and broke it. Sam was curious about this letter—but I still hadn't found the courage to tell him the truth about either Frederick or why I was staying in his apartment. I just didn't have the energy to get into any of it with him.

Bracing myself, I slid out the single folded sheet of stiff, off-white paper from the envelope and began to read.

*Dear Cassie,*

*I hope this letter finds you well.*

*I write to let you know that your belongings are right where you left them. When you fled, you said I could dispose of anything you left behind. That said, I suspect* that what remains in my home constitutes the bulk of your material possessions. I further suspect that you said what you did only out of fear and in the heat of the moment—and that you do, in fact, wish to have your things returned to you.

If I do not get a response to this letter within a week, I will assume you truly do not wish to have your things back and I will arrange with Gerald to have them donated to charity. (Gerald handles recycling for our building. I spoke with him for the first time yesterday. Do you know he has worked for the city's sanitation department for twenty-two years, and has two grown children? I did not. But you probably already do, as you took out the recycling several times in the two weeks we lived together and you are so warm and friendly with everyone.)

Please let me know at your earliest convenience if you would like your things returned to you. I can even arrange it so that you can collect them without having to interact with me, if that's what you want.

Despite how we left things, I want you to know it was truly a pleasure to have made your acquaintance and to have been your roommate for the short time we were together. I am so sorry to have upset and frightened you through my lack of full disclosure and my actions.

Yours,
Frederick

I swallowed the lump in my throat, then read Frederick's letter a second time.

*Yours, Frederick.*

He was just so . . . *earnest.*

And thoughtful. Beyond the compliment he paid me—*you are so warm and friendly with everyone*—he'd understood me well enough to know that after my panic had subsided, I'd likely want my stuff back.

Without him hanging around.

The vulnerability Frederick must be feeling all but jumped from the page. Yet I could tell he had taken great pains to try and hide it. I thought back to the evening he'd tried so hard to understand my art. In hindsight, of *course* my art made no sense to him. The man was hundreds of years old! But he'd tried anyway, listening attentively as I explained it to him—all because it was important to me.

Maybe Frederick was telling the truth when he said he never wanted to hurt me. It was seeming increasingly likely. He might not technically be alive—and yes, he was a vampire—but he was also . . .

Kind.

And thoughtful.

It's possible he'd been faking all that just to lure me in, but with some distance from the events of the other night, I didn't think that he'd been pretending.

"You planning to fill me in on what's going on?" Sam's sharp voice cut into my musings.

I bit my lip, looking away. "What do you mean?"

Sam set his bowl of oatmeal down on the coffee table and assumed what Scott and I secretly called his *Sam the Lawyer* posture: leaning forward in his chair, elbows on knees. I'd become so familiar with it over the years I had a feeling I knew what I was in for.

"You showed up at our apartment the other night with none

of your stuff, no warning, and no explanation," he started. "You looked like you'd just seen a ghost. You look that way right now, too, reading and rereading a letter that looks like it was written with a feather and quill."

I pressed the letter against my chest reflexively. "This is my private mail."

Sam rolled his eyes. "You're literally in my living room, Cass. My question stands. What is going on?"

I paused, trying to think through how to answer that question without raising any more red flags in Sam's mind.

"This letter is from Frederick," I said, very carefully. "He wants to return my stuff, but I . . ." I trailed off. Took a deep breath. "I think I need to talk with him. I might have been too hasty when I moved out."

Sam stood up abruptly. "What are you talking about?"

"You heard me."

"Cassie," Sam said. "You were so terrified of him the other night you ran here. Now he sends you one letter and you want to go back?" He shook his head. "This feels like a hypothetical they might use to train lawyers on how to file protective orders against abusive partners."

My heart leapt into my throat. "It's not like that."

"No?"

"No." I shook my head. "Frederick hasn't done anything wrong. He's been a great roommate. We just . . ." God. How could I possibly explain this situation to Sam in a way that made sense?

Sam put a hand on my shoulder, warm and reassuring. His face softened. *Sam the Lawyer* was gone now, replaced with *Sam the Life Counselor*. I'd seen a lot of him over the years, too.

"Let us help you find another place to live, Cass. Your arrangement with Frederick clearly didn't work out. And while you're welcome to stay with us as long as you like, at some point I assume you'd like to not be sleeping on our couch anymore."

I hesitated. The smart thing for me to do, of course, would be to try and find another place to live. That's what a rational, level-headed person who just found out their hot roommate was a vampire would do.

But I'd never once been accused of being rational or level-headed.

And now, after having some time to think it over, I believed him when he said he would never hurt me.

I thought back to how I'd basically lied to him, too, when I told him in my first email that I was an art teacher. I'd wanted to make the best impression possible when I applied for the apartment and when I moved in. I wanted him to *pick me.*

Could I really blame him for also wanting to hide the more unsavory aspects of his history, and his most unpleasant personality traits, from his new roommate? Granted, yes—being a vampire was a much bigger deal in the grand scheme of things than exaggerating my job history. But in that moment, I think I understood his reasoning for doing what he did.

"I need to talk to him before making a decision," I said to Sam. "When I ran out, he told me he . . . he wanted to explain a few things. I left without giving him a chance to do that."

The sound of running water floated out to us from the bathroom. Scott was awake now, too. He and Sam would soon be off to their respective offices.

"And now you want to give him that chance?" Sam asked, softly.

I nodded. "There are a few things I need to clear up with him."

"I don't feel good about this." Sam was staring at me now,

arms folded tightly across his chest. "I bet if you told me the whole story I'd feel even worse about it."

He was probably right about that.

I quickly kissed Sam on the cheek to distract him, then grabbed my phone and made my way to the front door. "I'm going to give him a quick call, then run a few errands. I'll be back later."

"You're not going to call him here?"

"Nah," I said, trying to ignore what sounded like alarm in Sam's voice. There was no way I'd be able to keep Sam in the dark about what Frederick was if I had this conversation in front of him. I pulled on the trainers I kept by the front door. "I want to go for a walk and stretch my legs while I'm talking."

"You hate exercise."

He was right about that, too. This time, the note of concern in Sam's voice was unmistakable. "I'll be right back," I promised again, before leaving.

......................

I DECIDED TO CALL FREDERICK FROM THE SOUTH SIDE RE- cycling center.

True, the recycling center was noisy. But I needed to make this call from a place of confidence and strength. I was only going to move back in with Frederick if I felt I could handle it, and if it served *me*. What better way to remind myself that this phone call was me taking active steps towards improving my situation than to have it while working on my art?

But by the time I'd gotten off the El stop by the recycling center, my nerves couldn't take the anticipation anymore. I stepped into a donut shop with a flashing neon sign over the door that said FRESH DONUTS. It was gloriously warm inside, and I was greeted by the mouthwatering smell of melting sugar.

I made my way to a table near the back, promising myself I could have a chocolate glazed donut if I made it to the other side of this phone call.

I pulled my phone from my bag, reminded myself that I could do hard things, and texted him.

**Hi Frederick**

**It's Cassie**

**Can I call you?**

Frederick—a man who hated texting, and who by all accounts should have been asleep at that hour—replied immediately. Like he'd been sitting there all this time, phone in hand, waiting for me to reach out.

**Yes.**

**I am available now if you are.**

I dialed his number. He picked up on the first ring.

"Cassie?" The note of hopefulness in his warm, rich voice was unmistakable.

I ignored the corresponding twinge in my chest.

"Yeah," I said. "It's me."

"This is a surprise. I was worried I wouldn't hear from you again."

"I'm kind of surprising myself right now, too," I admitted. "Until a few minutes ago I also thought you'd never hear from me again."

A long pause. "What changed your mind?"

Frederick must have been with someone, because I could

hear someone saying something I couldn't quite make out over the line.

"Shut up, you *imbecile*," Frederick muttered. And then, in a rush, he added, "Oh, Cassie—I apologize. That . . . wasn't directed at you."

I stifled a laugh in my palm. "Who's with you right now? Reginald?"

"Who else?" He sighed. He sounded exhausted. "Regrettably."

"I thought you hated him."

"I do hate him." More mumbled words from Reginald that I couldn't quite make out, followed by his raucous laughter and a loud *ow!* Did Frederick hit him? The idea was so ridiculous I almost laughed again.

"I see," I said.

"Yes," he sighed. "Alas, my options for companionship are limited."

I toed at the floor under my feet as a wave of irrational guilt rose up in me. The bell over the donut shop's door chimed as a loud group of customers came inside. Their laughter filled the small space as I worked up the courage to say what was on my mind.

"So. About our situation."

A pause. "Yes?"

I took a deep breath. "The other night, after you . . . before I ran out, you said you could give me an explanation."

"Yes."

"Do you still want to give it to me?" My heart was pounding. Was I really doing this?

His voice was quiet, guarded, when he next spoke. "I do." And then, after another long moment, he added, "But only if you want to hear what I have to say. I will not force myself, or my story, on you."

I took another deep breath. "I'd like to hear it."

"Wonderful. But, may I ask what made you change your mind?"

My breath caught at the hopeful note I heard in his voice. How should I answer that? Should I tell him the truth? That I'd been thinking about him more than was probably wise since I'd moved out—enough to start doing my own research into vampires? That the letter he sent was one of the sweetest letters I'd ever received?

No. I wasn't ready for that.

So I gave him part of the truth. "I feel bad about running out on you without giving you a chance to explain, when it was so obvious you had more to say. And I believe you, now, when you say you won't hurt me."

"I will *never* hurt you," he said emphatically. "*Never.*"

I swallowed around the lump in my throat, unsure what to do with the emotion I heard in his voice.

"I believe you," I said. "But I have a lot of questions."

"Of course. I understand this is a lot for any human to absorb. I will be at home all evening. Would you care to come by and talk then?"

"No." We needed a neutral meeting place. I still wasn't completely sure what my next move would be, and I didn't want the awesomeness of the apartment or my undeniable attraction to Frederick to sway my decision-making. Besides—if I was totally wrong about him and Frederick was playing a long game with respect to eating me, I wanted to do this in a public place. "How about Gossamer's?"

"Gossamer's?"

"It's the coffee shop where I work. I'll text you the address."

"Fair enough," he said. "When?"

I swallowed. No turning back now. "Tonight at eight?"

"Perfect." A pause. "I am very much looking forward to seeing you again, Cassie."

His voice was soft and sincere. I tried to ignore the way that made my stomach flip, but didn't really succeed.

"Me, too," I said, meaning it.

# EIGHT

**Letter from Mrs. Edwina Fitzwilliam to Mr. Frederick J. Fitzwilliam, dated October 29**

My dearest Frederick,

I am in receipt of your most recent letter. Reading it has done nothing to assuage my concerns. Your decision to remain in Chicago and to put your safety in the hands of a wastrel like Reginald and a young human woman is unwise at best—and DANGEROUS at worst. This poor decision-making is MOST UNLIKE the Frederick I once knew!

I fear it is but further evidence that your mental state is compromised from your century of slumber.

I would be remiss in my duties as the eldest remaining member of our family—and as someone who cares for you, DESPITE our history—if I allowed you to cancel our family's arrangement with the Jamesons. If Miss Jameson is sending you gifts I daresay that is a *GOOD* thing! It is a sign of her continued affection for you despite your continual rebuffs. You *MUST* open her gifts, and should send her some gifts *IN RETURN* as a sign of the long-standing goodwill between our two families.

Do not continue to vex me like this, Frederick.

Yours,
Mother

......................

Hey Freddy

Whats with the packages

They are from Esmeralda Jameson.

I do not want them.

Shes still sending you stuff?

Yes.

I have asked her to stop, to no avail.

Mother refuses to intervene.

She thinks it's a GOOD thing.

So you're giving them to me?

The ones I think you'll enjoy, yes.

> One of us might as well
> get use out of them.

What am I going to do with a cross-stitch
that says "Home Sweet Home" made
from what looks smells and tastes like
human entrails, Freddy

Why did you think I'd want this

> I thought it matched your decor, Reginald.

Okay, that's fair

FREDERICK WAS ALREADY AT A TABLE IN THE BACK WHEN I arrived at Gossamer's, taking in his surroundings with the dazed, wide-eyed wonder one might expect from a tourist visiting an exotic location halfway around the world.

He always looked good, but even by his own standards he looked like an absolute snack. A single dark lock of his hair fell beautifully over his forehead like he'd sprung fully formed from the pages of one of his Regency novels. Seeing him sitting ramrod-straight in his chair, wearing a three-piece suit that fit like he'd had it tailor-made, I began to doubt the wisdom of us meeting in public after all. Because other people were also noticing how good he looked. Two women wearing Northwestern University sweatshirts and drinking coffee at the table beside his kept stealing surreptitious glances in his direction.

A strange, unfamiliar possessiveness I neither recognized in myself nor liked swept through me.

What if one of those women started hitting on him?

I bumped their table a little as I breezed by them, telling myself it was purely accidental.

Frederick held my gaze as I approached him. His thick, long eyelashes were just as wasted on a man now as they'd ever been.

In truth, it was *strange* seeing him here. This was the first time we'd interacted outside of the apartment, and until now I hadn't realized how much I'd come to think of him as a fixture of the lavish place where he lived. Seeing him outside of it was as jarring as seeing a flamingo on the El.

His gaze slid over me, nose twitching a little when his eyes fell on my awkwardly bandaged left hand. Could he *smell* the cut on my hand? I didn't want to think about it.

His brow furrowed. "What happened to you?"

I hid my injured hand behind my back.

"It's nothing." It was the truth. That afternoon's trip to the recycling center had been productive, in the sense that I found several usefully large pieces of scrap I wanted to take back with me the next time I had access to Sam's car. But on my way out I snagged my hand a little on the jagged underside of an old bicycle seat. It barely even rose to the level of a bad paper cut, and it stopped bleeding almost immediately—but the guy working there had freaked, babbling about tetanus risk and liability. He insisted on bandaging me up before letting me go.

I'd been such a tangle of nerves on my way over, I'd forgotten to take off the bulky padded bandage and swap it for a more appropriately sized Band-Aid.

"It doesn't look like nothing," Frederick countered, still staring at me. He sounded genuinely concerned. "Show me."

He leaned in closer, and I could smell the shampoo he must have used that evening before arriving. Sandalwood and lavender. The scent-memory of that moment just outside his bathroom—

me, dripping wet, in just a towel—hit me like a tidal wave, crowding out more rational thinking.

I dug my fingernails into my palm before I could do something stupid. Like run my fingers through his thick, luscious hair in a public place.

Leaning in so that he could hear me but no one else would, I whisper-hissed, "I'm not about to show a vampire an injury that was bleeding an hour ago." My tone was harsher than I intended, and his face crumpled a little. I fought to ignore the pang of guilt that shot through me. "Just . . . just trust me when I tell you it's fine. Okay?"

His eyes fell to the table. "Okay."

I glanced back at the ordering counter, where Katie was grinding beans for the next morning's brew. It was a slow night, and no customers were in line.

"I'm getting a drink." I jerked my thumb towards the counter. "Want anything?"

Frederick shook his head. "No. I am unable to consume anything other than . . ."

He arched an eyebrow meaningfully rather than finish his sentence. The coffee bean grinder started up again behind the counter, loud and abrasive.

"Oh." I wondered if this was something I should have known. I couldn't remember if Spike or Angel ever drank coffee in *Buffy*. "Not ever?"

"It would be like you trying to consume metal," he said, quietly. "My body simply does not recognize anything other than *you know what* as sustenance."

I wanted to hear more about this. Had he really consumed *nothing* but blood since becoming a vampire? It was a hard thing to wrap my mind around. For starters, it seemed incredibly inefficient. Assuming his caloric requirements were roughly the same as a human of his size, how much blood did he have to drink every day?

More than anything, though, a diet consisting of only one thing for literally forever sounded terrible. And boring as hell.

I made a mental note to ask follow-up questions concerning his dietary habits later.

"May I come along with you while you purchase your drink?" He looked around at the other customers at Gossamer's, taking in how each of them had drinks or food in front of them. "As I will explain in more detail shortly, I need to learn how to blend in with modern society. I have not ordered coffee in over one hundred years. I suspect the process has changed."

My eyes widened.

*In over one hundred years.*

This was the second time he'd made an oblique reference to how old he was, but it was just as jarring hearing it now as it had been the other night. He didn't look a day over thirty-five. The cognitive dissonance required to look at him and believe he was centuries old was staggering.

My mind flashed once again to the moment before I fled his apartment. He'd said, *I need your help.* Sitting with him in Gossamer's—watching him regard our surroundings with equal parts confusion and fascination—I thought I finally understood the kind of help he needed.

And, perhaps, why he'd placed an ad for a roommate in the first place.

I fidgeted with my purse strap to disguise how rattled I was.

"Yeah, why don't you come with me?" I suggested. "Coffee shops are a big thing in Chicago. You said you want to blend in—"

"Yes," he cut in, emphatic.

I swallowed. "Okay. Well, if you want to blend in, you need to learn how to order coffee. Even if you never actually drink what you order."

He pushed back from the table without another word, the wooden legs of his chair scraping loudly against the linoleum floor. He followed so close behind me as we made our way to the register that I could feel his cool, solid presence at my back as we moved. I shivered—in part because his proximity was more exciting than I wanted to admit to myself, but also because his body radiated cold in a way I'd never experienced with anyone else.

I thought back again to when we'd collided outside of the bathroom. I'd been so mortified I hadn't fully registered just how *cool*, how unyielding his chest had been when my nose brushed against it.

I was thinking about it now, though. Just how many clues had I missed?

Katie looked up when we reached the counter, her yellow flowery *Gossamer's* apron as bright and chipper as her personality. She was easily the nicest supervisor I'd ever had, one of the few managers who didn't try and pull rank when it came time to clean the milk frother or handle obnoxious customers.

"Here on your night off?" she asked, clearly surprised to see me. Her surprise made sense. I rarely came here when I wasn't working.

"I was in the neighborhood," I lied. She didn't need to know I was meeting Frederick at a place I worked because it would make me feel more empowered for the conversation we were about to have. And because I wanted witnesses, just in case I was wrong about him being a friendly vampire and this went south in a hurry.

Katie nodded, then asked, "Can I get you something?"

Frederick was already staring up at the chalkboard menu

above Katie's head, with an intensity one might use to translate ancient hieroglyphics. The menu listed nearly two dozen drinks in chalk pastel lettering, written in Katie's flowery handwriting.

"*We Are Bountiful*," Frederick read, as slowly and awkwardly as though the words were in a language he did not speak. "*We Are . . . Soul Searching*." He turned to look at me, bewildered. "I thought you said this establishment served coffee."

"It's kind of a whole thing, the way we name things here." Katie rolled her eyes. "The owner attended a wellness seminar in Marin County a few years ago. When she came back all the drinks had to have *inspiring* names."

"They're the same drinks you'd get anywhere, though," I clarified. "So don't let the names throw you."

"The same drinks I'd get anywhere," Frederick repeated.

"Right," I said. "So just let me know if you want a translation."

He seemed to consider that, and then turned to Katie. "I would like to purchase *coffee*." He said the words slowly, carefully—and loudly. Like a stereotype of a stupid American trying to make himself understood in a different country to people who don't speak English.

"Coffee?" Katie asked.

"Coffee," Frederick confirmed, looking extremely pleased with himself. And then, as an afterthought, he added, "Please."

Katie looked at him patiently. We got people in there all the time who were conscientious objectors to our owners' naming system. She knew how to handle this.

"What kind of coffee?" she asked.

A beat. "Coffee," Frederick replied.

"But what kind?" With a practiced motion, Katie pointed to the menu above her head. "*We Are Sparkling* is our light roast, *We Are Exuberant* is our dark roast, and *We Are Vivacious* is—"

At some point, more customers must have shown up, because a line of people had formed behind us. Frederick paid them no mind as he turned to me. "These names are ridiculous."

"You still have to order something."

"I *never* drink coffee, Cassie," he reminded me, looking so affronted I had to bite the inside of my cheek to keep a giggle from escaping. "Maybe this wasn't a good idea."

"Just pick one," I advised. "If you're not going to drink it, it doesn't matter what you order. Right?" I leaned in closer so the people behind us wouldn't hear me and whispered, "It's good practice for blending in."

He tilted his head as he considered that. "You're right." He turned back to Katie. "I will have one—" He paused, looking up at the pastel lettering above her head, and grimaced. "I will have one *We Are Vivacious.*"

"One *We Are Vivacious.*" Katie pushed a button on the register. And then, with the patience she usually reserved for customers over the age of seventy-five—which, given the circumstances, was more appropriate than Katie realized—she asked, "What size would you like? Our *We Are Vivacious* comes in Moon, Supernova, and Galaxy sizes."

This seemed to be Frederick's limit.

"I recognize each of the words you just said as belonging to the English language," he said, looking dazed. "When taken all together, however, none of what you just said makes any sense whatsoever."

"Frederick—"

"A liquid expands to conform to the size and shape of the container it is placed in. Coffee does not have a *size.*"

Frederick's voice was getting louder. The line behind us was now five customers deep. I turned around and noticed that some of them were whispering to one another and staring at him.

I needed to intervene.

"What she means, Frederick, is what size *mug* of coffee do you want to order?" I pointed at the menu display hanging over Katie's head. At the bottom were little chalk-drawn cartoons of small, medium, and large coffee cups—or, Moon, Supernova, and Galaxy—and their corresponding prices. I'd drawn the mugs for that display menu my first week there. That had been fun. "The drinks here come in different-sized mugs depending on how much people want to drink. Each size has a corresponding space-related name."

Understanding dawned across his handsome face. "I see." He glanced at Katie. "You should have said as much from the beginning."

For the first time, Katie's patience was showing visible cracks. She glanced at me and murmured, "You know this guy?"

"Sort of," I admitted sheepishly. "Frederick, what size mug do you want Katie to get for you?"

He seemed to ponder the question very seriously. "What do *normal* people purchase here? That is the size I would like."

"He'll have a large *We Are Vivacious*," I blurted out before Katie had a chance to answer. This conversation needed to end as soon as possible. "Sorry—I mean, he'll have a Galaxy-sized *We Are Vivacious.* I'll have a Moon-sized *We Are Empowered*, with extra foam."

I dug into my wallet to pull out my credit card, but Frederick put his hand on my arm.

"I will pay for the drinks," he said, his tone brooking no opposition. Out of nowhere, he pulled out a neon-purple bag that looked a lot like the fanny pack my grandpa used to wear on our family vacations to Disney World. He unzipped its front pouch, and a motley assortment of coins—dozens, *hundreds* of them—spilled out of it and all over the counter in front of us.

I stared down at the pile in complete bafflement. There must have been at least fifteen different currencies on the counter. Some sort of looked like gold doubloons. Were those actually a *thing*?

Katie, to her credit, didn't even bat an eye. "Sorry. We're cashless." She pointed to the credit card reader in front of us.

Frederick stared first at it, then at her, with an utterly blank expression. "What is that?"

"I'll pay for the drinks," I said, hurriedly. Frederick allowed me to elbow him out of the way, still staring at the credit card reader in abject confusion.

"But—"

"You can pay me back later," I said, inserting my credit card in the machine. "With your gold doubloons."

.....................

FREDERICK GLANCED AT ME OVER THE RIM OF HIS *WE ARE Vivacious*. He sniffed its contents with obvious distaste.

"I remember loving coffee," he mused, setting it back down on the table. It was still full, and still steaming hot. "Now it just smells like dirt water to me."

He sounded sad. How much of his old self had he lost when he'd changed into what he was now? But there'd be time for exploring that question later. I needed other answers first.

I cleared my throat.

"So," I began. "Before I ran out the other night, you said you could explain everything. That you had more to tell me."

If Frederick was surprised by my sudden change of subject, he showed no sign of it. "Yes. It . . . is a long story," Frederick said. His eyes were sad and distant. "And one I should have shared with you from the outset. I apologize again for not telling you sooner, but if you are willing to listen, I would like to share it with you now."

"It's what I'm here for," I said. "I hope at least part of this long story has to do with why a centuries-old vampire with no apparent need for money placed a Craigslist ad looking for a roommate."

The corner of his mouth quirked up into a smile. I refused to be distracted by how handsome he looked when he did those half smiles. Especially when they made his dimple pop. "It does."

"I had a feeling," I said. "Go on, then."

"Perhaps I should give you a condensed version. Otherwise, we will be here all night."

I sipped my cappuccino (it was good—Katie made a mean *We Are Empowered*) and then licked my lips. Frederick's eyes tracked the movement of my tongue with interest. I pretended not to notice.

"A condensed version is probably a good idea," I agreed. "Gossamer's closes at eleven. Katie won't like it if we're still here."

"I wouldn't want to anger her," he mused. "I suspect she has had just about enough of me already."

I smiled. "Probably."

"All right, then." He sat up straighter and fixed me with a gaze so sincere it took my breath away. "Cassie, I need someone to live with me because one hundred years ago Reginald, while practicing his *turning wine into blood* charm, accidentally poisoned me at a costume party in Paris. Which subsequently sent me into something akin to a century-long coma. I woke up in my Chicago home one month ago, knowing nothing of the changes of the past one hundred years." He smiled again, but there was no humor in it. "I am as lost and helpless in the current era as a babe in the woods."

The room started spinning as I tried to process what he was telling me. My grip on my coffee mug tightened without my even realizing it until my knuckles went white.

"I see," I said, not seeing at all.

Frederick tilted his head to the side, gauging my reaction. "I believe I have surprised you. I understand. It was rather a lot for me to comprehend as well. And I was the one who went through it."

"Mm."

"Perhaps I should not have given you the condensed version after all," he mused. "Maybe a more nuanced, detailed description with dates, place names, and settings would have helped ground the story and made it easier to understand."

I doubted that. "I don't think there's anything you could have said or done that would have made that easier to understand."

His face fell. "Perhaps not."

"And so," I said, piecing everything together. "You need a roommate because you need someone to help you navigate the modern world."

"Yes," he agreed. "But I need to do more than just navigate it. It is imperative to my survival that I blend into my current surroundings as best as possible. Or at the very least, that it is not *too* obvious that I am an anachronistic vampire living in the entirely wrong century."

"Because . . ."

"Because it can be . . . *dangerous*, for someone like me to stick out too much. Deadly, even."

What could be dangerous to a vampire? Weren't vampires supposed to be powerful immortals who killed humans for sport? I waited for him to clarify, and for a moment he looked like he wanted to say more. Ultimately, though, he must have decided against it, because he simply leaned back in his chair, eyes on his untouched coffee.

I still had a zillion questions, though.

"Okay, but . . ." I shook my head. "Why *me*? Why am I the roommate you chose to live with you?"

His eyes widened.

"Isn't it obvious?"

"No."

He shrugged. "Who better to teach me about life in the twenty-first century and help me adapt to a modern Chicago than a young human like you who glides effortlessly through it?"

He met my gaze. His dark brown eyes were so soft and inviting.

I could get lost in them, I realized. My stomach did something that felt like a somersault.

*Dangerous.*

No, I yelled at myself. *We are not going to be thinking about how hot and sad Frederick looks right now.*

"Also," he continued, "you were the only person who replied to the ad."

Of course. The two-hundred-dollar price tag probably scared everyone else away.

"Okay, but . . ." I cleared my throat, trying to pull myself together. "Why couldn't you just live with Reginald? He seems to be managing the world okay."

"Unthinkable," he said, flatly. "Reginald may be more familiar with the modern era than I am, but he is also the reason I am in this predicament. Additionally, he is chaos incarnate. Before you moved in with me, I was entirely dependent on his assistance. It was at least as terrible for both of us as you might imagine. The practical jokes he played on me, even while I was still in a coma . . ." He shuddered, then shook his head. "Though I concede that without him, I would likely have starved during my century of slumber. Or been run over by a car within an hour of my reawakening. Or been captured by vampire hunters."

The room started spinning again. "Vampire hunters are real?"

"They were real a century ago. But in Chicago? Today?" He made a seesawing motion with his hand. "There are rumors that they are still out there. Though I admit I do not know how reliable those rumors are, especially since I suspect Reginald started most of them."

"Ah."

"Right," Frederick agreed. "Cars, however, are absolutely real. I wish very much to avoid being struck by one while going for my nightly constitutional."

"Would . . . would that kill you? Getting hit by car?"

His mouth quirked into another half smile. He *had* to know how potent those were. "Probably not. But I suspect it would not feel very good."

I couldn't help but smile back at him at his dry attempt at humor. "Yeah, I can't imagine it would feel good for anyone."

"Maybe I should suggest that Reginald attempt it and ask him to report back."

That got a small laugh from me despite everything. Frederick's posture visibly relaxed, and his smile grew. He really had such an incredible smile. It lit up his entire face and made him seem . . .

More human, I realized suddenly.

That brought me back to reality.

This was ridiculous. I couldn't let myself get distracted by my attraction to him. I still had so many questions, and it felt like the more answers he gave me, the more questions I had.

"I should have told you the truth from the outset," he said again, eyes on the floor.

The contrition in his voice was unmistakable. "Yeah. You should have. My roommate was a *vampire*, Frederick. And I had no idea."

His eyes fluttered closed, the corners of his lips turning down a little. When he looked at me again his dark brown eyes were apologetic. "I hope you can understand why I was initially reluctant to share the truth of my situation with a complete stranger." He paused. "Or, at the least, that you will one day find it within yourself to forgive me for starting things off so badly."

He looked away again, chastened.

"I . . . think I understand," I began. "And I might be willing to help you, if you still want my help."

He sat up straighter in his chair. "Really?"

"Possibly," I clarified, holding up a hand.

I thought of how he had made me feel while we lived together—with his gifts of fruit and cookware, his warm glances, and his sincere interest in my art. And my financial situation was no better now than it had been when I moved in with him two months ago; the two-hundred-dollar rent would come in just as handy now as it had before.

Even still, I needed to do some more thinking. This whole situation was objectively surreal.

"I understand," Frederick said.

"Good," I said. "I need to think about whether providing live-in, hands-on life instructions to a vampire is something I can deal with before committing to doing it."

Frederick held his hands up in front of his face, frowning at them. "*Hands-on?* I will admit I had not imagined using our hands as a part of the instruction process. But if you think *touching* would help . . ."

If I'd been drinking my cappuccino at that moment, I'd have spat it out all over the table. Suddenly, it felt like the temperature in Gossamer's had increased by ten degrees. "Oh my god. No—it's just a figure of speech."

He looked at me. "It's a figure of speech?'"

"Yeah. *Hands-on* just means learning by doing."

A pause. "Learning by doing?"

"Yes," I said. "The way you ordered your drink tonight, for example. I'd consider that *hands-on* instruction. You learned how to order a drink by ordering a drink."

Recognition dawned on his face. "Oh, yes. I see." His eyes dropped to his mug.

And then, he leaned in a little closer to me across the table.

A smart person in my situation would probably have reacted to that by backing away and putting more space between us. I couldn't bring myself to do it. It wasn't just that he looked incredible, though that was certainly part of it. Despite everything—who and what he was, and the fact that he hadn't been totally honest with me when I'd moved in—I wanted to trust him.

I *did* trust him.

But I didn't trust him enough to let myself be drawn in like that again. Deliberately, and with more difficulty than I would have liked, I made myself shift back in my chair to increase the distance between us again.

He seemed to understand my intent, because he added, "I understand if you still need time to think things through."

He didn't sound happy about it at all.

Which made no sense.

"Even if I can't live with you again, Frederick, you'll just find someone else who can."

His eyes went hard. "Impossible. I . . ." He trailed off, then shook his head. "While yes, I suspect I could find another room-mate, given adequate time, I will not find anyone who can in-struct me so well as you."

That surprised me. "I'm nothing special."

His brow furrowed. Something about what I'd said bothered him, though I couldn't imagine what it might be.

"Over the past two weeks I've discovered that in this city of millions, you are one of a kind." His words carried a quiet inten-sity I could feel in the pit of my stomach. Suddenly, there was no one in that noisy place but the two of us. The din of the room dropped away, inaudible over the sudden rush of blood in my ears. My eyes dropped reflexively to the table.

The Galaxy-sized coffee mug he was cradling looked posi-tively tiny in his hands.

I cleared my throat. "I'm sure that's not true, Frederick. I'm—"

"Do not think for one moment that you are replaceable, Cassie Greenberg," he said. He sounded almost angry. "For you are anything but."

......................

I TURNED MY CONVERSATION WITH FREDERICK OVER AND over in my head all the way back to Sam's place.

The apartment was dark when I let myself inside. I vaguely remembered Scott mentioning an event that night at his univer-sity for faculty and their partners. That must be where he and Sam were.

Given how muddled my thoughts were, I was grateful to have the apartment to myself. I wouldn't be able to handle it if Sam were there with his nosy but well-intentioned questions.

If I was being honest, I was already leaning towards moving back in with Frederick. But I didn't want to rush this decision, no matter how badly he seemed to want me to live with him. If I said no, he'd be fine. Regardless of what he'd said, he'd easily find someone else just as qualified to do . . . whatever this was.

He was distraught when I suggested it, even though it was true. Because of that, I owed it to him to give him an answer as soon as I had one and not just sit on this decision.

I glanced at my phone. It was nearly eleven at night. Frederick wouldn't think it was late if I called him, though. Eleven at night was basically late morning for him. He *might* think I was being a bit pathetic and overeager, though, since we'd just said goodbye an hour ago.

Then again, maybe he'd be glad I'd made up my mind so quickly.

I took a deep breath and closed my eyes.

On the train ride back home I decided that if he could reassure me about one *very* specific thing, I'd be satisfied. The rest of my questions could wait.

I counted to ten, willing my racing heart to slow. Then I called him.

He picked up on the first ring.

"Cassie." His voice was bright with surprise. "Good evening."

"I have one more thing I want to go over with you," I said, leaping right in. This was not the time for small talk. "If we can agree on a few parameters now, I can agree to move back in."

The sound of street traffic—a honking car horn, someone laughing—filtered in from Frederick's side of the phone. He must be out, doing . . . whatever it was he did at night.

I didn't want to think about what that might be.

"What is it?" he asked, unable to hide the eagerness in his voice.

I closed my eyes again, trying to steel my nerves.

"We need to discuss food," I began. "Specifically, *your* food."

"Yes. I had assumed you would want to discuss this eventually."

"You assumed correctly." I bit my lip, trying to think how to phrase what I wanted to ask him. "I believe you when you say you don't feed from living humans—"

"Good," he said, emphatically. "Because I do not."

"You get food from blood banks, then?"

A pause. "Usually, yes."

I made the intentional decision not to think about what *usually* meant. Or about the ethical dilemma stealing from blood banks raised. Drinking blood meant for human patients who needed it would also lead to human deaths, even if indirectly. But I supposed Frederick was just doing what he needed to do to survive in as humane a way as possible.

"I think I can handle the fact that you drink blood, given how you limit yourself."

"I am very glad to hear that."

"But," I continued. "I cannot handle another experience like the one I had the other night. Where I open the fridge and, *bam*—blood." I paused, trying hard not to think about the sickening smell of all that blood in the place where I kept my food. The way Reginald had sucked it down like a kid digging into a juice box at recess. "If anything like that happens again, I'm gone for good."

"I understand," Frederick said, very quickly. "You neither want to see blood in the apartment nor see me eating it."

"That's right."

"I will make it so," he promised. "All kitchen food storage space will be for your use only. I will store my food in a special refrigerator I will keep in my bedroom for this express purpose. Or else keep it out of our home altogether."

*Our home.*

I ignored the warmth that flooded me at those words.

"That should work," I agreed, glad he was not there to see how flushed my face was.

"Good." He paused, then added, "Please believe me when I tell you I never meant for you to see the blood. Or to see one of us eat. I swear I believed you would not be home that night until much later."

I believed him. "What Reginald did wasn't your fault."

"Either way, I will only eat in the apartment when you are not around to see me do it."

"Thank you."

"It is no hardship. There are only a few hours each day when we are both at home, and even fewer when we are both awake."

"You really aren't awake much during the day, are you?"

He paused, and then sighed. "An aftereffect of having been asleep for a century, I'm afraid. I was once able to be awake during daylight hours like any mortal human, even though being in direct sunlight has always been mildly unpleasant. But . . ." He trailed off and sighed again. "I am still regaining my strength, Cassie. For now, the best way for me to do that is to minimize the time I am awake during the daylight hours."

"Of course," I said, as if I understood. But I didn't. I still had so many questions about how his life—or, nonlife—worked. Everything I had ever learned about vampires was from fictional sources. Even among the fictional vampire worlds I'd seen or read about there were a lot of inconsistencies. The vampires in Anne Rice novels, for example, didn't act like the vampires in *Buffy* or *True Blood*.

I assumed Frederick didn't sparkle in the sun like the vampires in *Twilight*, though even that was just a guess. Beyond that, I had no idea how any of it worked.

I figured there'd be time to puzzle it all out later, though. For the time being, I put a mental check mark beside *Food*, reasonably satisfied by what he'd just promised me.

"I still have a lot of questions," I admitted. "And concerns, too. But I'm willing to take a lot on faith, assuming you're up front with me about the big stuff going forward."

"If you agree to live with me and help me adjust to life in the twenty-first century, I will never again omit anything about myself that might impact your life in a significant way."

"Good," I said. And then, before I could stop myself, I added, "I will move back in tomorrow."

I couldn't know for sure, but when Frederick said good night to me a few minutes later I thought I could hear him smiling.

# NINE

Hey Frederick

Cassie. Hello.

Is everything all right?

You are still planning to move in, I hope?

Oh yeah for sure

I just wanted to let you know I'm
arranging to have WiFi set up at
your place

My treat

WiFi?

Yeah. If I'm moving back in
I'll need internet.

Everything I have heard about
the internet makes it sound like a
cancer upon the modern world.

I am not certain I want it.

Well I want it

I need it to watch my shows
and do email and stuff

You're gonna love it
I promise

I can assure you I will not

But if it is something you require
to be happy I'll allow it

IT WAS SURPRISINGLY GOOD TO BE IN FREDERICK'S APART-
ment again. It was three in the afternoon, so just like the last time
I moved in he wasn't there to greet me. He had, however, left the
curtains covering the lake-facing windows open—presumably for
my benefit. The bright autumn sun glinted off the water so enticingly it almost felt like the view was welcoming me back home.

Or maybe I'd just gotten tired of camping out on Sam's sofa.

I quietly entered the apartment, doing my best to ignore the
bizarre decor. The too-dark walls, the creepy stuffed wolf's head
over the mantel, the way the hall closet I was forbidden from
entering smelled vaguely of fruit—it was all just as odd, and still
gave off every bit as much of the *rich people have more money
than sense* vibe as it had a few days ago. The only difference now

was that by knowing he was a centuries-old vampire it all made a bit more sense.

I yawned as I made my way towards my bedroom. I'd stayed up late the night before trying to convince Sam that yes, I was certain moving back in with the same roommate I'd fled from the other day was what I wanted to do. I couldn't blame Sam for his concern; I understood that from all outside appearances I was behaving erratically.

But Frederick's secret wasn't mine to share.

Hopefully, in time Sam wouldn't worry quite so much about me.

As soon as I entered my room my breath caught. Frederick had left my Saugatuck landscapes hanging in the exact same spot they'd been when I moved out. Even though I knew he didn't really understand them.

Two envelopes with my name on them waited for me on the thick mattress of my four-poster bed. Beside them lay a wooden bowl filled with more of those mouthwatering little orange kumquats he'd given me the first time I'd moved in.

I opened the first envelope and out slid two sheets of crisply folded off-white paper, bearing handwriting that at this point I'd recognize anywhere.

*Dear Cassie,*

*Welcome back. I am very glad you decided to move in with me again and hope you are glad as well.*

*I have begun preparing a list of potential lesson topics for us to cover together. Enclosed please find said list, submitted for your approval. Please note that I am so uneducated in the ways of the modern world that I likely*

*do not even know what it is I do not know. If you can
think of any serious omissions from this list, please advise.*

*Yours,
Frederick*

*ps: As you may have noticed, I included "coffee shops and
how to navigate them" in the list. After what happened at
Gossamer's when I tried to order a beverage, I thought you
would agree further education is required.*

I huffed a laugh when I got to the final line.

*Good call, Frederick.*

I reviewed the list he'd included with the letter, worrying my bottom lip as I pondered what he'd jotted down.

*Frederick J. Fitzwilliam's Proposed
Modern Day lessons list*

1. *Coffee shops and how to navigate them.*
2. *General conversation tips (with specific focus on how to
   converse with others in such a way that it is not
   immediately apparent I was born in the eighteenth century).*
3. *Public transportation: how, where, and when?*
4. *The internet (since you insist I learn about it).*
5. *"Tick Tock"*
6. *A brief summary of all major historical events that have
   transpired over the past one hundred years.*

Leaving aside the fact that there was no way I could summarize one hundred years of world history, Frederick's list was incomplete. If he wanted to blend in with Chicago in the twenty-first century, one of the first things he needed to do was ditch the three-piece suits, the cravats, and the wing-tipped shoes and pick up some more modern, less formal clothing. I'd assumed he already knew he dressed like an extra from an old *Masterpiece Theatre* episode and that big changes were necessary—but *Teach me what to wear* wasn't anywhere on this list, so I must have assumed wrong.

I quickly jotted down *Fashion lessons—shopping spree?* at the top of his list so I'd be sure to remember it.

The rest of his list would do, for a start. With some tweaking, I thought I could address his biggest concerns without much difficulty. I didn't know much about TikTok, but I could show him Instagram. Teaching him about the internet might even be fun. I folded up his letter and his list and put them back into their envelope, already thinking through how best to teach him the things he most wanted to know.

As I pondered, I picked up the second envelope where it lay on the mattress. Beneath it was a long, slim, rectangular silver-and-gold foil-wrapped box that looked suspiciously like a gift.

Did Frederick get me another moving-in present?

I slowly opened the second envelope and pulled out the slip of paper inside.

This letter was only three words long.

*Dear Cassie,*

*For your art.*

*Yours,*
*Frederick*

Swallowing, I picked up the box and tore open its careful wrapping. The paper he'd wrapped it in was thick and butter-soft.

The box inside was pale cream in color, its bottom stamped with the famous Arthur & Bros. forest-green logo. Arthur & Bros. was an art supply store based near the University of Chicago that shipped internationally and made some of the nicest paintbrushes I'd ever personally used.

I opened the box. Inside was a set of forty-eight beautiful colored pencils, ranging in colors from pale pink to a blue so dark it was nearly black. I hadn't used colored pencils in any of my work since I was in high school and wasn't certain I'd find a use for these.

The thoughtfulness of this gift, though, was undeniable. I wondered how he'd managed to even get them, given how far away Hyde Park was from his apartment—and how he seemed to have no idea how to pay for things.

I told myself I had to push aside any thoughts of what a generous, thoughtful gift like this might mean.

But I didn't quite manage it.

I grabbed a pen and a scrap of paper from my bag, and scratched a hasty note for him.

Hi Frederick,

Your list looks good to me! It's a place to start anyway. But we also need to work on your clothes. They're very nice but they make you stand out in a way I don't think you want. We should go shopping together soon. What do you think? I'll show you exactly what to buy so no one thinks anything's off about you when they see you in public.

And thank you so much for the pencils. They're beautiful.

Yours,
Cassie

I stared at the way I'd signed the note for a long time before I could convince myself to leave it for him on the kitchen table.

There was nothing weird, nothing worst-idea-in-the-world about signing a note *Yours, Cassie,* in reply to a note signed *Yours, Frederick*—right?

I was just being polite. Doing what any good, friendly roommate would do. There was no reason at all for my heart to be racing when I imagined him reading my note after I'd gone to sleep, grinning so broadly at the way I'd signed it that it activated his killer cheek dimple. No reason whatsoever.

My heart *was* racing, though, all the same, when I left the note on the kitchen table five minutes later.

......................

BECAUSE SO MANY OF THE ARTISTS WHO SHARED SPACE AT Living Life in Color had day jobs during traditional business hours, the studio was always busiest on evenings and weekends. When I got there a few hours after moving back into Frederick's apartment, it was seven o'clock and the studio was packed. There was no space left for me at the big communal table—my favorite spot to work when I made it in.

"There's still an open carrel in the back," Jeremy, a painter who all but lived there from what I could tell, said from his position at the head of the big table.

"Is it the one with the good lamp or the broken one?"

"Oh, Joanne got the broken one fixed on Tuesday."

"Really?" That was a surprise. It was no secret that the studio barely earned enough money in artist rental fees to cover its rent. Joanne generally viewed any repairs that were not absolutely required to keep the building up to code as something she could put off indefinitely.

"I know, I was surprised, too." Jeremy chuckled. "Anyway, it's the carrel that up until Tuesday had a broken lamp but that works just fine now."

The project I wanted to create for my submission had been coming to me in bits and pieces over the past few days. It had solidified that afternoon when I'd walked into my bedroom and saw my Lake Michigan landscapes hanging in the place where that awful oil painting of the fox-hunting party had once been.

Frederick's old painting was hideous. But not all art depicting life in the eighteenth-century English countryside was bad—at least if those classes I took while studying in London when I was in college were halfway accurate. What if I created something inspired by that era, but without the grisly hunting stuff? A manor house, set in the Lake District, with leafy green trees in the background and a babbling brook in the foreground? I still needed to think through exactly how I'd subvert the image through found objects—how to make it modern, how to make it mine—but that would come to me. In the meantime, the sort of image I was imagining would really get me to stretch my oil-painting muscles in a way that excited me.

I dug through my bag for my sketchpad—and for my newest gift from Frederick. Normally I just used a regular old graphite pencil for my preliminary sketches, but for this project, I would draw my planning sketches in color.

# TEN

*Text messages between Mr. Frederick J. Fitzwilliam and Mr. Reginald R. Cleaves*

Can I ask your honest opinion?

Always

What do you think of my clothes?

The way I dress, I mean.

Do I dress stylishly?

Stylishly?

Yes.

I think you dress great buddy

Good.

I do too. Thank you.

I think my clothes look very refined.

> I mean I kept all your clothes carefully
> preserved for you while you slept right?
>
> So I might be biased

Perhaps, but I also happen to think that
in this isolated instance, you did well.

> Awwww thank you 😃
>
> But hey why do you suddenly
> care about your clothes 👀

I always care about my clothes.

> Ummmmm in the three centuries Ive
> known you youve never once asked my
> opinion on your clothes or appearance
>
> Why are you asking now? 👀 👀 👀

I was just . . .

Curious.

> Lolllllll u sure it doesnt have anything
> to do with that GIRL moving back
> in with u 👀 👀 👀

**I haven't the slightest idea**
**what you're talking about.**

THE NEXT EVENING—AFTER THE SUN HAD SET, AND FREDER-
ick had welcomed me back to the apartment in person with a
small smile playing on his lips—we found ourselves huddled together at the kitchen table in front of my laptop.

Frederick was scowling, arms folded tightly across his chest as
he glared at my screen.

"What am I looking at, Cassie?"

"Instagram."

"Instagram?"

"Yes."

Frederick pointed at the filtered picture of a breakfast Sam
had, according to the caption, eaten a few months ago on his
honeymoon in Hawaii. "Instagram is . . . pictures of food?"

"Sometimes, yeah."

Frederick scoffed, clearly unimpressed.

"Reginald really didn't show you anything on the internet
before now?" I asked, a little incredulous. But it was a rhetorical
question. It couldn't have been clearer that before I got Frederick's internet up and running that afternoon, he'd never been
exposed to anything online.

Frederick shook his head. "He didn't."

"How did you know to ask about TikTok, then?"

A pause. "I thought it was a new kind of music," he admitted,
a bit sheepishly.

I couldn't help but smile at that. He really was adorably clueless. "Really?"

"It's called *TikTok*," he said. "That's the sound a clock makes,
is it not? I think it was a reasonable guess."

He had a point there. If I'd just woken up from a century-long nap, I might have reached the same conclusion. As it was, I was born just a few decades ago and I barely knew what TikTok was, either.

"Well, either way, being connected to the internet is essential in the twenty-first century," I said. "It's the only way people get their information now."

"That's probably why Reginald didn't connect me," Frederick said, darkly. "He fed me for a century and made sure my bills got paid so I wouldn't waste away or be homeless when I woke up. But if, upon waking, I had reliable access to information at my fingertips it would have impeded his ability to play practical jokes on me."

I snorted. "I think I'm going to be a nicer life assistant than he was."

"There's no question in my mind about that."

He turned his attention back to my laptop. Earlier, I'd explained to him that while I wasn't familiar with all corners of the internet or all social media platforms—for example, I'd only joined TikTok for funny cat videos and barely understood it—I *was* regularly on Instagram and could show him around.

He'd agreed readily enough, though in hindsight I realized that that was because he hadn't known what Instagram was. Ever since I'd pulled up Sam's page Frederick had made it abundantly clear he regretted that decision—and possibly regretted asking we engage in internet lessons together at all.

"What is the point of technology dedicated solely to sharing pictures of breakfast foods?" He sounded so baffled—almost offended, really—that I had to bite my lip to keep from laughing. He was the broad-chested, gorgeous, not-quite-living embodiment of the *OK boomer* meme. The fact that he looked like a man in his mid-thirties only made it funnier.

And more adorable.

"Instagram isn't just pictures of food," I countered, trying to keep a straight face.

He pointed an accusing finger at the screen. "Your friend's account seems to be entirely pictures of food."

"Sam likes taking pictures food," I admitted. "But Instagram lets you share pictures of anything you want with people all over the world. Not just pictures of food."

He seemed to consider that. "Oh?"

"Yes," I confirmed. "You can share pictures of important news events, or of beautiful places. And, yes, okay—sometimes people share pictures of meals they've enjoyed. Especially if they were somewhere special or exciting when they ate it."

"Why would people all over the world care what your friend Sam ate while on holiday?"

I opened my mouth to respond, but then realized I didn't have a good answer for that.

"I . . . don't really know," I admitted. "But we could take a picture of that bowl of oranges you keep on the counter for me and post that if you want. They're pretty."

He glanced over his shoulder at the oranges in question, then shook his head disapprovingly. "I simply do not understand this modern urge to share every errant thought one has with the entire world the instant it happens."

"I can't say I completely understand it, either," I admitted. "I use Instagram to promote my art. Other than that, I don't use social media much."

"Then why are you insisting I learn how to use it?" He sounded petulant, like a small child on the verge of throwing a tantrum over having to do his math homework. "If this is social media, social media seems like nothing but a noisy, invasive waste of time."

As he continued to scowl at my laptop, I became nearly over-whelmed with sympathy for him. When Frederick fell into his century-long sleep, he'd left behind a world of handwritten letters and horseback riding. Waking up to social media and the Kar-dashians had to be an incredible shock. He was like an octoge-narian learning how to use a computer—only worse.

Octogenarians were more than two hundred years younger than he was.

I was determined to stick with this lesson, though. Frederick may not have intended to ask me to teach him about social media when he asked about TikTok, but honestly? It was a good idea. Now that we were doing this, I wasn't going to let him get in his own way.

"You don't have to use social media," I said, keeping my voice gentle. "But if you want to blend in, you need to at least know what social media *is*."

"I am not certain that is true."

"It is."

His full, plush lips turned down into a pout. My centuries-old vampire roommate was *pouting*. It was as ridiculous a sight as it was riveting. He bit his lip, and my eyes fell helplessly to his mouth. His front teeth looked no different from anyone else's. Did Frederick have fangs somewhere, the way Reginald did?

If he pressed those beautiful lips to my throat, would he be able to feel my heart beating beneath the skin?

I still had so many questions. Some of which I didn't dare admit even to myself.

"The clarity of the photographs you can see on the internet *is* astounding." Frederick's grudging compliment of Sam's pictures cut into my daydreams, saving me from myself. Thinking about his mouth on my neck—on any part of my body—would lead to nothing good.

I sat up a bit straighter in my chair, feeling a bit flushed. "I'm pretty sure Sam used a filter on that."

"A what?"

I shook my head. A lesson on Instagram filters could wait for another day. "Never mind."

Fortunately, Frederick let it drop. "My understanding from Reginald is that there is a way to interact with images you see on social media. How do I do that?"

"Oh. Well, on Instagram you can like a post by clicking that little heart, or you can leave a comment."

Frederick frowned. "A comment?"

"Yeah."

"What sort of comments does one leave on Instagram?"

I thought for a moment. "I mean, people say whatever they want. Usually people try to be funny. Sometimes they might try to be mean, I guess. But that would be a dick thing to do."

"A . . . dick thing to do," he repeated slowly, sounding confused.

"Exactly."

Frederick shook his head and muttered something under his breath that sounded a bit like *incomprehensible modern slang*, though I couldn't be certain. Then he asked, "May I leave a comment on this picture your friend has posted of his breakfast?"

His question surprised me, after how openly hostile he'd been to the very idea of social media. It was good that he wanted to learn, though. "Sure." I pointed to the comment box. "Just type whatever you want to say right here."

He stared at the keyboard, then began to peck at the keys very slowly with two large index fingers.

"I am still unfamiliar with modern keyboards," he admitted as he painstakingly crafted his message. "They differ so much from the typewriters I am used to."

I thought of the old typewriters the Art Institute of Chicago had in its collection, and tried to picture Frederick in his old-fashioned clothes, using one of them.

"You're pretty good at texting," I said. "I'd think a phone would be even harder to use."

Frederick shrugged. "I discovered a feature called *talk to text*," he said, as he continued typing. For someone who usually moved so fluidly, who seemed so at ease in his own body, he was a clumsy and graceless typist. It was oddly endearing. "Without it I would never use my phone at all."

Talk to text would explain the length of some of the texts he'd sent me. Smiling a little, I glanced up at my laptop's screen. My smile vanished when I read what Frederick was writing.

While this photograph is nice enough, I fail to see the point of using advanced technology for such pedestrian purposes. Why did you share it? Yours in good health, Frederick

I stared at him. "You can't post that," I said, at the exact same time he hit *send* and the message posted.

"Why not?" Frederick sounded genuinely confused. "You just said people could leave whatever messages they wanted on Instagram."

"Not when you're signed in with my account." I batted Frederick's hands away from the keyboard, ignoring his protests. "Delete it. That was a mean thing to say."

"It was not. I was simply asking for clarification."

"It *was* mean. Sam will think you're a dickhead." Of course, Sam already didn't like Frederick. I still hadn't explained why I'd fled this apartment and showed up on his doorstep with no notice, or why I went back to Frederick just as quickly. Knowing my history with terrible living situations and terrible men, Sam was almost certainly drawing the worst conclusions.

The pensive look on Frederick's face suggested he'd somehow guessed what I was thinking. "Your friend already has plenty of reasons to mistrust me," he said. "If I were him, I probably wouldn't trust me very much, either. I suppose you're right. I do not want to make matters worse by insulting his choice in breakfast photography."

"No." I shook my head. "You don't."

"Very well," he said. "You can take the comment down." He closed his eyes, his long, thick eyelashes fanning out along the tops of his cheeks. I found myself transfixed by them, and by the slow, steady rise and fall of his chest as he breathed.

"I . . . was once known for my straightforward demeanor," he said, his voice just above a whisper. "It was an admirable trait among men at the time. I gather that now, one must mince words often in order not to offend." He paused again. "None of this is intuitive to me. I feel I shall forever be a bumbling idiot in public."

His shoulders slumped, making him look so sad my heart ached. The enormity of what he faced, what he was trying to do—and everything he had lost over the long centuries of his life—hung unspoken and heavy in the air between us.

"I'll do what I can to help." My words, the offer I was making, felt inadequate. Too small.

Slowly, he opened his eyes, a quiet smolder in them that hadn't been there before.

"I know you will." A beat. "Will you show me *your* Instagram account?"

I blinked at him. "What did you say?"

He frowned. "Did you not hear me?"

"I heard you. I'm just surprised."

"Why?"

"I didn't think you wanted to look at Instagram."

"I don't want to look at Sam's breakfasts on Instagram," he corrected. "But if it's so important I learn about social media and the internet I would at least like to see something interesting."

I hesitated.

"My account's boring."

"I am certain it's not."

"Instagram has zillions of hilarious cat reels," I hedged, my cheeks going hot. "Let's look at one of those."

I leaned forward to click on one of my favorite cat accounts. The inside of my arm brushed up against his forearm in the process, sending an involuntary shiver down my spine. I closed my eyes against the unexpected rush of sensation that coursed through me, just from that.

"Cassie."

Tentatively, he placed one of his hands on top of mine, stopping my scrolling—and my breathing—instantly. His hand was cool, his palm smooth against my knuckles. I glanced down at our hands, marveling at the contrast between them as I fought to steady my breathing. Warm, and cool. Small, and large. Tanned, and pale.

It was the first time he had ever intentionally touched me. This seemed to occur to him in the same moment it occurred to me, and it surprised him just as much. His eyes widened, pupils dilating as he regarded me.

It took an embarrassing amount of willpower not to twine our fingers together, just to see what that would look like, too.

"Please stop distracting me."

Frederick's voice was at my ear, tickling the little hairs at my nape, causing my forearms to erupt in a riot of gooseflesh.

I swallowed, trying to focus on the cat on my laptop screen. The kitty was cute, and really good at snowboarding. He deserved my full attention.

"Distracting you?" I breathed. I could barely hear my voice over the rush of blood in my ears.

"Yes." Frederick removed his hand from mine. I tried to tamp down an irrational wave of disappointment at the loss of contact. "I want to see your Instagram account. You are trying to distract me with cats."

I took a deep, steadying breath, and chanced a glance at his face. His eyes sparkled with amusement.

"It's not working?" I managed.

"No. I like cats well enough. But I have seen cats before. I have never seen your page." And then, almost as an afterthought, he added: "Please show it to me."

Did vampires have magical powers that made humans want to do their bidding or something? I wasn't sure. All I knew was one moment I was about to tell him that while he may have seen cats before, there was no way he'd seen one *snowboard*—and the next I was loading up my Instagram, just like he'd asked me to.

Maybe it wasn't magical power at all. Perhaps it was the lingering effects of how it had felt, having his hand on mine.

I blinked up at the monitor, and at the goofy selfie from five years ago that served as my profile picture.

I cleared my throat. "Here it is."

He hummed in appreciation. "How do I look through the pictures?"

"Like this," I said, showing him how to scroll through. "I

mostly post things I've made, but it isn't a *true* art account because there are also selfies and pictures of friends mixed in."

"Selfies?"

"Oh." Of course he wouldn't know that word. "Selfies are pictures you take of yourself."

"Ah." He nodded. "*Self*-ies."

He figured out how to maneuver through the photos on my Instagram quickly enough. He looked at the pictures I'd taken in Saugatuck of me, Sam, and Scott, our arms around each other as we smiled up at the camera. He took in pictures of the beach trash I'd collected to make the canvases in my bedroom—and the pictures of me, grinning like a proud fool in pigtails and flip-flops, standing in front of it.

Frederick went through the pictures, looking at each one with mild interest.

Until, that is, he came to a picture Sam had taken the last day of our vacation: me, on the one day that entire week that could have been accurately described as hot, wearing the only bikini I owned. It was bright pink, the bottoms covered in white daisies.

It wasn't anything special.

As far as bikinis went it wasn't even all that revealing.

Frederick paused his scrolling. His eyes widened, his free hand clenching into a tight fist at his side.

He looked like he was about to have an embolism. Or whatever the vampire equivalent of an embolism was.

He pointed a shaking finger at the picture.

"What are you *wearing*?" His jaw was clenched, the tendons of his neck standing out in sharp relief.

"A bathing suit."

He shook his head. Closed his eyes. The whirring of the refrigerator clicked on, filling the room with white noise.

"That," he said, his voice a gravelly rasp, "is *not* a bathing suit."

I was about to ask what he was talking about—because yes, clearly it was a bathing suit. And then I realized he was likely used to women's bathing suits that covered you from head to toe.

But why would he care what I wore on a beach vacation years ago?

"It *is* a bathing suit, Frederick." I glanced at the image of myself, smiling at the camera. "I know it's different from the bathing suits you're used to, but . . ."

The rest of my words died in my throat as I took in his expression. The glint in his eyes, the tight set of his jaw . . .

I'd been wrong. He didn't look angry.

He looked *murderous*.

I licked my lips, casting about for something to say, trying to make sense of his bizarre reaction. "You don't like the picture?"

His scowl deepened. Clearly this was the understatement of the century. "No."

A hard little knot formed in the pit of my stomach. I knew I hardly had a supermodel's body. My curvy hips and long torso made wearing a bikini a bold choice. But did he have to be so mean about it?

"You . . . don't think I look good in it?" As soon as I asked the question, I felt silly for caring. What did it matter if he thought I looked good or not? It didn't matter.

Except for some reason . . . it did.

"That is not what I said," Frederick muttered.

I frowned at him, puzzled by how he was acting. "I don't understand."

Silence stretched between us, punctuated only by the ticking of the grandfather clock in the living room.

When Frederick opened his eyes again they were full of a fiery possessiveness that stunned me. He pushed back from his chair with so much force he nearly knocked it to the floor.

"What I said, Cassie, was that I did not like the *picture*." He was facing the window that looked out over Lake Michigan now, his back to me. Which was just as well. If the look on his face was even half as heated as the tone of his voice, I wasn't sure what I would do. Probably something Sam would lecture me for later. Possibly I'd burst into flames.

His hands were still clenched at his sides, his whole body taut as a bowstring.

"Perhaps young, beautiful women *do* routinely dress in next to nothing at all when they go to the beach. Perhaps my reaction to seeing you dressed this way is incredibly old-fashioned." He paused and turned to face me. His eyes were full of torment—and something else I didn't have words for, but which my body somehow recognized all the same. My heart sped up at the way he was looking at me now, my breathing coming short and too quick.

"I'm allowed to dress how I like, you know."

"You are," he conceded. "I have no right to dictate how you dress or live your life. My opinion does not—and should not— matter. But the idea of other people being able to see so much of your body . . ." He looked away again, then sighed. "Perhaps I have lived too long."

By the time I managed to gather my wits about me enough to respond, he'd turned and stalked out of the room, leaving palpable, unbearable tension in his wake.

# ELEVEN

**Diary entry of Mr. Frederick J. Fitzwilliam,
dated November 4**

Cassie went to bed two hours ago.

Every time I close my eyes I can still see her—beaming up at the camera in that flimsy excuse for clothing, her hair a golden halo around her head, her body backlit and glorious.

I am filled with rage.

At the photographer for taking that picture.

At Cassie for allowing so many others to see her practically naked.

At all seven billion people on this planet who have the theoretical ability to see that picture of her with a few simple clicks of a button.

At myself.

As I sit hunched over my desk I try desperately to ignore the urgent, now-familiar ache in my loins. As Cassie sleeps innocently, unknowingly in the next room, I clutch at what remains of my sanity and of my self-control.

Because God's thumbs—when I saw that picture of her all I could think was how badly I want Cassie to wear that "bathing suit" of hers for <u>me</u>.

If I had been there when it was taken, it would have been all I could do to keep myself from easing those delicate little straps of fabric off her shoulders and baring the rest of her beautiful body to my eyes.

I am a reprehensible creature.

Cassie is a young, vibrant, <u>human</u> woman who does not deserve to be the object of my lustful imaginings. Tomorrow, she is taking me shopping to help me pick out what she insists will be more suitable casual clothing than my current wardrobe. I expect this will involve her evaluating my body and the way it looks in various outfits. What if she needs to <u>touch</u> me as part of this process? I am harder than a rock just imagining it.

If I were not already damned for all eternity I certainly would be now.

I am, as Reginald might say, in <u>way</u> over my head.

FJF

"SO. YOUR ROOMMATE NEEDS A MAKEOVER, HUH?" SAM fought to keep the amusement out of his voice but wasn't managing it well. He was biting the inside of his cheek, clearly fighting a smile. "Must be urgent if you called for my help."

The mall was crowded, full of noisy suburban teenagers and frazzled parents with kids in tow. I proposed Frederick meet me there on a Tuesday evening because I'd assumed the mall would be relatively quiet and empty midweek. But ten minutes earlier I was nearly run over by a woman pushing a stroller, and I realized a person like me who rarely went to malls had no basis for making assumptions.

"Not so much a makeover as a new wardrobe," I said. I took a bite of the pretzel I'd just bought from a mall kiosk, marveling at the way its chemical deliciousness melted on my tongue. I had no idea what actually went into those pretzels. It was probably better that way.

"A new wardrobe?"

"Yeah. He needs new clothes pretty urgently. That's why I asked you to join us. You're a man and I'm not. You'll know more about men's fashion than I do."

In truth, Sam didn't know more about men's fashion than many people. His approach to clothes hadn't really evolved past what he'd worn in college, except for the suits he wore to work. I mostly asked Sam to join us at the last minute in the hopes he'd serve as a buffer between Frederick and me as we picked out clothes and he tried them on. Because now that I was at the mall, I realized it was one thing to tell your extremely handsome, off-limits, vampire roommate that he needed to dress differently— and an entirely different thing to actually *take* your extremely handsome, off-limits, vampire roommate to the mall, help him pick out clothes, and then evaluate how they all looked on his gorgeous body as you helped him make decisions.

Especially given how our Instagram lesson had ended.

It had been two days, and I still wasn't certain what his reaction to my bikini picture meant. Not for lack of thinking about it endlessly from every possible angle, of course.

I'd thought about it at work. While trying to work on my submission for the art show. While trying to fall asleep at night, hyper-aware that he was awake and in the next room over from me, going about his nightly routine.

I'd spent more time than I wanted to admit to myself reliving exactly how he'd looked at me before storming out of the room—his eyes flashing with, what? Anger? Jealousy? Or something else?

We hadn't spoken since then, save for a handful of notes back and forth coordinating this shopping trip. If I was going to survive two hours of looking at Frederick in jeans and Henleys, I needed my best friend with me.

"I thought your roommate dressed well, though." I could hear the teasing smirk in Sam's voice as I leaned against a large white pillar bearing a perfume ad on one side and a floor plan of the mall on the other. "I thought he was a *dreamboat*."

My cheeks flushed with embarrassment over the situation and mild annoyance with my friend. "He does. He is. But . . ." I bit my lip, trying to think through how to describe Frederick's *dresses-like-he-lived-one-hundred-years-ago* problem without also outing him as a vampire.

And then Frederick chose that moment to stride into view, sparing me from having to say anything at all. As always, he was dressed like he was on his way to meet Jane Austen, with an expensive-looking dark gray three-piece wool suit and black shoes that had been polished to a shine.

He'd left the cravat at home, which was a good thing. But I'd been hoping he'd leave his suit jacket at home for this errand, too. It would only get in the way when he tried things on. That said, he looked incredible—even if more out of place than ever at this suburban mall.

One glance at Sam told me he agreed with my conclusion. Frederick looked good. It was the first time he'd ever seen Fred-

erick in person, and I could all but feel my best friend warring
with himself as he fought to keep his eyes trained on Frederick's
perfect, chiseled face, rather than let them trail over his broad
shoulders and at the way his perfectly tailored clothing fit his
body.

Frederick nimbly stepped around a clutch of teenagers chatting animatedly to one another with an ease I wouldn't have expected of him, and then joined us where we stood by the mall
floor plan. He looked at Sam, stopping just short of turning his
back on me completely. The heated intensity in his eyes from the
other night was gone, replaced with a pleasant, blank expression.
To see him, you'd never imagine that two nights ago he'd completely lost his shit at a picture of me in a bikini.

He had, though.

If the way he was standing there, avoiding my gaze, was any
guide, he didn't want to unpack what any of that meant just then.

Come to think of it—neither did I.

"Hello. I am Frederick J. Fitzwilliam," he said, extending a
hand for Sam to shake.

Sam took it eagerly. I had to stifle a laugh in my palm. Who
was this person, and what did he do with my friend who'd been
so opposed to me moving back in with Frederick?

"Nice to meet you, Frederick," he said. "I'm Sam."

"It is nice to meet you as well. Cassie told me you will be joining us tonight to help me select clothing." Frederick gestured to
me without looking at me, his eyes still trained on Sam. A wave
of irrational disappointment went through me when I realized he
was just as glad to have a human buffer for this as I was.

"I hope I can help," Sam said, too cheerfully.

"As do I. I know little about modern fashion." He gestured
vaguely to himself. "As I'm sure you can see."

By this point Sam had completely lost the battle on checking out the way Frederick filled out his suit. He was openly staring at him now. He swallowed hard, then rubbed the back of his neck. "Oh, I'm sure you know . . . some things."

"I do not," Frederick insisted. If he noticed how not-surreptitiously Sam was ogling him, he showed no sign of it. "I trust Cassie when she tells me I must dress more casually as I go about my daily activities. But it has been my lifelong instinct to dress as formally as possible for every occasion."

"Yeah," Sam agreed. "You can't wear a suit like that to, like— the grocery store. Or to take out the garbage."

Frederick sighed and shook his head. "As it happens, I wear this exact suit to take out the garbage every Wednesday evening."

"And that's a problem," I reminded him, inserting myself into the conversation for the first time since Frederick showed up. Frederick still wasn't facing me, but his entire body tensed when I spoke, as if just the sound of my voice was enough to cause him anxiety. I ignored the confusing jumble of emotions that elicited in me and pressed on. "If you want to . . . be more comfortable, you should wear T-shirts and jeans occasionally."

I raised my eyebrows meaningfully, so he'd know that *be more comfortable* was code for *less like a centuries-old vampire*. "You're right." Frederick's look of resigned determination made him look like someone had just volunteered him to chaperone a middle school dance or told him he'd been elected to the board of directors of a homeowners association—and that while he'd rather do anything else, he was too honorable to back out now.

I turned to Sam. "Should we start at Gap, or somewhere else?" It had been a while since I'd been shopping anywhere that wasn't online, but I seemed to remember Gap was good at this mall.

"It depends what your budget is. The Nordstrom here also has nice things."

Frederick looked directly at Sam and asked, "Between Nordstrom and Gap, which would you say has *nicer* casual men's clothing?"

"Nordstrom for sure."

"Then Nordstrom it is." That decided, Frederick pulled out an honest-to-god pocket watch on a chain from his pocket. Checking the time he said, "I believe we have two hours before the mall closes and our errand ends. Shall we begin?"

"Wait, hold on." Now Sam was pulling his phone from *his* pocket. "Shit, it's my firm."

He put his phone up to his ear. "Sam Collins." His voice was so different—stiffer, more formal—than it was when he spoke to me. It must be one of the partners calling him.

Frederick frowned at me. "His employer calls him in the evening?"

"Sam's a lawyer," I explained. "He's in his first year and he works absolutely inhuman hours. His husband Scott told me he's at the office close to seventy hours a week right now."

Frederick looked horrified. "That's horrible."

"I know."

Sam had pulled a notebook from his bag and was jotting things down as he listened to whatever the person on the other end of the line was telling him. "I don't understand why Kellogg is panicking over the merger. It's happening next week, I understand that, but . . ." Another pause. "Yes, of course. I'll draft that memo as soon as I get into the office." He glanced at his wristwatch. "I'm out in Schaumburg right now but I can be there in forty-five minutes."

Sam hung up, then looked at me, eyes apologetic.

My stomach plunged somewhere in the general vicinity of my shoes. "Do you have to go now?" I asked, my panic rising.

"Yeah. I'm really sorry. This merger we're handling is . . ." He trailed off, shaking his head. For the first time I noticed the dark circles ringing his eyes. "There are no problems whatsoever with this merger. It should go off without a hitch next week, but our client is panicking and I need to go calm them down."

And then, he raised an eyebrow and leaned in a little closer before adding, in a low voice, "I am *especially* sorry I'll miss Frederick trying on clothes."

That was almost enough to distract me from the terror I was feeling over the fact that I would soon be alone with Frederick in various states of dress and undress for an entire evening. I swatted my best friend. "You are a *married man*, Sam."

"Married, not dead." He paused, then added, "In all seriousness, he seems like an okay guy. A bit strange, but . . ." He shrugged. "I'm no longer convinced you're making the worst mistake of your life in living with him."

I snorted. "Good. Now go be a lawyer. We'll be fine." I looked over at Frederick, who looked anything *but* fine with this change in plans. His eyes were saucer-wide, making him look nearly as terrified at the idea of doing this alone with me as I felt.

"Text me if anything comes up or if you have any questions," Sam said, shouldering his messenger bag. "I'll get in touch with you tomorrow to see how it went."

And then, he was gone. Leaving me alone with Frederick, to go try on casual men's clothing.

This was going to be great.

Absolutely great.

Frederick cleared his throat beside me. His eyes were on his shoes, the left fingers of his hand drumming rapidly on his upper thigh.

"I am . . . glad you don't work as hard as he does, Cassie." His voice was so quiet I had to strain to hear him over the din of the crowded shopping mall. "I would worry a lot, I think, if you did."

His eyes met mine, soft and so warm, before flitting away again a moment later.

He cleared his throat. "Shall we go to Nordstrom, then?"

Nordstrom. Right.

"Yeah," I said, feeling breathless and a little dizzy at the abrupt change in subject. How on earth was I going to survive this? "Nordstrom it is."

. . . . . . . . . . . . . . . . . . . .

THE LAST TIME I'D BEEN IN A NORDSTROM WAS NEARLY twenty years ago, when I'd come to this same mall with my mom to try on dresses for my bat mitzvah. Given how long ago that was, it was astonishing how strong the feeling of déjà vu was the moment I walked into the store. The perfume that seemed to permeate the air, the fluorescent lighting—all of it brought me right back to being thirteen years old, miserably uncomfortable in my own skin, and wishing I were just about anywhere other than where I was.

From the way Frederick's hands kept clenching and un-clenching at his sides, I suspected that he was feeling much as I had all those years ago.

"I had not expected this establishment to be so . . ." He trailed off, his dark eyes wide and showing how overwhelmed he was as he tried to take everything in.

"You hadn't expected it to be so what?" I asked, as I guided him past the ostentatious shoe department that had its own wine bar.

He stopped abruptly when we reached the display of five-thousand-dollar winter coats that looked like they'd been cobbled together from rhinestones and trash bags.

He frowned at them. I could only guess at what he was thinking right now.

"I hadn't expected this establishment to be so . . . *much*."

He didn't elaborate. But he didn't have to. I understood what he meant perfectly.

My hand was still on his elbow as I steered him towards the men's department, applying only the gentlest pressure to encourage him to move to the left. It was noisy in there, the store filled with shoppers and salespeople and piped-in generic background music—but even still, I heard the way his breath hitched at my touch as easily as if there'd been no one else there at all.

I tried to follow the signage for the men's department, but there were so many *other* departments in that massive store it was a challenge. There were also way too many other people. It was nearly as crowded in there as it was in the main area of the mall. It felt like we were bumping into yet another well-dressed shopper every ten feet.

We must have wandered around Nordstrom for a solid ten minutes before finally finding the men's department. It was on the sixth floor, past the home goods section, and at the very opposite end of the store from the mall entrance. It was so much smaller than the cumulative parts of the store dedicated to women's clothing that it felt a bit like a forgotten stepchild.

What they did sell to men, though, looked just as expensive as everything else Nordstrom sold. Racks of suit jackets in conservative colors, adorned with thousand-dollar price tags, greeted us. Just behind them was a silk tie display that took up an entire wall.

Fortunately, they did seem to sell more casual stuff as well. A little further into the section we found jeans that would make Frederick stand out a lot less the next time he went out.

"Can I help you?"

A slender woman in a black sheath dress, with her dark hair pulled back into a severe but elegant bun, appeared at Frederick's elbow. I noted her name tag—this was Eleanor M.—and the fact that she looked about my age, albeit far more put together. I wondered if Nordstrom required employees to buy the clothes they wore to work the way The Limited did when I worked there back in college.

"Yes," Frederick said. "My name is Frederick J. Fitzwilliam. I require clothing."

The salesperson's eyebrows shot up. "Clothing?"

"Yes."

She continued to look expectantly at Frederick, as if waiting for clarification. When none came, she pivoted on one of her expensive-looking, three-inch heels to face me.

"What he means," I began, feeling a bit awkward, "is he wants to try on some jeans. And some casual shirts. He already has a lot of suits but wants some clothes he can wear, like—around the house, or to a coffee shop. Things like that."

"Ah." She gave me a knowing smile. And then, in a conspiratorial stage whisper she added, "Your boyfriend's a real workaholic, always-at-the-office type, isn't he?"

*Boyfriend.*

My heart lodged itself in my esophagus at the same time my stomach did a not entirely unpleasant somersault. I glanced at Frederick. From the thunderstruck look on his face, I could tell he'd heard exactly what she'd just said.

"Oh . . . he's . . . ," I stammered. I tried to laugh. "He's not my—"

But she wasn't there to hear the end of my sentence, already walking away and gesturing for us to follow her away from the suits and towards the men's section's more casual clothing. I glanced at Frederick, following just behind me. I didn't think a person's eyes could even *get* that wide.

"Our store's men's department is the largest one out of all the Nordstroms in the Chicagoland area," she boasted, oblivious to my rioting thoughts. "Our suiting options are especially robust. But I gather you aren't here for that."

"No," Frederick agreed. He gestured to me, adding, "Cassie says I need to wear more casual clothes in order to blend in with modern society."

The salesperson hummed, nodding sagely. "Yes. Well, you've come to the right place." She stopped walking when we reached several racks of jeans. "Are you interested in distressed jeans or a more classic look?"

Frederick raised a suspicious eyebrow at the salesperson. He gingerly plucked at a pair of jeans that were so distressed they looked like they'd soaked in a vat of acid for two weeks.

"I am *not* wearing this," he said, flatly. "God's thumbs, Cassie. This garment is more hole than fabric."

"He'd like a more classic look," I said, very quickly, to the salesperson. I steered Frederick to a rack of jeans that I thought he might find more acceptable.

He blinked. "These?"

"These," I agreed.

He considered me a moment before asking, "How do I know which of these will fit me?"

At this, the saleswoman turned to Frederick, letting her eyes trail down his long form and then back up again. They lingered on his chest a few beats longer than strictly necessary, given that we were talking about jeans. My hands clenched into involuntary fists at my sides, an unpleasant, hot sensation I was absolutely *not* going to parse filling my chest.

"What is your inseam?" she asked. "What about your waist measurement?"

Frederick worried his lower lip, looking like he was trying to work out the answer to a difficult math problem in his head.

"It has been some time since I had my measurements taken," he admitted. "I'll admit I don't remember them."

"I'm happy to measure you," Eleanor M. offered. She pulled out a fabric measuring tape from somewhere and approached him.

Frederick looked as terrified as if he'd just tripped over a hornet's nest. He took a reflexive step back and away from the salesperson. "That's *quite* all right," he said, sounding scandalized. He looked at me, then at the rack of jeans. He picked up five pairs at random, holding each of them up to his body in turn. "Which of these do you think look most like they will fit me?"

I considered each of them as he held them up to himself, fighting hard against the instinct to imagine him in that dressing room, taking his trousers off and pulling on the jeans he was holding. "It's . . . hard to say," I hedged. "Why not take all of them with you into the dressing room and see?"

He nodded, like this made a lot of sense to him.

"I will be trying these on," he informed the salesperson. "If you could bring me casual shirts in every size and color available that would be a good use of your time."

. . . . . . . . . . . . . . . . . . . . .

"DON'T LOOK."

"I'm not looking."

"Are you *certain* you are not looking?"

I rolled my eyes but kept them closed. "The door is closed, Frederick. Even if my eyes were open I couldn't see you. But yes, I swear on my father's kombucha that I am not looking."

A pause. I could hear fabric hitting the floor from within the dressing room. "You swear on your father's . . . what?"

I huffed a laugh. "It's this thing my mom and I say when we want to make fun of my dad. In his retirement he's gotten very into brewing it."

"Brewing . . . what?"

"Kombucha. It's this naturally fermented tea stuff. It's pretty good, but Dad is obsessed with it now. There are dozens of bottles in his garage in various stages of consumption readiness."

"I see," he said, though I was certain he didn't. A loud zipping sound came from within the dressing room. Frederick must have been trying on the jeans. I squeezed my eyes shut tighter, trying not to imagine the denim sliding up his bare legs, the waistband settling low on his hips.

"Yeah," I breathed, shaking my head to clear away unnecessary images. "Anyway, whenever Mom and I want to tease Dad, we'll preface something mundane with 'I swear it on my father's kombucha.' Mom and I laugh, Dad gets annoyed; it's a great time."

Silence from inside the dressing room. More rustling fabric. A hanger being taken from the wall.

The lock on the dressing room door turned. The door opened.

"Not one word of what you just said made any sense whatsoever," Frederick said, stepping out of the dressing room. "But you can open your eyes now."

I did.

My mouth fell open.

Frederick looked great in the parade of old-fashioned suits I'd seen him in since we'd met, of course. More than great. But I realized now that his consistently too-formal, out-of-date attire served as a constant reminder to me that Frederick was out of my league in every imaginable way—and completely off-limits.

Untouchable. And *other*.

Now, though . . .

"What do you think?" he asked. "Do I look like I fit in with modern society now?"

With difficulty, I tore my eyes from the broad expanse of his chest now covered in a forest-green Henley that fit him like a glove and met his gaze. He was fidgeting a little as I looked back at him, drumming his fingertips against his upper thigh again, and looking at me with a nervous intensity that stole the breath from my lungs.

I let my eyes trail slowly down his body, drinking him in, taking in his new shirt and the dark blue jeans that fit him so well you wouldn't have guessed he'd had no idea what size he was twenty minutes ago. The other jeans he'd tried on lay folded in a pile on the chair beside him; his suit hung neatly on a hanger in the dressing room.

I focused on these other details to distract myself from how Frederick not only looked just as hot in more casual clothes as he did in his stuffy suits, but also how he now looked *attainable* in a way that was dangerous to me, specifically.

I had to avert my eyes. Looking right at him felt a little too much like looking directly at the sun.

"You look great. You look unbelievable, actually." I heard his sharp intake of breath, only then realizing that that hadn't quite been what he'd asked me. All he'd asked was whether he looked like he fit in. My stomach swooped, my face suddenly feeling like it was on fire. *Idiot.* "That is . . . that is to say—"

"You think I look great?" He was looking at me with an expression that fell somewhere between surprise and pleasure. He stepped from the dressing room, stopping when he was only a few inches away from me. I took an involuntary breath, breathing in the scent of lavender soap and new clothes that clung to him. "Really?"

His tone was so hopeful. It set off a wave of butterflies in my stomach that I tried to ignore.

I nodded—though *great* didn't begin to do justice to how he looked.

"Yeah. Really."

He gave me a bashful, lopsided smile that activated his killer dimple, then looked down at his arms. He rubbed one of his thumbs along his collarbones, and then across his chest. "The fabric feels nicer than I expected. Softer."

I watched as he ran his hand over the material. "Oh?"

"Yes." He paused. "Would you . . . would you like to touch it, too?"

My eyebrows shot up so high they nearly met my hairline. "What?"

"I am curious whether most shirts made in this era are as soft as this one. I thought if you touched my shirt . . ." He trailed off. "I thought maybe you could tell me whether this particular shirt was representative."

He was staring down at his shoes like they were the most interesting things in the entire world.

I gazed up at him, blood rushing in my ears.

He . . . wanted me to touch him.

Here.

Outside of a Nordstrom dressing room.

I swallowed hard.

"Would it be . . . educational? For you?"

He nodded, still staring at his shoes. "I think so. But—" He looked at me, expression unreadable. "But only if you want to, Cassie."

In the end, I didn't need to think it over for too long. If it were anyone else but Frederick making this request, I'd assume this was the most transparent excuse in the world to get someone to touch them.

But this wasn't anyone else.

This was Frederick, someone who was so formal, so prim and proper, he only stopped calling me *Miss Greenberg* and began referring to me by my first name after I'd asked him to several times. This was the same person who was so overcome by the sight of me in a bikini he couldn't bring himself to speak to me for two days.

Frederick might have been the most gentlemanly person I'd ever met. If he'd wanted to find some flimsy excuse for me to put my hands on him, he'd have done it long before now.

Besides—I *wanted* to touch him. A lot, in fact. Whether it was a good idea to touch him was a separate matter, and one I would have ample time to think about later.

I stepped closer and put both of my hands on his chest. Part of me still half expected to feel a heartbeat, a warm and yielding male body beneath my palms. But Frederick's chest was cool and almost unnaturally solid where I touched him, no rhythmic thumping where one would have been if he were still human.

Fortunately—or, unfortunately—my heart was beating more than enough for the both of us.

Frederick was right. The fabric of his shirt *was* soft. I slowly slid my hands back and forth over the waffle-knit material, reveling in how silky it felt beneath my fingertips, how delicious the contrast was with the hard planes of the chest beneath.

Now that I had the answer to his question, I probably should have stopped touching him. I should have stepped away from him and kept my hands to myself the rest of the night.

But I didn't.

The shirt he was wearing was nice enough. But that wasn't what kept me rooted to the spot, what kept my hands on his body long beyond what he'd probably imagined when he asked me to do this. I'd known he was muscular, but now that I was actually touching him I realized he was all but *made* of muscle. Had he been this physically fit when he was still human, I wondered? Or was being built like a professional athlete a physiological peculiarity unique to vampires? Either way, I could feel his pectorals bunch and flex beneath my palms as I touched him, could feel his sharp intake of breath when I grew bolder and started gently tracing his collarbones with my thumb.

His eyes were still trained on me, but growing glazed and unfocused.

"How . . ." He stopped, his eyes drifting closed. When he opened them again there was a heat in his gaze that made the department store, the rest of the world, fall away. He inclined his head towards me, his mouth scant inches away from mine. I could feel each one of his breaths against my lips, cool and sweet. My heart raced. My knees wobbled. "How does it feel?"

"Wow! Your boyfriend looks great in everything, doesn't he?"

We flew apart at the sound of the salesperson's voice, coming from right behind me. Frederick—now standing at least a foot away—stuffed his hands into the pockets of his jeans, eyes downcast. He wasn't blushing—*could* vampires blush? I wasn't sure— but I sure was.

I was too shell-shocked to respond.

Fortunately, Frederick seemed to recover his wits faster than I did. Or maybe he had never lost them in the first place. Though he didn't correct her, either.

"Thank you," he said, his voice strained. His eyes never left my face. "Cassie likes this shirt. I will take one in every color."

# TWELVE

Letter from Mr. Frederick J. Fitzwilliam to
Miss Esmeralda Jameson, dated November 7

Dear Esmeralda,

I am in receipt of your most recent correspondence. As a
rule, I am loath to repeat myself, as doing so is generally a
waste of time. However, your latest missive shows me I
have no choice.

As I have said multiple times before, to both you and
my mother: I do not believe a marriage in which one
partner is an unwilling participant would be a happy one.
Additionally, since my last letter to you, I have developed
feelings for someone else. I doubt anything will come of
them for a variety of reasons I will not bore you with.
Either way, you deserve far more than marriage to a man
who pines for someone else. I will not sentence you to a
life of that kind of misery.

It has been over one hundred years since we last spoke

*in person, but I remember you not only as a reasonable*
*woman but also as an admirably independent one. You*
*cannot possibly want an arranged marriage to a man who*
*doesn't love you. Please help me convince our parents this*
*plot of theirs is the mother of all bad ideas.*

*With kind regards,*
*Frederick J. Fitzwilliam*

......................

## ART TEACHER WANTED FOR UPPER SCHOOL—
## HARMONY ACADEMY

*Harmony Academy, a K–12 coeducational private school lo-*
*cated in Evanston, Illinois, dedicated to fostering moral integ-*
*rity, intellectual vitality, and compassion among our diverse*
*student body, seeks an art teacher for its Upper School. Posi-*
*tion to begin in the spring semester. Qualified applicants will*
*have a BA in an art discipline from an accredited university,*
*1–3 years of experience teaching fine arts in an educational*
*setting, and excellent references. MFA strongly preferred.*
*Working artists are especially encouraged to apply.*

*The ideal candidate will, through their professional history*
*and art portfolio, demonstrate sincere commitment to Har-*
*mony Academy's above-stated values. For consideration, please*
*email your CV, cover letter, and portfolio to Cressida Marks,*
*Harmony Academy Head of School.*

I STARED AT THE HARMONY ACADEMY JOB DESCRIPTION,
trying to decide what to do with it.

Ordinarily, I would just delete it—the way I deleted all emails from my alma mater's career office. A one hundred percent rejection rate from all Younker-referred jobs I'd applied for my first two years post-MFA had taught me that continuing to beat my head against that particular wall wasn't worth my time.

But I was feeling good. I'd spent most of the day in the studio working on my project for the art exhibition. It was exciting how quickly it started coming together once I realized the found object materials needed for it were wrinkled cellophane and Christmas-colored tinsel glued together with epoxy. The piece's working title was *Manor House on a Lake,* and though I was seldom satisfied with my oil paintings I felt this project represented some of the best work I'd done in years. The cellophane-and-tinsel mixture emerging from the canvas made the water look like a three-dimensional neon-colored fever dream—and in a good way.

Overall, I thought *Manor House on a Lake*—by marrying traditional paints and modern synthetic materials—was at once classic and postmodern. It was the perfect subversion of the exhibition's Contemporary Society theme.

It had been a while since I could truthfully say I *liked* what I was creating.

So, yes. In general, I was feeling optimistic.

Optimistic enough that I decided I might as well apply for this Harmony Academy job. I couldn't see a downside. The worst thing that could happen would be I wouldn't get the job—but I was basically a professional at not getting jobs. Given everything else that was happening, that near-constant voice in the back of my head that told me I was doomed to fail was easier than usual to ignore.

A good old-fashioned rejection letter might be just the thing to get me to stop ruminating on what had happened with Frederick at Nordstrom the other day. To stop thinking about the feel of his solid, broad chest beneath my fingertips. To stop reliving his raveling composure as I touched him.

Yeah. Maybe applying to Harmony Academy was exactly what I needed.

Determined, I pulled up the last cover letter I'd written for a teaching position and gave it a quick once-over. My job situation hadn't changed much since the last time I'd applied to a job like this one, so updating it took less than ten minutes.

Before I could talk myself out of doing it, I emailed the cover letter, my CV, and photographs of several recent projects—including an in-progress shot of *Manor House on a Lake*—to Cressida Marks, Harmony Academy's head of school.

There. Done.

With that out of the way, hopefully I'd be able to dedicate the rest of the evening to drawing and mindless television.

I leaned back against the black leather couch, where my sketchpad rested beside me. Before finding out about the Harmony Academy job I'd been half watching an old *Buffy the Vampire Slayer* episode on Frederick's new flatscreen television, letting it play in the background as I drew. I'd seen this episode already—in the days since finding out Frederick was a vampire, I'd binged most of the first two seasons—but it was comfortable background noise, helping me focus as I thought through some final fiddly details to *Manor House*.

"May I join you?"

I startled at the sound of Frederick's deep voice, accidentally jostling my notepad off the couch with my knee. It fell with a loud rustling of pages, landing upside down on the floor.

I hadn't even heard him enter the room.

In fact, before now, I hadn't seen him at all since our shopping trip a couple days earlier. Part of me suspected he'd been intentionally keeping his distance after that moment we'd shared outside the dressing room. But I couldn't let myself think about that. I wasn't ready to admit to myself that I had enjoyed touching him as much as I did.

Or that it had even happened at all.

He was looking directly at me with a laser-sharp gaze, wearing one of the sweaters we'd picked out at Nordstrom. The pale green pullover perfectly accentuated his broad chest, and the dark-wash jeans fit him just as well.

I swallowed and fumbled for my notepad, willing my suddenly racing heart to slow. Could he hear my heart beating? The way his eyes flicked down to my chest before quickly shifting back up to my face made me wonder.

"Of course you can join me," I mumbled to the floor. I motioned to the spot next to me on the couch without looking at him.

He hummed, then sat down, leaving enough space between us that no parts of our bodies were touching—but not so much space that I couldn't smell the lavender soap he liked to use in the shower.

We sat together in silence for a long moment, watching as Buffy Summers single-handedly beat up and then staked a string of vampires, one right after the other. This was one of the earlier episodes, back when Sarah Michelle Gellar still had some roundness to her cheeks and the show's special effects budget was lower than Xander's IQ.

Buffy's fighting moves and her outfits were something to behold, as always. Even still, it took more concentration than it really should have to keep my eyes trained on the screen rather than on the person beside me.

"Have you ever seen this show?" I blurted out. It was a dumb question. Frederick had been asleep for a century and had only gotten Wi-Fi a few days ago; surely he hadn't found the time to watch a campy show from the nineties about fictional vampires. But I was desperate for something to say to break the awkward silence.

He ignored my question. "Do you think Angel or Spike is more handsome?" he asked instead, with all the seriousness of an NPR journalist. His eyes were on the screen, not on me—but his tone, his ramrod-straight posture, and the steady, rapid way he drummed his fingers on his thigh gave away his keen interest in my response.

I was completely thrown. Whatever I'd expected him to say when he joined me on the couch, it wasn't that. I had no idea how I was supposed to answer it—partly because it felt extremely loaded, but mostly because I'd never been particularly into either of *Buffy*'s bad boy vamps.

After a bit of somewhat frantic consideration, I gave him the truth.

"Giles is the hottest man on this show."

"Giles?" Frederick spluttered in what sounded like genuine surprise. He turned to face me, eyes boring into mine with an expression that bordered on outrage. "The *librarian*?"

"Yeah." I pointed to the screen, where Giles was presiding over a meeting of teenagers in the high school library. He looked supremely put upon and hot in his unique, middle-aged, glasses-wearing librarian way. "I mean, look at him."

"I am looking at him."

"He's objectively attractive."

Frederick grunted something unintelligible. He folded his arms tightly across his chest, his mouth turning down in a scowl.

"Also, of all the men on this show—alive and undead—he's the only one who's already processed and dealt with his shit." I shrugged, turning back to the television. "Everyone else has way too much baggage."

Frederick looked unconvinced. "But Giles is just so . . ." He trailed off, shaking his head and closing his eyes. His scowl deepened.

"He's just so what?"

"*Human*," he spat, the single word laced with bitterness and disapproval.

I gaped at him. But Frederick wasn't looking at me anymore. His eyes were back on the television, staring at it with an intensity that could burn a hole through paper.

Was Frederick jealous of a fictional librarian from an episode that aired almost twenty-five years ago? Was that what was happening here?

Impossible.

Stupidly, my heart sped up a few beats at the idea of it all the same.

"What's wrong with being human, Frederick?"

He muttered something under his breath I couldn't make out but didn't otherwise acknowledge he'd heard me.

"To answer your earlier question," Frederick said eventually, sidestepping the issue of hot librarians, "I have seen this show. Reginald recommended it to me."

"Really?" That surprised me.

"Yes. Although the version we watched at his home had frequent interruptions from companies wanting to sell things. *Commercials*." He shook his head. "Annoying."

I guess Reginald didn't spring for commercial-free streaming platforms. "They usually are," I agreed.

"I couldn't even tell what I was meant to buy half the time," he complained. "Though I did enjoy singing along to some of them. The music was often quite good."

The idea of buttoned-up Frederick singing along to a car insurance ad—or, god, an ad for one of those sexual enhancement meds—was so ridiculous I nearly burst out laughing.

"What . . . what did you think of the show itself?" I asked, trying to recover.

If Frederick noticed I was on the verge of dissolving into giggles he showed no sign of it. "It's a bit silly," he said, thoughtfully. "Though I enjoyed what I saw."

"How accurate would you say it is?" I was probably crossing a line, but I couldn't help myself. I'd been wondering this ever since learning he was a vampire.

He hesitated, pondering the question. "The show's writers got a few things wrong about my kind. For example, I have no penchant for leather jackets, and I don't burn to ash when exposed to sunlight. Additionally, my face doesn't change in a cartoonish way before I feed. But they also managed to get a number of details correct." He paused, then added, "Which is surprising. As far as I know no one on the writing team was a vampire."

My eyes widened. I hadn't expected this much honesty when I'd asked the question. Was this my chance to finally get more information about him?

"What did they get right?" I prompted, unable to hide my eagerness.

"I, like Angel, do enjoy a good brooding stare."

"I've noticed that."

"I'd imagine it would be hard to miss," he conceded, his eyes twinkling.

"Anything else?"

He considered that. "I require express permission before entering someone's home. Some vampire legends are nonsense and others are legitimate, and I have to say the show handles that detail quite well. Also, I cannot sweat, I never blush, and my heart hasn't beat since I turned." He glanced at me from the corner of his eye. "You likely noticed I had no heartbeat when we . . . when you touched my shirt at the department store."

He might not be able to blush anymore, but at the reminder of that moment we shared outside the dressing room I was blushing more than enough for both of us.

"Oh," I mumbled. "Yes. I . . . I noticed."

He nodded, his eyes inscrutable as he held my gaze. "If you ever find yourself lacking in diversion you could do worse than *Buffy the Vampire Slayer.* Especially if you wanted to know more about me." A pause. "Not that you would necessarily want to know more about me, of course. I am . . . merely stating a hypothetical."

"I will," I said, the room feeling suddenly a bit too warm. "I mean . . . I do want to know more about you."

On screen, Buffy's mom was lecturing her about staying out all night again, but I wasn't paying attention to the show anymore.

. . . . . . . . . . . . . . . . . . . .

I DIDN'T REMEMBER FALLING ASLEEP ON THE COUCH BE-side him.

One minute Spike and the other monsters from Sunnydale were getting up to their usual antics. I'd been laughing; Frederick had been staring intently at the screen, as if he were watching an important university lecture and didn't want to miss a word.

The next minute I was blinking up at the side of Frederick's face from where my head rested on his shoulder.

Instinct told me to move away. Frederick would be horrified when he realized what had happened. But as consciousness slowly returned, I realized he had to be fully aware of the situation. He might be a vampire, but as far as I knew he had nerve endings in his shoulder. Surely he could feel it when a heavy object like my head was resting there.

I looked down. The careful inches he'd left between our bodies when he joined me on the couch had evaporated as I slept. Our thighs were pressed together now, knee to hip.

My hand rested lightly on his upper thigh, just above his knee. His leg was muscular and solid, his body unnaturally cool beneath my palm.

My mind raced through all options available to me. Jumping away from him and apologizing was appealing. But so was staying right where I was, admiring the sharp angle of his jaw, and the way his shirt smelled enticingly like laundry soap and cool, male skin. It felt *good*, being close to him like this. Exciting, yet comfortable. Our bodies fit together so perfectly.

Just as I'd decided to stay right where I was, Frederick spoke, his voice a low rumble against the top of my head I could feel more than hear.

"Your art is remarkable, Cassie."

That was unexpected enough to make me forget about this awkward situation. I shifted away from him—and noticed the soft, resigned sigh that escaped his lips when I did.

Maybe he'd enjoyed my falling asleep on him as much as I had.

The idea thrilled me. But unpacking that would have to wait. I had too many questions about what he'd just said.

"My art?"

"Yes." He pointed to the glass-topped coffee table beside the couch. My notebook was spread open to a page of doodles I'd made early in the planning stages for *Manor House on a Lake*. "Your art."

A flare of something—part embarrassment over someone seeing my incomplete sketches, part genuine irritation at his intrusion— shot through me.

"That's not for you to look at!" I leaned forward and flipped the notebook closed. I knew he didn't understand my art. His earlier abject confusion over my Saugatuck piece rang in my ears. Was he making fun of me now when he said my art was *re-markable*?

"I apologize for invading your privacy," he said sheepishly. He sounded genuinely sorry, but that didn't excuse his snooping. The cuddly feelings from a few moments ago were gone. "I should not have looked through your notebook."

"Then why did you?"

He said nothing for so long I assumed he wasn't going to an-swer my question. When he finally did, his voice was quiet and a little strained. "I have grown . . . *curious* about you and the inner workings of your mind. I thought looking through the sketchbook you spend so much time with would provide insight with rela-tively minimal disruption." He paused. "I should have asked your permission first, and I apologize for not having done so."

Confusion mixed with my irritation. "You've been curious about how I think?"

"Yes."

The single word hung in the air between us. I paused, feeling as if the ground were shifting beneath my feet. "You've been curious about how I think because you . . . want to learn as much as you can about the modern world and . . . learning more about how I think will help on that score." I paused, evaluating his reaction. "Right?"

He didn't answer me right away. His dark eyes grew pensive, his face adopting an odd expression I couldn't read.

"Of course." He nodded brusquely. "That is the only reason why I've been curious about what's on your mind."

But his eyes were so soft, his voice a gentle caress, belying his claim. My heartbeat kicked up and . . .

Frederick's eyes flicked down to my chest again, the same way they had the last time my heartbeat started racing when I was with him.

Maybe he *could* hear my heart beating.

My cheeks grew warm again at the thought of it.

"I apologize again," he said. "But please believe me, Cassie. Your drawings are excellent."

"They're just rough sketches."

"Do not downplay your talents," he said, scowling as though the idea of me selling myself short was offensive to him.

He leaned forward to grab the notebook, then paused, looking back at me over his shoulder before his fingers closed around it. "May I?"

I nodded, unable to think of a reason to tell him no when this time, he was asking permission.

He opened the notebook to the page I'd been working on when he joined me on the couch, moving a little closer to me in the process.

Our thighs were touching again. My insides were quivering at his nearness, at the solid musculature of his thigh beneath his clothes. It didn't seem to have the same effect on him that it had on me, though. His eyes were fixed firmly on the art on the page.

"This is fascinating," he breathed, gesturing to my designs. This early version of *Manor House* was nothing but the barest outlines of a house and the general impression of a lake. Arrows pointed from the middle of the lake out to the edge of the page to represent motion and modernity; the idea of combining tinsel and cellophane had not yet occurred to me when I'd drawn it.

"You don't have to say that." Years of kind words from Sam and other well-meaning friends who didn't get what I did made it so that false compliments hurt almost as badly as negative—but honest—feedback. "I know you don't understand what I do."

"That . . . might be true," he admitted. He touched the top of *Manor House*'s roof with his right index finger. "But that does not mean I do not find it fascinating."

I watched as he traced over every single line on the page, from top to bottom, not skipping over any part of it, with deliberate care. The house. The lake. The barely intimated trees blooming as rough graphite swirls on either side of the page. The memories of his large hand covering mine as we explored Instagram together— the way my hands had looked pressed up against his chest in the Nordstrom dressing room—rose unbidden, sending a delicious shiver down my spine.

I'd always felt my art was an extension of my innermost self, and the sight of his large, graceful hands touching every single part of this early drawing felt almost unbearably intimate.

"What do you find fascinating about it?" I couldn't tear my eyes away from the sight of his hands touching my work. I felt moments away from melting into a puddle at his feet.

"All of it." His hand left the page. I *felt* him withdraw as much as saw it and exhaled for the first time in what felt like minutes. An unexpected, indescribable feeling of emptiness coursed through me. "I do not claim to understand what you see when you draw and build these things. But the intricacy of your detailing suggests that whatever it is, it is big and deliberate. This is *intentional*. It means something to you. I cannot help but respect it."

His eyes met mine, his gaze so piercing it punched the breath from my lungs.

It took a moment for me to remember how to form words.

"Yeah," I said. Like a moron.

His expression went suddenly distant and wistful. "There was an artist in the village where I was raised. She drew the loveliest things. The sunset in winter. A child playing with a small toy." He paused. "Me, when I was just a child myself, laughing with friends."

I bit my lip, trying to ignore the sudden stab of irrational jealousy that went through me at hearing the word *she*.

*Get a grip, Cassie.*

"Your girlfriend?"

His smile slipped. "My sister."

I winced, feeling like an asshole. She had to have been dead for hundreds of years.

"I'm sorry."

"Don't be." He shook his head. "Mary lived a long, rich life, full of art and other beautiful things. The village she married into was small and close-knit. I don't doubt she lived happily until the end of her days."

These details about his sister were the first personal details about his life he'd given me, beyond the basics of how he'd ended up in his current situation. I wasn't sure why he'd chosen to share this with me now—but the decision felt momentous.

In truth, I still knew almost nothing about my weird, fascinating roommate. This small tidbit was like a dam breaking on my curiosity about him.

Suddenly, I was greedy to know more.

"Where did you grow up?"

"England." He rubbed at the back of his neck, his eyes distant as though he were picturing the town in his mind's eye. "About an hour south of London by car if you were to make the journey today. When I lived there, though, the journey to London involved nearly a full day of travel."

England? That surprised me. "You don't speak with an accent at all."

"I have lived in America for much longer than I lived in England." He gave me another small smile. "It doesn't matter where you were born, Cassie. After you're gone from a place for a few hundred years the accent's barely detectable anymore."

*After you're gone from a place for a few hundred years.*

I bit my lip, gathering the courage to ask something I'd wondered about ever since I found out what he really was.

"You've . . . been gone from England for a few hundred years?" I asked, dancing around it.

He nodded. "I have not been back to where I was born since just before the American Revolutionary War."

"How old are you, exactly?"

He looked at me for such a long, heavy moment before answering that I began to worry I'd overstepped. Before I could apologize for prying, though, he said, "I am not entirely certain. My memories before I turned in 1734 are . . . opaque." He swallowed and looked away. "There was a vampire attack on my village that year. Most of us were either killed or turned. I believe I was in my mid-thirties when it happened."

1734.

My mind was reeling as it tried to process the fact that the man sitting beside me on the couch was more than three hundred years old.

"And that is precisely why I have not returned in so long," he continued. "All the people I knew from before I turned are long gone, except for—" He abruptly cut off, as though he'd been about to say more but decided against it at the last minute. He shook his head. "All the people I knew and loved from my childhood are dead."

The firm set of his jaw told me there was more he wanted to say, but he simply pressed his lips together and looked again at the art notebook spread open before us on the coffee table. For the first time, it occurred to me that it must be incredibly lonely to live forever while everyone around you aged and died.

Maybe this was why he kept Reginald around. Having one constant from his past must be a comfort to him—even if said constant was also kind of an ass.

"What was your hometown like?" I asked.

He'd already shared more about his past in these few minutes than he'd done the entire time I'd known him, and part of me wondered if asking for more was pushing it. But he was still such an enigma, even after all these weeks with him. Now that we were talking about his past, I couldn't help myself.

If he minded my question, he didn't act like it.

"I don't remember much," he admitted. "I remember feelings. My family, some of my closer friends. Some of the things I liked to eat. I used to love food." He smiled wistfully. "I remember the house I lived in."

"What was it like?"

"Small," he said, chuckling. Looking around his spacious living room, he added, "You could probably fit three of them in this apartment. And there were four of us living there."

"No McMansions in England three hundred years ago?"

He shook his head, still smiling. "No. Certainly not in the

small village where I was raised. No one had the money or the resources to build anything bigger than what was absolutely required to keep a family protected from the elements."

I thought of what little I'd learned of the architecture in eighteenth-century England from my art history classes. I could almost picture Frederick's little house in my mind's eye. A thatched roof, possibly. Floors made of simple wood.

How did a boy raised in a place like that end up here—in wealth and splendor, in a fabulous apartment across the ocean— hundreds of years later? The details he'd shared with me only whetted my appetite for more information about him. But he leaned back against the couch cushions then, arms folded across his chest, signaling that he was done sharing for the evening.

I didn't have to be done talking, though. After sharing with me what he had about his sister, the urge to reciprocate and share something of my own life was too strong to resist.

"I'm glad you had your sister, for a time," I said gently.

"Me, too."

"I don't have any siblings."

His eyes—which had once again been resting on my opened art notebook—flicked to mine. "You must have been very lonely growing up."

"I wasn't." It was the truth. "My imagination and my friends kept me company." The only *real* problem with having no siblings was there was no one else around to distract my parents from me—and my many failings. But I wasn't about to complain, given what he'd just shared. My dumb only-child guilt was more than Frederick needed to know.

We sat together in comfortable silence after that. Frederick's eyes drifted once again to my art notebook, but his gaze was unfocused.

"I would like to hear more about your life, Cassie." He swallowed, his Adam's apple bobbing in his throat. "I wish to know more about you. I wish . . . I wish to know everything."

The quiet intensity of his tone shot straight through me. The atmosphere in the room seemed to shift, the nature of what we were to one another suddenly tilted on its axis.

I looked at my notebook, which had suddenly become the only safe place in the room for either of us to rest our eyes.

# THIRTEEN

## *Mr. Frederick J. Fitzwilliam's Google Search History*

- how do you kiss if it has been three hundred years since
- how can you know if she wants to kiss you
- is it a bad idea to kiss your roommate
- is it bad to think about or have sex with your roommate
- age gap relationships
- best breath mints

......................

## *[EMAIL DRAFT, UNSENT]*

From: Cassie Greenberg [csgreenberg@gmail.com]
To: David Gutierrez [dgutierrez@rivernorthgallery.com]
Subject: submission for Contemporary Society art show

Dear David,

I wish to submit for consideration my three-dimensional oil and plastics mixed-media piece, *Manor House on a Placid Lake*, for River North Gallery's Contemporary

Society art exhibition in March. The dimensions of the canvas itself are three feet by two feet, with a cellophane-and-tinsel sculpture attachment extending out from the canvas another ten inches.

I have attached five JPEG images of my completed piece to this email for your consideration. Pursuant to the parameters set out in the Request for Submissions, the finished piece will be available for display in your gallery upon request.

I look forward to hearing from you soon.

Cassie S. Greenberg

BY THE TIME I GOT TO THE ART STUDIO, SAM AND SCOTT were already there, standing in front of *Manor House* and staring at it with matching expressions I couldn't parse.

They didn't look horrified, at least. That was something.

I dropped my bag off at an empty cubicle and stood beside them. "Thanks so much for taking pictures for me," I said to Scott. He had a fancy camera with a name I didn't recognize and was a great amateur photographer. I was grateful he was available to do this. I was planning to submit to the River North Gallery art exhibition that evening, and while I'd already drafted my email to David, I needed to attach five pictures of my piece to it to be considered.

"It's my pleasure." Scott lifted his camera—worn suspended on a strap around his neck—without taking his eyes off what he was there to photograph. "Where should I . . . um." He paused, then looked to Sam, wide-eyed, for help. Sam shook his head and chuckled quietly before turning back to whatever he was reading on his phone. "Where should I stand?"

I pointed to a spot about two feet away from where *Manor House* hung on the studio wall. "Start there. I think that'll capture the light as it streams in through the window. Hopefully it'll reflect off the tinsel-cellophane sculpture and really make the pictures pop."

Scott's mouth twitched. "Got it."

"The manor house itself isn't quite as large as I'd originally planned," I mused. The explanation was probably unnecessary— Scott was a trooper to do this for me at all and probably didn't really care. But I was excited about the finished project and needed to tell someone.

"Oh?" Scott moved around the piece, snapping a new picture every few seconds. "You'd initially wanted to make something bigger?"

"Sort of," I admitted.

As I'd put the finishing touches on it over the past few days, my mind kept revisiting my conversation with Frederick about his past. In the process I'd inadvertently incorporated some of the details he'd shared about his old home. By the time I was finished with *Manor House*, the home it showed was smaller than what I'd originally planned, the plain wooden floors he'd described could be seen through the windows, and the roof had taken on a more thatched appearance than had been my original idea.

"The lake and the tinsel sculpture coming out of it are both bigger than I'd originally planned to compensate for the smaller house," I added, as Scott continued to snap photos.

Scott grinned at me. "The plastic sculpture is the coolest part of it anyway."

I couldn't tell if he meant that or if he was just being nice. Either way, I definitely agreed.

"I hope the judges like it."

What if they didn't, though? I'd been so preoccupied with

simply finishing this piece I hadn't let myself think about what I'd do if it was rejected.

It would be okay, though. Eventually. It would suck in the short term, just like all the rejections I'd gotten over the past ten years had sucked. But I *liked* this piece, even if I was the only person who ever would. That had to count for something.

As Scott resumed taking pictures, I went back to the cubicle where I'd stashed my things and pulled out my laptop so I could review the email I'd drafted to David before I sent in my application.

And I nearly jumped out of my chair when I saw the email I'd just received.

From: Cressida Marks [cjmarks@harmony.org]
To: Cassie Greenberg [csgreenberg@gmail.com]
Subject: Interview—Harmony Academy

Dear Cassie,

I am writing to let you know our hiring committee has evaluated your materials and would like to bring you to campus for an in-person interview. We are conducting interviews the last week of this month, and every Friday in December. Please let me know at your earliest convenience whether you are still interested in the position and, if so, what your availability is on these dates.

Sincerely,
Cressida Marks
Head of School
Harmony Academy

I read the email from Cressida Marks again, too stunned to believe that what I'd just read was real.

"Are you okay?" I startled at the sound of Sam's voice. He peered at me from where he stood by Scott, worry lines notched between his brows. "You look like you've seen a ghost."

"Not a ghost," I assured him. "I just found out I got a job interview I wasn't expecting." That was the understatement of the year. I'd only applied to Harmony Academy because I was having a good day and I'd had all the application materials on my hard drive. I hadn't expected anything to *come* of it.

And now, just a few days later, Cressida Marks, the head of school at Harmony Academy, actually wanted to interview me for a job.

How was this real?

"That's great news," Sam said. He smiled, pulling out a chair from the main table and sitting down. "What's it for?"

I hesitated. This situation was surreal enough as it was. It felt like if I told another living person about it, the opportunity would vanish in a puff of smoke. I didn't have a teaching credential. That might not matter to Harmony; some of my classmates from Younker had been able to get teaching positions at private schools without one. But the fact that my entire portfolio was light-years away from what parents wanted their kids to learn in art class would almost certainly matter to a school looking for someone to educate their students.

Sam, though, didn't seem to pick up on my self-doubt.

"It's a position at a private school up in Evanston," I eventually said. "Teaching art at their high school."

"That's fantastic!" Sam's smile grew. "You're so talented, Cassie. And you've seemed to enjoy art nights with the library kids, right? That school would be lucky to have you."

"You really think so?"

Sam walked over to *Manor House* and paused, studying it. "I do," he confirmed. "Of course, I know more about corporate mergers than I do about art. I admit I don't know exactly what I'm looking at, but I can tell, just from looking at it, that *you* know." He smiled at me. "You are someone with vision, and who is passionate about that vision. Who better to teach young people about something than someone who cares passionately about what they do?"

His words surprised me. Sam had always been supportive of me and my goals, but in a vague, *I-love-you-but-I-don't-really-understand-you* kind of way. This might have been the most effusively he'd ever praised my skills in all the years I'd known him.

"Thank you," I stammered, at a total loss. "That . . . really means a lot to me."

"If you need to give them references, you can give my name if you like."

I snorted. "You're my best friend, not my current employer."

"The offer stands," he said, with conviction.

"Thank you, Sam," I said. "I . . . just, thank you." And then, without thinking, I added, "I can't wait to tell Frederick the news."

Sam looked at me, one eyebrow raised. "I'm sorry. Who can't you wait to tell? I didn't quite catch that."

"Um." I reached up and tucked a lock of hair behind my ear. "Just Frederick."

Sam was smirking at me now. "Just Frederick, huh?"

"Yes," I said. "Frederick. My roommate." Roommates told each other things, right? Why was Sam acting like this?

"Why are you blushing?" Now even Sam's *smirk* was smirking.

"What? I'm not blushing. It's just . . . warm in here."

Meeting Frederick in person had apparently put Sam's mind at ease that I wasn't living with a serial-killer monster. Which was great, of course. Even if a bit ironic, since Frederick was a *literal* monster.

Only right now it wasn't so great. Sam was acting the way he did every time I'd ever confessed a crush to him. And that just wasn't what was going on here.

Or, even if it *was* what was going on here, it wasn't like anything was going to come of it.

I rolled my eyes at Sam, my irritation with him growing, then walked over to Scott, hoping that would be the end of this conversation. Fortunately, Scott was looking at his camera, not at me.

"Could I look through the pictures you took?" I asked, trying to ignore how flustered I was. "I'd like to send my application to the show organizers tonight."

"Sure," Scott said. He leaned closer to me so I could see his screen, and then gave me a wide, shit-eating grin. "I won't even give you grief over how much you're blushing over your *roommate* while we do it, either."

......................

THERE WAS A NOTE FROM FREDERICK WAITING FOR ME ON the kitchen table when I got home that afternoon. My heart skipped a beat, and I felt my lips curve into a smile as I unfolded the now familiar sheet of crisp white stationery.

*Dear Cassie,*

*What are your favorite foods?*
*I haven't asked my personal question yet today, and I would like this to be today's question.*

*Yours,*
*FJF*

This *one-personal-question-per-day* thing was something new we agreed to try after the night we'd stayed up too late watching *Buffy*. After he said he wanted to know more about me so he could learn about the modern world, we decided one personal question per day would be a good way to accomplish that.

I knew, on some level at least, that the *learning more about the modern world* bit was just a ruse we were using to get to know each other better as people. But I tried to shut down that line of thinking whenever it cropped up.

I wasn't quite ready yet to ponder what that meant was happening between us.

With each subsequent question he asked, though, the truth of what we were doing was getting harder to ignore.

*Dear Frederick,*

*I have a lot of favorite foods! Lasagna, chocolate cake, honey nut cheerios, eggs benedict, and chicken noodle soup are probably the top 5.*

*Also, this doesn't answer your question, but guess what? I got a job interview today! There's probably no chance in the world I'll get the job but it's still exciting.*

*Cassie*

*Dear Cassie,*

*Wonderful news about the job interview! Why do you think you would not get the position? If it were up to me, I would hire you in a heartbeat (if you will excuse the figure of speech).*

Thank you for answering my question about your favorite foods. That helps my understanding of what humans in their 30s enjoy eating in the early twenty-first century. My question for today has to do with color. Specifically: What is your favorite color?

FJF

Dear Frederick,

That's very kind of you to say you would hire me in a heartbeat. But you can't mean that. You don't even know what the job is! It could be something I have zero qualifications for. In fact, it is.

I have two fave colors: carmine (which is a specific shade of red) and indigo. How about you? Do you have a favorite color?

Cassie

Dear Cassie,

This is probably extremely cliché, but my favorite color is red.

And I meant exactly what I said. I _would_ hire you in a heartbeat. For any job.

I still need to think of a good daily question to ask you, but in the meantime I want to let you know that last night while you slept I visited an all-night cafe with Reginald called "Waffle House." I think you would be proud of how well I managed to order our food and beverages without either mishap or drawing undue attention to ourselves. I daresay even Reginald was impressed with how fluidly I managed to extract my new credit card from my wallet and pay for everything. (As you may have guessed, impressing Reginald is nearly impossible.)

We did get a few stares from the table of young people adjacent to ours, but I suspect that may have been a side effect of the substances I could smell on them and not due to anything anachronistic Reginald and I were doing. In either case, I am eager to travel to another cafe soon to practice my fledgling skills.

Given that I would not have been able to order that chocolate chip and peanut butter waffle last night without your unending patience with me I wanted to let you know. I couldn't eat it of course; but it still felt like a small victory.

Yours,
FJF

I picked up the pen that now lived permanently on the kitchen table and pondered what to write in my note back to him.

Sam had just texted me earlier in the day to invite me to a party he and Scott were throwing on Friday evening. Maybe Frederick could come with me. He could practice interfacing with people in public there.

I dashed off a quick note to him before I could talk myself out of it.

*Hey Frederick,*

*Great job at Waffle House. Yeah, I'm sure those kids were*
*only staring at you because they were high as hell (though I*
*may be projecting a little from my own teenage years).*
*     Unrelated—my friend Sam is having some people*
*over Friday night. Do you want to come with me? It could*
*be another opportunity for you to practice your*
*<u>talking with people skills</u> around someone other than*
*me and Reginald.*

*cassie*

I read over my note, torn between leaving it on the table for
Frederick and tearing it into a thousand pieces.

In truth, bringing Frederick would probably make the night
more fun for me, and could be a great distraction from all the
awkward questions I would inevitably get about what I did for a
living from Sam's law school friends and Scott's English department colleagues. I'd have to pay attention to him, and possibly
run interference if things went sideways and he tried to pay for
something with gold doubloons or something.

And the more chances Frederick had to put it all into practice, the better.

It was normal for roommates to invite each other to things,
right? Just like it was normal for roommates to tell each other
about job interviews and their favorite foods, and to semi–feel
them up outside a Nordstrom dressing room when they needed
new clothes.

But then, a small part of me wondered—would falling for him
really be so bad? Sure, there was the whole drinking blood thing,

and the whole *hundreds-of-years-older-than-me-and-also-immortal* thing. But he was being really good about keeping his promise to never eat in front of me. And I'd dated guys with much bigger strikes against them than immortality.

Before I could talk myself out of crumpling up my note, I sketched a quick picture of the two of us, dancing, amidst a sea of floating musical notes. I drew the cartoon version of him with a smile on his face—because he really did have such an incredible smile.

I left the note on the kitchen table before I left for my evening shift at Gossamer's, not sure if I hoped he'd say yes to the invitation or turn me down.

......................

WHEN I GOT BACK HOME AT MIDNIGHT FROM MY SHIFT, Frederick was at the stove, his back to me as he stirred something that smelled suspiciously and deliciously like chicken soup.

This was the first time I'd seen him so much as stand in the kitchen since my first night there, when I'd gone on that futile search for cookware. I'd certainly never seen him *cook* anything. I didn't know why he was doing it now; his food preparation routine was, as far as I knew, limited to cutting into bags from the blood bank.

He didn't seem to notice my presence, so I decided to just stand there in silence and watch him for a while. He really did have an incredible build for men's T-shirts. And an amazing ass for jeans.

Taking him to the mall and getting him new clothes hadn't only been a favor to him. It had been a favor to humankind.

"Frederick?"

He whirled around at the sound of my voice, a wooden spoon with something dripping from it clutched in one hand and a sheet of paper in the other. He wore a black apron over his clothes with the words *This Guy Rubs His Own Meat* in large white Comic Sans lettering.

I huffed an involuntary laugh, momentarily forgetting what I'd been about to ask him. "What are you *wearing*?"

He looked down at himself, then back at me. "It's an apron."

"Yes, I can see it's an apron, but . . ." I managed to convert the giggles threatening to escape me into a cough, but barely. "Where did you get it?"

"Amazon." He set his wooden spoon down on the stove and smiled at me, clearly proud of himself. I made a mental note not to let Frederick navigate Amazon on my laptop without supervision anymore. "I saw this apron and immediately thought, *This message conveys competence in the kitchen.* Which is exactly what I'd hoped to convey as I prepared your meal."

My eyes went wide. "You're cooking something for me?"

"I am."

I didn't know what to say. "But why?"

He shrugged. "To thank you for helping me. I see what you feed yourself, Cassie. All those snacks and ready-to-grab things you keep in the fridge." He looked back over his shoulder at me. "It's important to get adequate nutrition, you know."

I stood there, heart in my throat, struck dumb at the idea that a centuries-old vampire was lecturing me on the importance of three squares a day.

No one had cooked a real meal for me since I'd left my parents' house. Not even Sam.

"And so you're making me—"

"Chicken soup." He gave me a shy smile. "I might have had an ulterior motive when I asked you for your favorite meals. I also cut up some fresh fruit for you. Pineapple and kiwi. There's a bowl of it on the counter."

"Thank you," I murmured, my chest tight. I was an adult and had been taking care of myself for years. But the idea that he wanted to care for me . . .

It did something to me.

Trying to distract myself, I turned and sat at the kitchen table. My laptop was there, and I decided I might as well check my email while waiting for Frederick to finish the soup.

I grabbed a slice of kiwi from the bowl of fresh fruit, popping it into my mouth and enjoying the bright burst of flavor on my tongue. Humming appreciatively, I clicked the mouse button on my laptop.

The screen lit up, and—

### HOW TO KISS: TEN FOOLPROOF TIPS TO HAVE YOUR PARTNER CLAMORING FOR MORE!

I stood up from the table so quickly I knocked over my chair. I rubbed my eyes with my fists, thinking maybe I'd just hallucinated the Buzzfeed headline in thirty-six-point font I'd just seen on my laptop.

I checked again, and . . .

Nope.

There was definitely a kissing-tips article pulled up on my laptop.

I was one hundred percent certain I had not Googled anything that would yield a result like this the last time I'd used my computer.

I had, however, given Frederick permission to use my laptop whenever he wanted to.

"Um. Frederick?"

"Hm?"

I bit my lip. Should I admit to what I'd just seen?

If he wanted to read internet how-to articles about kissing, he had every right to do exactly that. My flushed cheeks and racing heart needed to stay out of this situation entirely, as it had *nothing* to do with me.

My lack of response must have clued Frederick in to what made me jump out of my chair, because two seconds later he inserted himself like a six-foot-tall vampiric shield between me and the kitchen table. His hands shot out, gripping my upper arms like twin iron vises, cool fingertips digging into my warm flesh.

"Laptop." His voice broke on the word. "Did you—"

No point in denying it now. "Yes."

"Um," he said. He licked his lips, and—look, after finding that article on the computer, it wasn't *my* fault that my eyes fell reflexively to his mouth. "Listen—"

"You don't have to say anything," I said very quickly. "I said you could use my laptop and . . . it's none of my business what you use it for. I'm sorry. I shouldn't have looked."

"You have nothing to apologize for," he said, his fingertips flexing a little on my arms. "It's your laptop. You don't need my permission to use it. I'd meant to put that article away before you came home, but I got caught up in preparing the food, and . . ." His eyes dropped to the floor. "I must have forgotten."

We stood like that for a long moment, his hands still on my arms. The soup was still bubbling away on the stove, but we both ignored it. It felt like I was supposed to say something—something to defuse the situation, probably—only I wasn't certain what it should be.

So I said the first thing that popped into my head. "Are you . . . curious about kissing?"

Probably a stupid question, given what I'd found on my laptop. But he looked surprised all the same. His eyes snapped to mine. "What makes you think that?"

I huffed a laugh. "Your browser history."

I could all but see the wheels in his mind turning as he cast about for how to reply. But after an interminable moment he seemed to regain some of his composure.

He stepped a little closer to me. At the heated look he gave me, all rational thought fled.

"I know about *kissing*, Cassie."

He sounded genuinely affronted, and I cringed at what I'd just implied—even as my knees went weak at the implication of what he'd just said. He'd been alive—or, his equivalent of alive— for hundreds of years. He'd probably kissed hundreds of people. Maybe thousands.

In fact—he was probably *really good* at kissing.

"I'm sure you do," I said, too flustered to look at his face anymore. My gaze drifted down to his ridiculous apron. *This Guy Rubs His Own Meat.* I flushed deeper with the awkwardness of this entire situation. How was any of this happening? "It's just . . . well. That website." I paused. "You can see why I might think that—"

"Right, right," he said, impatiently, waving a dismissive hand. "I understand what it must look like. But I swear, my only reason for reading that was . . . that is to say, I just wanted to see if . . ."

He trailed off.

He dropped his grip on my arms and ran an agitated hand through his hair.

I peered at him. "You just wanted to see if . . . ?"

His expression was unreadable. "I just wanted to see if anything . . . *significant* . . . had changed."

What? "You wanted to see if . . . anything had changed?"

He nodded. "Yes. It has been a while, since I . . ." He shook his head and shoved his hands deep in the pockets of his jeans. "Over the years there have been . . . *trends* in this area, you see. What is desirable in a kiss in one era may not be pleasurable in another."

Oh.

*Oh.*

"And you're curious about what those trends are right now?"

He swallowed. "Yes."

I had no reason to think his curiosity about modern kissing trends was anything but purely intellectual. He was curious about a lot of things in the twenty-first century—everything ranging from urban sewage systems to Midwestern politics. But something about the way he was now steadfastly looking at everything in the room but me made my heart knock hard against my rib cage—and gave me the courage to admit something very stupid.

"I'm curious, too."

His eyes snapped to mine. "What?"

Operating on pure nerve, I clarified. "I've never kissed a vampire before." I didn't have to admit that I'd wondered what it would be like to kiss him specifically, right? "So I'm curious about what it's like." At the thunderstruck look on his face I added, "Purely from an intellectual standpoint."

A beat. "Of course."

"For science, honestly."

"Science."

"Comparison purposes."

"What other purpose could there be?"

We stood there in the kitchen for what felt like entire minutes, just staring at each other. The soup was still bubbling on the stove. It sort of smelled like it was burning at this point. I didn't care.

I took another step closer, until we were near enough to one another that I could see all the variations of color within his dark eyes. They weren't a monochromatic brown, like they appeared from a distance. His irises contained very subtle pinpricks of hazel as well, combining with the brown to create the richest, most beautiful eye color I'd ever seen.

I licked my lips. His eyes fell directly to my mouth.

"What do you think about us showing each other what it's like?" His voice was barely above a whisper. "For science. And comparison purposes."

I nodded. "I'm hardly an expert, but I'm probably at least as knowledgeable about modern kissing trends as that article."

His jaw tightened. "Probably."

"And given that I *am* your point person for lessons on living in the modern era—"

"It only makes sense that it should be you," he agreed. "Likewise, I do not claim to be an expert at vampire kissing, but . . ."

He trailed off. His eyes were still focused on my mouth.

The offer was out there, now—for both of us. There was no taking it back now.

Before I could remind myself that kissing this gorgeous, undead man who wanted to make me chicken soup and said he liked my art might end up being the worst decision I'd made in a lifetime full of not-great decisions, I placed my hand on his chest, right over the place where his heart would be beating if he were human.

He closed his eyes, taking several very deep breaths. He inclined his head a little towards me, again making me wonder if he could hear, or even smell, my heartbeat.

He covered my hand on his chest with one of his own. His palm was so cool against my heated skin. He squeezed my hand gently, making me shiver, and shifted even closer to me.

And then he kissed me, just a gentle, barely there press of his lips to mine. He pulled back a half moment later, ending the kiss as soon as it began. To give me an out if this wasn't what I wanted.

"I—we—kiss like this," he whispered. I traced his plush bottom lip with the tip of my index finger, thrilling at the way his eyes fluttered closed at my touch. Slowly, as though moving through a dream, I cupped his cheek in my hand, tilting his face a fraction so he had to look me in the eyes.

His eyes were heavy-lidded, unfocused.

He needed no further encouragement.

The second brush of our lips was chaste and unhurried, his free hand coming up to cup my face in a mirror image of how I was now touching him. His mouth *was* as soft as it looked, in sharp contrast with the rasp of his stubble against my palm and the hard lines of his body as it pressed against mine. From a distance I could hear the grandfather clock down the hall marking time, but it felt like time had stopped—Frederick's arms slowly coming around my body to pull me closer, the steady beat of my heart an indelible reminder of just how long I'd wanted this to happen.

My fingers soon wound their way into his hair, carding through his impossibly soft locks. The tug of my hands seemed to unlock something inside him. He pulled me closer, allowing me to feel every cool, unyielding inch of him against the front of my body. His breath hitched as he tilted his head again and kissed my mouth with intentionality and considerably more pressure than he'd used before. I opened to him instinctively, his quiet, needful intensity parting my lips before I even realized it had happened.

And then it was over. He pulled back abruptly, resting his forehead against mine, breathing very hard for someone who didn't technically need oxygen to survive. He shook his head minutely and then squeezed his eyes tightly shut, like he was trying to regain control over a situation that was rapidly slipping through his fingers.

"*That*," he breathed, "is what it is like to kiss a vampire."

From a technical standpoint it turned out to be not much different from kissing anyone else. And yet I'd never experienced anything like it. He still held on to me, his arms wound just as tightly around my body as they'd been while we were kissing— which was a good thing, as my knees felt moments away from buckling under my weight. As he worked to calm his breathing I detected the faint but unmistakable metallic scent of blood on his breath. I wondered if self-consciousness over a recent meal was why he'd ended our kiss so abruptly.

When he opened his eyes, his expression was so guarded I knew both that the mutual kissing lessons were over, and that whatever the reason for it was, I shouldn't pry.

"You did well, too," I said, trying to sound—*feel*—detached about the whole thing. The reality, of course, was that I felt anything but detached. I wanted to kiss him again. Right then. With a reserve of will I didn't know I possessed I stepped back, but not before I registered the flash of disappointment that crossed his face when I moved away. "You've got the modern trends down, I'd say. You're a quick learner."

Frederick straightened, then gave me a self-possessed smile that stole the breath from my lungs.

"So I've been told," he said.

# FOURTEEN

Lord and Lady James Jameson XXIII
and Mrs. Edwina Fitzwilliam
Do Hereby Request the Honor of Your Presence at the
Wedding of Their Children

MISS ESMERALDA JAMESON
and
MR. FREDERICK J. FITZWILLIAM

~ Date and Time to Be Determined ~
The Ballroom, Castle Jameson
New York, New York
Light refreshments and bloodletting will be provided

~ The couple is registered at Crate & Feral ~

"ANSWER ME THIS," I SAID, STARING AT FREDERICK. "FOR SOME-
one who claims to be clueless about modern society, how did you

pick up on how to dress so well from one measly little trip to Nordstrom?"

Frederick seemed genuinely surprised by my comment. "*Do I know how to dress well?*"

I huffed a laugh. If I didn't know better, I'd have accused him of false modesty. He was wearing dark blue jeans and a light blue button-down over which he'd pulled a deep burgundy sweater—none of which we'd purchased at the mall the previous week.

Even if I hadn't kissed him the other night—for science and comparison purposes, of course—it would have been all I could do to keep my hands off him. I was almost afraid to take him to Sam's party looking like this. I didn't know Sam's or Scott's friends well enough to know how they might respond to Frederick walking into this party like the world's most oblivious sex on a stick.

"You do know how to dress well," I confirmed. "You look like you just walked out of a J. Crew photo shoot."

He raised an eyebrow at me. "What is a *J. Crew photo shoot?*"

I waved my hands. "You know what I mean. How could you *possibly* not know exactly what you're doing, dressing like that?"

He paused, considering my question.

"Maybe when a person turns into a vampire, they acquire an encyclopedic and instantly updated understanding of how best to dress for purposes of blending into modern society and attracting victims." He gestured to himself, giving me a broad, dazzling smile. His eyes twinkled with amusement. "What you see before you is the result of millennia of vampiric genetic evolution, Cassie. Nothing more."

I raised a skeptical eyebrow at him and folded my arms across my chest. "Spare me," I said, though I was on the verge of laughing. "There is no such thing as vampire osmosis or I wouldn't be here. And we *didn't* buy you those clothes at the mall."

He gave me another smile, more bashful this time. "Fine, fine. You've got me." He pointed at the television. "I've been watching subtitled Korean dramas on Netflix."

A pause. "Korean dramas?"

"Yes," he confirmed. "Did you know that about a decade ago, South Korea's government began investing massive sums in its entertainment industry? It's an entertainment powerhouse now. It has made a science of dressing its actors and actresses attractively. Between our trip to the mall and *Crash Landing on You,* I've learned an incredible amount."

I hadn't seen any Korean television before. But if Frederick had learned how to dress by watching it, I wasn't about to complain.

"*Crash Landing on You?*" I asked. "Is it good?"

"If vampires were capable of producing tears I would have cried my eyes out." Then he glanced at his new wristwatch— something else we definitely didn't buy together. He'd gotten alarmingly good at online shopping—especially for someone who'd originally been so dead set against connecting to the internet. "It's time for us to leave for your friend's party. Shall we go?"

I nodded and grabbed my purse, trying hard to tamp down the irrational wave of possessiveness that suddenly came over me at the idea of sharing Frederick for an evening with Sam and his friends.

"Oh, before I forget—I want to reassure you that I have given some thought to possible conversation topics for this evening."

"Oh?" This was good news. I'd hoped tonight would be an opportunity for him to practice interacting with people in a relaxed setting. If he'd thought things through a bit, so much the better.

"Yes. I spent four hours on the internet after you went to sleep last night, researching topics of most interest to people between the ages of twenty-five and thirty-five. I noted my findings on a scrap of paper." He patted the front pocket of his jeans nodding proudly. "I am bringing the list with me in case there is time on the train for me to study before we arrive."

My stomach sank. I'd wanted him to have enough familiarity with current events that he would be able to vaguely follow conversation. Maybe even make a casual reference to current music, or skyrocketing rents in the city, or the slow, inexorable decline of capitalistic society. If one of those topics happened to come up, of course.

But it sounded like he'd sat up all night on Wikipedia. That hadn't been my intent at all.

"You didn't actually need to memorize anything," I said. "Or really study anything at all."

His smile slipped. "Oh."

"I'm sure it'll be fine," I said quickly, hoping I sounded more certain of that than I felt. In truth, I was suddenly very concerned Frederick was about to become an in-the-flesh embodiment of the *How do you do, fellow kids?* meme. "Always better to be over-prepared than underprepared, right?"

He straightened a little at that. "True."

Worst-case scenario, I told myself as we made our way down the stairs, Sam and Scott would just become further convinced I was living with a weirdo.

....................

IT WAS IMMEDIATELY OBVIOUS THAT I WAS NOT THE ONLY one who thought Frederick looked good that night.

Or, at least, it was immediately obvious to me. Frederick, on the other hand, seemed completely unaware of the effect he had on the people we passed on the street. His eyes seemed to be everywhere all at once as we walked through the frigid late-autumn evening towards the El, studying our surroundings like he expected to be quizzed on everything later—but the appreciative once-overs and open-mouthed stares he earned from passersby went right over his head.

"Is this how you get to work every day?" His voice was full of wonder as we descended into the underground El station. Frederick seemed to be the only person not bundled up like a shapeless potato against the cold. It hadn't occurred to me before now that he didn't get cold the way humans did, though in hindsight it probably should have. Either way, the lack of extensive bundling up only enhanced his attractiveness. A group of young women making their way up the stairs stopped mid-conversation and turned to watch him as he and I approached the ticket vestibule.

"Sometimes I take the El to the library, yeah," I said, clenching my jaw a little and fighting against a wave of irrational jealousy. Everyone was right to think Frederick was hot, of course. I had no business being jealous. I had no claim on him. "Other times I take the bus."

When we got to the crowded platform, Frederick stared anxiously up at the sign flashing the names and wait times of the different trains that were due to come through the station.

"You really haven't taken the El before? Or a bus?" I knew he hadn't, but I still couldn't fathom someone living in Chicago for any length of time without at least occasionally taking public transportation.

"Never." His eyes widened when the flashing *4 minutes* by the name of the northbound Red Line train changed to *3 minutes*. "I haven't been on any kind of train in over one hundred years and . . . well. It worked differently back then."

"How do you get around, then?"

He gave a one-shoulder shrug, eyes still on the sign. "I get around in a few different ways. Vampires can run very fast, you know. Also, if necessary, vampires can fly."

Frederick could freaking *fly*? That was news to me. I glared at him and said, "You told me you wouldn't hide anything important anymore."

"I didn't think knowing how I got around Chicago was important." A corner of his mouth ticked up. "I am also joking about being able to fly."

I rolled my eyes. "Joking, Frederick? Twice in one evening?"

His eyes twinkled with amusement. "Well. *Partially* joking."

I was about to ask what *that* meant when our train surged into the platform. Everyone except Frederick instinctively stepped back from the platform's edge as it hurtled into view. I grabbed him by the arm to get him to step away.

The feel of his biceps beneath my fingertips triggered my body's memory.

It was the first time we had touched since we'd kissed in the kitchen two nights ago. His strong arms pulling me impossibly close. His lips, soft and pliant, brushing against my own.

I shook my head. Now was not the time to dwell on something we hadn't even talked about since it happened. We were about to get on the Red Line at rush hour—a stressful endeavor even if it wasn't your first time on public transportation. And Frederick was counting on me to guide him through it.

"This is an assault on the senses, Cassie," Frederick said, shouting to be heard over the din of the station and the *whoosh* of the approaching train.

"You're not wrong about that," I shouted back. Sam's party started at seven, and the platform was packed with people—some heading home from work, some on their way to a Cubs game (if the sheer volume of Cubs hats and jerseys people were wearing were any indication), and still others who, like us, were simply going out on a Friday night.

The noise and the crowds that went along with riding the El at rush hour on a Friday were a lot to handle, even for someone who did this almost every day. In hindsight, I probably should have introduced Frederick to public transportation at a saner hour. But he wanted to learn about life in the twenty-first century. Might as well throw him into the deep end of the pool.

The train cars opened with a loud *ding-dong* sound. I kept my hold on Frederick's arm, wordlessly signaling him to wait until everyone who wanted to get off had left the train.

"One small step for vampire, one giant leap for vampire-kind," I murmured into his ear as we stepped aboard, pleased at my little joke. But his forehead creased in confusion. He looked like he was about to ask what that meant when a loud group of guys in Cubs jerseys shoved past us from behind and muscled aboard the train.

"*Oh!*"

Frederick's hands flew up to grip my arms, steadying me as I nearly toppled to the floor. The train lurched forward a moment later—and while usually I prided myself on my ability to ride public transportation without losing my balance, the suddenness of Frederick's fingertips digging into my upper arms caught me completely by surprise.

I quickly regained my footing, averting my eyes as a warm flush crept up the back of my neck. I tried not to think about how close he was but pretty much totally failed. He relaxed his grip a little once it became clear I wasn't going to fall, but even though I was clearly totally fine now, he seemed not to know what to do with his hands once he'd put them on my body.

Which just made things that much more awkward when the train jerked unexpectedly, one of the Cubs fans stumbled into me from behind, and I fell directly into Frederick.

"*Shit!*" My exclamation was muffled by his broad chest. His burgundy sweater was so soft it might as well have been made of angel kisses. I breathed in, deep and reflexively, and then immediately wished I hadn't because, god, he smelled good.

Beyond good.

I had no idea if it was some sort of expensive cologne, or the soap he used—or if all vampires smelled this amazing if you breathed them in right at the source. All I knew was that the scent of him made me want to crawl inside his soft, fitted shirt and wrap myself up in it. Right there, on the crowded Red Line train, all the other passengers be damned.

"Cassie?" Frederick's voice rumbled in his chest. "Are . . . are you okay?"

He sounded concerned but made no move to disentangle himself from me. Not that he could have; the wall of the train was at his back and we were packed in there like sardines. However, he could have at least *tried* to put some space between us.

But he didn't.

Instead, he slowly slid his hands from where they still rested on my shoulders down to the small of my back, enveloping me in his arms in the process.

He pulled me closer.

"It isn't safe in here," he murmured, his breath fanning cool and sweet across the top of my head. "I will hold on to you. For your own protection, I mean. Just until we reach our destination."

What he was saying was just an excuse to keep holding me. I knew that. But I didn't care. I shivered, tucking myself closer to him before I could remind myself that cuddling in public with one's vampire roommate was probably not a smart idea. But his body just felt so delicious against mine. Despite the chill he radiated, I felt nothing but heat suffusing me, excitement racing down my spine as he pulled me closer and rested his cheek against the top of my head.

The rest of the train ride simultaneously took far too long, and by passed in an instant.

# FIFTEEN

**Letter from Mrs. Edwina Fitzwilliam to
Mr. Frederick J. Fitzwilliam, dated November 11**

My dearest Frederick,

I will not beat around the bush with you.

I have it from the Jamesons directly that you have continued to ignore my entreaties and are still returning Miss Jameson's gifts to you unopened.

This will not stand.

I have booked passage on a direct flight from London, where I am currently on holiday, to Chicago next Tuesday evening. Given that the mail is not a speedy business, I suppose there is a chance that I will arrive in Chicago before this letter does. If that happens, so be it. Perhaps it would be better if you have no forewarning before I arrive. That way I will be able to see for myself the mess you have made of your life.

*Despite all, I do love you, Frederick. In time I*
*hope you come to understand I have only ever had*
*your best interests at heart.*

*With kind regards,*
*Your mother,*
*Mrs. Edwina Fitzwilliam*

AFTER FREDERICK AND I GOT OFF THE TRAIN WE WALKED
towards Sam's apartment in lockstep. Even though we sprang
apart the instant the train stopped moving I could feel his touch
as acutely as if we were still embracing.

Frederick drummed the fingers of his right hand rapidly
against his leg—what I'd come to recognize as his most obvious
nervous tell. He kept his eyes straight ahead, not sparing me so
much as a sideways glance.

"I have made a list of several topics of conversation for this
party," he said, repeating himself from earlier in the evening. He
slid his hand into the front pocket of his slacks and extracted a
small, folded piece of paper. His hand was trembling. He must have
been affected by what happened between us on the train, too—
because his hands rarely shook, and he never repeated himself.

The thought was both exhilarating and terrifying.

"You already told me that," I said.

A car drove by us, its windows rolled down. Hip-hop music I
didn't recognize blasted on its radio.

"I already told you that?"

"You did."

"Oh."

Fortunately, it wasn't far to Sam's building. When we got
there I pushed the buzzer on the front door panel to let Sam and

Scott know we'd arrived. The door lock clicked a moment later, and I grabbed the door's handle to pull it open.

Frederick put his hand on my upper arm, stopping me. The urgency of his touch cut through my thick winter coat like a knife.

"Remember? I need explicit permission from them before I can enter their home."

I blinked, trying to understand what he was saying. "What?"

He looked away, sheepish. "Remember, when we watched *Buffy*, how I told you that some vampire legends are rubbish while others are legitimate? This one is legitimate."

Then it clicked. That evening with him on the couch, when we'd discussed *Buffy*—shortly before I fell asleep with my head on his shoulder.

"Oh," I said abruptly, warming at the memory. "Yes, of course. I'm sorry I forgot about that." I pointed at the button I'd just pushed. "But they unlocked it for us. Isn't that enough?"

"No." His eyes were on his shoes. He was embarrassed, I realized. My heart clenched. "It . . . must be a direct, explicit invitation. Could you possibly text Sam or Scott and ask them to invite me in?"

Laughter drifted down to us from an open window. The party was already in full swing. "They're going to think that's weird, Frederick."

"Be that as it may, I don't have much of a choice."

Just then, a guy I recognized as Sam's downstairs neighbor appeared in the doorway, dressed in a bright pink leather minidress that stopped about six inches above his knees. He had an occasional gig as a burlesque dancer at a club in Andersonville, if I remembered correctly.

He was fumbling around in a purse he carried that matched

his outfit. Out of the corner of my eye I could see Frederick gaping at him and his outfit in stunned silence, his dark eyes wide as saucers. I ignored him.

"Jack!" I exclaimed, hoping to get his attention, and hoping that was actually his name.

He looked up.

"Cassie?"

"Yeah, hi." I looked over my shoulder at Frederick, who nodded encouragingly. "Can we come inside?"

"You heading up to Sam's?"

"We are."

He opened the door wider for us and motioned for us to come inside. "Sure. I'm just on my way out."

I glanced questioningly back at Frederick, who gave me a subtle nod that I interpreted to mean *good enough for me.*

"Thanks, Jack," I said. I made my way across the threshold, Frederick close behind me. He let out a quiet sigh once we were both safely inside.

Fortunately, Scott was already waiting for us in the doorway to his second-floor apartment.

"Can we come in?" I asked, hoping my voice didn't betray how nervous I suddenly was. A loud cacophony of voices and some kind of avant-garde house music poured out into the hallway from inside.

"Of course," Scott said. He gestured to the apartment behind him. "I'm just waiting for Katie to get here, then I'll go back inside."

My eyebrows shot up. "Katie? As in, Gossamer's Katie?"

"Yeah," Scott said. "We got to know her from all those nights visiting you at work. I was happy when she said she could make it."

I wished I was happy, too. Katie and I got along well—but

Frederick had made such a weird first impression on her the night he'd tried to order coffee and then pay it with his fanny pack of gold doubloons.

He'd made real strides towards passing as normal the past few weeks. He'd learned how to order clothes online. He'd ridden the El without anyone thinking he didn't belong there. The last thing he needed was to see Katie at this party and have her ask uncomfortable questions.

But I supposed there was nothing to be done for it.

I turned to Frederick. "Want something to drink?"

His brow furrowed. "No. I ate before we got here. You *know* I can't—"

I grabbed his lapel and tugged him down until his ear was at a level with my mouth. I resisted the urge to just stand there, breathing him in—but barely. "You have to do some pretending tonight for this to work."

He swallowed, then straightened.

"Right." He nodded. "Let's get a drink."

As we made our way inside, I turned to him and asked, very quietly, "By the way, what happens if you don't get permission?"

"I beg your pardon?"

"You said you can't enter someone's home without an invitation," I reminded him. "What happens if you try?"

"Oh. That." He quickly looked over his shoulder to make certain no one was within earshot, and then leaned in close. "Instant disintegration."

I stared at him. "You're kidding."

He shook his head gravely. "When I first heard about this phenomenon, I thought it was a joke, too. But not long after I was turned, I saw another vampire try and break into a local farmer's house while he and his family were out of town." He paused, then leaned in closer before adding, "Vampire bits *everywhere*."

I shuddered, though I was somewhat distracted from the graphic story by both the fact that in telling it, Frederick had chosen to share with me another closely guarded detail of his prior life—and the fact that his mouth was now just a hairs-breadth away from mine.

"How awful," I said, trying to keep it together.

"Yes," Frederick agreed, somberly. "It's not a mistake you make a second time."

"Cassie."

I looked up to see Sam, striding towards us from the kitchen. He had a beer in one hand and a glass of white wine in the other.

He handed the wine to me, but his eyes were on Frederick.

My stomach was suddenly a hard, tight knot of anxiety. It had been one thing for Frederick to interact with my best friend for two minutes at the mall the other day. It was another thing for them to spend an entire evening together. From the look on his face, Sam seemed to have gotten over whatever *oh no he's hot* moment he'd succumbed to during their last brief meeting and was prepared to come to a final decision about whether Frederick was a creep or was trustworthy.

I fidgeted with the stem of the wine glass and inclined my head towards Frederick. "Sam, you know Frederick."

Sam extended his hand. "Nice to see you again."

Frederick clasped Sam's hand in his and gave it a firm shake. "Thank you for extending us this invitation to your home. It is nice to see you again as well."

"Can I get you something to drink?" he asked. "Wine? Beer?"

Frederick was quiet as he pondered how to answer that. He

may have studied for tonight but he and I hadn't actually gone over small talk at parties. Which, in hindsight, was an incredibly stupid oversight on my part. I braced myself for Frederick's answer, hoping it would be at least somewhat within the realm of normal.

"I . . . cannot decide," Frederick eventually said. "What would you recommend?"

I let out the breath I hadn't known I'd been holding. Since joining his law firm Sam had become the world's biggest lawyer cliché by getting into different kinds of fancy wines. He loved boring everyone else with endless details about his latest discoveries.

I gave Frederick a small nod, which I hoped conveyed *That was the right thing to say.* His rigid posture relaxed slightly.

"That depends on your preference. I have a bunch of different reds," Sam said. "Do you like Malbec?"

Frederick glanced at me, his eyes a question. I gave another small, encouraging nod.

"Yes," Frederick said with the conviction usually reserved for questions about Halloween candy preferences. "Yes, I do like red wine. Very much so. In fact, Malbec is my favorite."

"Mine, too." Sam grinned at him, and if I weren't so relieved that Frederick was doing so well, I'd have laughed at how easy it was to play my friend. "Come into the kitchen and I'll get you set up."

Frederick stared at him like a deer caught in headlights.

"Go get a drink," I encouraged. And then, gesturing towards Sam, I added, "Sam will make sure to get you something good."

"Something good," Frederick repeated, an eyebrow raised. I winced, kicking myself for not warning him ahead of time that if he went to human parties he'd be expected to walk around with a drink he wouldn't want for most of the evening.

Once Frederick and Sam left for the kitchen I glanced around the room, trying to see if there were familiar faces. I vaguely recognized some guests from other get-togethers Sam and Scott had thrown over the years, but then I saw David—Sam and Scott's friend who was involved with the River North Gallery art exhibition—sitting on the couch beside Sam's sister Amelia.

My heart sped up. Professional networking was just above tooth extraction without Novocain on my list of favorite activities. Chatting with Amelia, Sam's extremely competent and put-together sister, was only marginally more enjoyable. But David was right there, less than ten feet away, chatting with a perfectly dressed, not-a-hair-out-of-place Amelia as he sipped from his glass of Chardonnay.

It had been forty-eight hours since I'd emailed David my submission. The River North Gallery was making their decisions within the coming week. A person in charge of her life would take this opportunity to talk with him, right?

Might as well pretend I was in charge of my life and do the same.

I squared my shoulders, reminded myself that I did hard things *all the time*, and approached them.

"Hi," I said.

David and Amelia looked up at me at the same time.

All at once, I remembered I wasn't remotely in charge of my own life and this was probably a terrible mistake.

"Cassie," Amelia said. Her tone was bright, and she smiled at me—but even over the din of the party I was reminded of how condescending she used to be whenever she deigned to speak with me back in high school. "It's so nice to see you again."

"It's been a long time," I said. I would make an effort tonight for Sam, I decided. "How have you been?"

Amelia shook her blond head and sighed, then took a sip of her white wine before setting the glass back down on the coffee table.

"Busy," she said. "Not as busy as I'll be in the spring, but busier than I want to be."

I tried to think of a time when Amelia *wasn't* so busy with her accounting practice that she was utterly miserable. My mind drew a blank.

"That sucks," I said, meaning it.

Amelia shrugged. "It is what it is, I guess. It's what I signed up for when I joined the firm. But enough about me," she said. "Sam says you've been really throwing yourself into your art again."

I nodded, too proud of what I'd been doing lately—and too cognizant of the fact that someone on the River North Gallery committee was sitting beside Amelia—to feel self-conscious.

"Yeah," I said. "I have been. In fact—"

I was cut off from finishing my sentence by Sam—who was now rushing over to Amelia's side with a petrified-looking Frederick in tow.

"Amelia," he said, laughing. "You have *got* to talk with Cassie's new roommate."

Sam's words distracted me completely from my anxiety over talking with Amelia and David, catching my attention as effectively as a record scratch in a quiet room. Alarmed, I turned to look at Frederick, whose wrist was in Sam's iron grip.

He was staring, wild-eyed, down at his shoes.

Before I could ask what was going on, Sam turned to me and said, delighted, "You never told me Frederick was such a big Taylor Swift fan."

I choked on my sip of wine.

"I'm sorry," I said, once I recovered. "But . . . Taylor Swift?"

Frederick shuffled his feet awkwardly. "I . . . might have mentioned a few things I knew about Taylor Swift to some people in the kitchen."

"A *few* things?" Sam laughed again and shook his head. "Don't be so modest. Your knowledge of her 1989 era is encyclopedic."

I had to stifle a laugh in my palm. "Is that so?"

"It is!" Sam gushed. "Like I was saying, Frederick—you need to talk with Amelia. She loves meeting other Swifties, especially when they're people who don't fit the usual stereotypes."

"Oh, yes," Amelia said. She was beaming now. I'd never heard her sound so delighted. "When people outside the expected demographics are really into her, too, it just proves how broad Taylor's appeal is, and how deep her talent."

I stared at her. It hadn't occurred to me that an accountant could *have* opinions on music. Though perhaps that was just me being overly judgmental. "You're a Taylor Swift fan?"

Amelia shrugged. "I mean, what's not to like?"

"I agree," Frederick said, with an enthusiasm that stunned me. "Taylor Swift, who was born in West Reading, Pennsylvania, in 1989, has won eleven Grammy Awards from the National Academy of Recording Arts and Sciences."

Amelia stood up and, still grinning, smoothed her hands over her wrinkle-free skirt. "Let's go into the kitchen and fangirl together," she proposed to Frederick.

Frederick's eyes widened. "I beg your pardon, but . . ." He glanced at me. "*Fangirl?*"

I leaned over a little and murmured, "It just means to get excited about something."

"Oh."

"I'll get another glass of Malbec," Sam suggested. "I won't be able to contribute much to the conversation, but I always enjoy watching Amelia in her element."

Frederick cast a helpless glance at me over his shoulder as Amelia guided him back into the kitchen.

With Amelia gone, the only person left for me to talk to was David. He looked up at me with a smile of recognition.

I swallowed, my nerves from a few minutes ago racing back now that the twin distractions of Frederick and Taylor Swift were out of the room.

"Cassie." David motioned to the empty spot on the couch beside him. I took it, feeling both eager and terrified. "Nice to see you. It's been a while."

"Nice to see you, too." I started fidgeting with the hem of my skirt as I tried to decide whether I should just tell him I'd submitted something for the art show, or if I should be more subtle about why I wanted to talk with him. "How are things going?"

"Busy." David laughed, and then—perhaps realizing that's exactly how Amelia answered that same question a few minutes ago—he rolled his eyes. "*Busy* is such a bullshitty small-talk non-answer of a way to answer that question, isn't it?"

I stifled a laugh. "Maybe?"

He waved a dismissive hand. "Yeah. Well, in my case, at least, it's true."

"Getting ready for the art exhibition?" Might as well get it over with.

"Yeah, actually." His smile grew. "I've never been involved in a juried show before from the administrative side of things, but it's a lot more work than I expected it to be."

"I can imagine it would be a ton of work." I swallowed, then mustered up my courage to ask for the information I really wanted. "Are you seeing a lot of good submissions?"

"*So* many." He shifted uneasily on the couch beside me. "I think the committee has made its final decisions on who to invite."

My heart was suddenly hammering so hard inside my rib cage it felt on the cusp of breaking bone. I set my wine glass down on the coffee table in front of us; my hands were shaking too badly to trust I wouldn't spill Chardonnay everywhere.

"Oh?"

"Yes." David was looking at the beer in his hands like it was the most interesting thing in the room. "Cassie, I don't know if I should be the one to tell you this, or if I'm supposed to wait to let the committee get in touch with you, but seeing as we're both here . . ."

He trailed off without finishing his sentence. But I could tell by the way he wasn't meeting my eyes that whatever he'd been about to say next, I wouldn't like it.

I took a deep breath, preparing myself for the worst. "I promise I won't tell them that you told me."

He nodded. "Everyone agreed your piece was terrific, but the committee decided your take on the Contemporary Society theme was too abstract and attenuated to accept into the exhibition. A classic painting subverted with such modern materials just wasn't what they were looking for." He paused before adding, "I'm sorry, Cassie."

Time seemed to stop. All the noise of the party fell away as what David had just told me slowly sank in.

"The judges had mostly finalized their decisions before we got your application," David continued. My despair must have been written all over my face because he reached out and gently put a hand on mine. "You know how it goes with these things. Unfortunately, your piece didn't grab them enough for them to change their minds."

Tears prickled at the corners of my eyes. I'd known there was no guarantee that my piece would be accepted, and of course I knew that most of the slots would likely go to people who were already established names in the art world. So, really, I had no idea why I was reacting like this.

But I was, all the same.

I turned and looked at the floor so David wouldn't see me cry.

"I understand," I mumbled.

"I'm sorry," David said again, his hand still resting on mine. "We're going to be doing another show next fall. You're *really* talented, Cassie. I hope you'll consider submitting something else when that request for submissions goes live."

"Okay," I said. I turned to smile at him, but his face was blurry. The tears were threatening to fall in earnest now.

Why I'd ever thought I'd be anything but a complete and to-tal fuckup was beyond me. I would always just be Cassie—the quirky eccentric who couldn't hold a job or even an apartment for more than a few months. The girl who would never achieve her dreams or amount to much of anything at all.

I glanced around the room. More guests had arrived. Sam and Scott were talking with a group of people I vaguely recog-nized as Sam's law school classmates. One of them was laughing at something Sam had just said.

Frederick and Amelia were nowhere to be seen.

Even a centuries-old vampire had his shit more together than I did.

I had to get out of there.

"Excuse me," I said to David in a watery voice, keeping my face turned away from him. "I . . . need to go check on something."

Sniffling, I quickly made my way out of the room, heading straight for the bathroom.

I was on the cusp of a full-on pity party.

Nobody needed to see that.

.....................

I STARED AT MY FACE IN THE BATHROOM MIRROR. FOR THE first time in I couldn't remember how long I'd decided to wear mascara, and I regretted that decision now. A raccoon's face stared back at me from the mirror, eyes ringed with smears of black makeup and cheeks splotchy with tears.

It made me feel like an even bigger idiot than I had when I'd ran in here to hide ten minutes earlier. Which was saying a lot.

A quiet knock on the bathroom door startled me out of my self-pity.

"Cassie? Are you in there?" Frederick's voice. It was low and full of concern. A gentle, reassuring warmth flooded me at the sound of it.

"No." Without thinking, I scrubbed away my tears with the back of my hand. It came away streaked with black.

"I just spoke with someone who said she saw you rush in here. I'm concerned. May I come in?"

"I said I'm not in here."

A quiet huff of a laugh. "Clearly you are."

I shut my eyes and leaned my forehead against the door separating us. The smooth wood felt refreshingly cool against my flushed skin. "I am *such* an idiot."

"You are not."

"You have to say that." Fresh tears pricked behind my closed eyelids. "You don't know how to ride the El by yourself and you'll be stuck here at this party forever if you aren't nice to me."

Another quiet laugh, then more firmly, "Move away from the door, Cassie. I'm worried about you. I'd like to come in."

His slightly authoritative tone flipped some sort of switch inside of me. "Okay," I said, sniffling.

He stepped inside the small bathroom—all six feet two inches of him, broad-shouldered and beautiful—before quietly closing the door behind him. All of a sudden I was reminded of just how small this space really was.

He seemed to notice it the same instant I did, his eyes widening as they darted over the shower stall behind me, the toilet, the sink. But then he saw my face, and the mess I'd made of it—and then his attention was all on me.

"Who did this to you?" His voice was low, but urgent. "What happened?"

"Nothing happened." I tried to turn away from him, but he grabbed hold of my arm, keeping me in place. I shivered, the chill from his touch burning its way through the fabric of my shirt and creating a stark contrast with the rush of warmth I suddenly felt everywhere else. "I'm a failure, is all."

"You are *not* a failure," he said firmly. "Anyone who made you feel like one will have *me* to deal with."

I smiled a little at the idea of Frederick threatening anyone at all. He might be an undead creature of the night—but as undead creatures of the night went, he was a marshmallow.

I sniffled. "That person, unfortunately, is me."

"You?"

"Yeah." I closed my eyes. "I submitted a piece I've been working on for weeks to an art exhibition. I was really excited about it, but I just found out it's been rejected."

"Oh, Cassie," Frederick said, his tone laced with sympathy. "I am so sorry." His hand was still on my arm. His touch was grounding. I hoped he wouldn't pull it back anytime soon. "Is that all?"

I sighed. "I'm such a fuckup, Frederick."

"People are rejected from things all the time, Cassie." He paused, thinking. "In a way, I was rejected from the entire past century."

I rolled my eyes. "Not the same thing."

"You're right. What I did was worse."

"How is it worse?"

His eyes twinkled. "I drank something Reginald offered me at a party. *Like an idiot.* Talk about being a fuckup."

I hiccup-laughed a little in spite of myself. Hearing Frederick use modern slang was like seeing a toddler with a fake mustache. He smiled at my reaction, clearly pleased with himself.

And then, all at once, his expression grew serious. "If anyone *fucked up* here, Cassie, it was the committee that refused to accept a visionary artist into the exhibition."

I blinked at him, stunned at the intensity of his praise.

"You don't have to say that."

"I never say things I don't mean."

Before I could decide how to respond to that, Frederick pulled a square of fabric from the front pocket of his jeans. Muttering something under his breath I couldn't make out, he turned on the faucet and ran the fabric beneath it.

"What are you doing?"

"No one seems to carry handkerchiefs anymore," he mused. "It's a pity. They work so much better than the thin paper tissues used nowadays. Now close your eyes."

He turned to face me with a look of quiet concentration. His eyes flicked to mine. Or, more specifically, to the mess of black eye makeup smeared beneath them.

Embarrassment flooded me. "Frederick, you don't have to—"

"Close your eyes, Cassie." His tone brooked no opposition, his stern insistence touching some raw, primal part of me that was helpless to do anything but obey.

His free hand cupped my cheek, gently tilting my face upward so he could look at me more clearly. Suddenly, it felt like all my nerve endings centered right where he touched me.

My eyes slid closed of their own accord.

"What is this black substance you have used to paint your face?" His voice was quiet, curious, as he tenderly wiped away the remnants of my mascara with his handkerchief. His face was so close to mine I could feel each of his shallow exhalations of breath on my skin. "I've not seen this sort of cosmetic before."

My mouth went dry. "It's . . . called mascara."

"Mascara." He said the word with obvious distaste, but I only dimly registered it. It was hard for me to focus on much of anything at all but the gentle swipes of his fingers beneath my eyes and the press of his free hand to my cheek. All the oxygen seemed to have vanished from the too-small room. My heart was thundering in my ears.

"It's vile," he added.

"I like mascara."

"Why?" His handkerchief dipped into the corner of my right eye, where the smudges were the worst. He leaned in even closer—probably to give himself a better view of what he was doing. He smelled like red wine and the fabric softener he used on his clothing. My lungs seemed to have forgotten how to breathe.

"It . . . makes me look good."

His hands stopped moving. When he spoke again, Frederick's voice was so low I almost didn't hear him. "You do not need cosmetics for that, Cassie."

All at once, the noise from the party, the slow drip of water from the shower behind me—all of it melted away. There was nothing but Frederick's tender hands, touching my face so gently I could hardly bear it—and the steady, rapid beat of my heart.

After what might have been a few minutes, or an hour, Frederick dropped the handkerchief onto the counter. I could feel him shift even closer to me, in the small, confined room, until our knees touched.

My eyes stayed closed. My stomach tightened with anticipation and nerves. I suspected that once I opened my eyes again everything between us would change.

I licked my lips without thinking—and registered his sharp intake of breath.

"Are . . . are the smudges gone?" My voice was shaky. I felt moments away from flying apart at the seams.

His hand was steady against my cheek. "Yes. They're gone." Frederick was standing so close to me now his words were cool puffs of air on my lips. I shivered, the need for him to move even closer nearly overwhelming. "Open your eyes, Cassie."

His mouth was on mine before I had a chance to comply, the gentle pressure of his lips stealing the breath from my lungs and pushing out any worries I might have had about whether this was a good idea. His hand slid down to my chin, gently tilting it up a little to give him better access. I was so overwhelmed with sensation that I was helpless to do anything but let him kiss me, and to kiss him back. My hands slid up his broad chest of their own volition, the fabric of his shirt soft beneath my fingers as I clutched at the ends of his collar with both hands.

My touch elicited a quiet moan from the back of his throat that made me dizzy with a spike of searing desire.

"We can't do this here," I mumbled against his lips. Mostly because it felt like something I was *supposed* to say, given that this was Sam's bathroom and an entire apartment full of people was having a party on the other side of the door.

But I knew, even as I said the words, that we were *absolutely* going to do this here.

It didn't seem like Frederick even heard what I'd said. If he did, he certainly wasn't paying it any mind. His kisses grew bolder, the exquisite pressure of his mouth increasing until I parted my lips for him on a ragged sigh. He tasted like breath mints and the wine he must have pretended to drink earlier this evening. I wanted to lose myself in it—in the way he slid his tongue along mine, coaxing a whimper from my throat; in his strong arms, as they encircled me and pulled me closer. I could feel his sharp, prominent canines against my tongue as I kissed him, something I'd certainly never noticed before when I'd seen him smile. A thrilling flash of heat shot through me, the visceral reminder of who and what he was startling me for only a moment before I lost myself in the kiss again.

"I have not done this in over one hundred years," he breathed, pulling away. He looked so dazed I didn't know if he was telling me this or saying it to himself. "Not since the other night."

He didn't wait for me to respond, only quickly maneuvered me away from the sink until I felt the bathroom wall pressed firmly against my back. He loomed closer, crowding me, leaning forward against the wall himself until his forearms bracketed my head. His dark eyes were all pupils, blown wide with the same desire I could feel coursing through my bloodstream. His mouth was less than an inch from mine. It took all my self-control not to lean forward right then and capture those plush lips of his in another kiss.

"Cassie," he breathed. "I—"

Whatever he'd been about to say was interrupted by a series of very loud, insistent raps on the bathroom door.

Frederick jumped back and away from me as if I'd scalded him.

"Anyone in there?" A woman's pleasant voice cut through the haze of lust like a knife.

*Oh no*, Frederick mouthed, his eyes wide.

"Just a minute," I yelled, trying not to laugh at how horrified Frederick looked. "We're almost done in here."

"All good!" the woman said, a bit too loudly. "I'll come back in a few minutes."

"Why did you say *we* are almost done in here?" Frederick whispered hoarsely. He looked like he was about to throw up. Could vampires throw up, I wondered? Something to think about later. "There are at least two dozen other people out there. And now, they will all know we were in this very small bathroom together all this time. Alone."

"So?"

"*So?*" He stared at me, incredulous. "What will they *think*, Cassie?"

If Frederick had pearls to clutch, he certainly would be clutching them now. He looked so petrified I had to bite the inside of my cheek to keep from laughing.

"Who cares what they think?"

"Your *reputation*, Cassie!" He shook his head. "The *conclusions* they will likely draw!"

I raised an eyebrow at him. "What sort of conclusions? That you were drinking my blood?"

His eyebrows shot up his forehead. "No! That we were . . . that we were . . ."

I slowly crossed the room until I was standing just a few inches away from him. I placed my hands flat on his chest. He made a little pained noise in the back of his throat that only spurred me on. If I had my way, he would be making that noise for me again and again that night.

"That we were what, Frederick?"

He swallowed. I tracked the movement of his Adam's apple, fighting the sharp urge to trace its shape with my tongue.

"That I was debauching you."

It was only the deadly serious expression on his face that kept me from laughing out loud.

"They might assume we were making out in here, yeah. But who cares?"

He looked horrified. "*Cassie—*"

I placed a finger to his lips, silencing him. "Things have changed in the past hundred years. It doesn't matter what anyone thinks."

He didn't seem to believe my assertions that he didn't need to worry about protecting my virtue or my honor. But when I grabbed his wrist to pull him out of the bathroom, he followed me all the same.

"Let's say goodbye to Sam and Scott and thank them for inviting us," I said. "Then let's go home."

# SIXTEEN

*Excerpt from Chapter 17 of*
**Making Love to Humans in the Twenty-First Century:**
**A Definitive Guide for the Modern Vampire**
*(Author Unknown)*

*If you have read this far, you now understand the full extent to which sexual mores and expectations have changed since the era when everyone simply pretended to wait until marriage to have sexual intercourse. There are certain acts your twenty-first-century human lover will likely expect that may catch you by surprise if you have not engaged in sexual congress in some decades.*

*This chapter describes several of the most popular modern methods for bringing a human to orgasm using one's mouth. The key, as we will discuss in more detail below, is to obscure your fangs. At the end of this chapter, you will be guided step-by-step through a series of practice exercises that, when implemented in bed, will leave your human lover immensely satisfied.*

FREDERICK CONVINCED ME TO TAKE AN UBER WITH HIM back to the apartment. Though *convincing* was an overstatement; I'd agreed as soon as he'd suggested it. After all, he'd done amazingly well picking up the public transportation basics on our earlier El adventure. If he felt uncomfortable with the process of riding the train, we could try again another time.

More to the point: Uber would get us home faster than the train. After what had just happened at Sam's party, I was eager to get home as quickly as possible.

It was obvious Frederick felt the same way. Once we were in our seat belts and our driver pulled away from the curb, Frederick's hands were on me again—touching my shoulders, in my hair. He looked at me with a guarded, hopeful expression.

I was only too ready to pick up again right where we left off. But first, I had some questions.

"Taylor Swift, huh?" I smirked at him, enjoying the way he fidgeted in his seat. "You're a Swiftie?"

He winced a little at the term. "No. It's like I said earlier. I just studied before the party."

"I guess you did."

He nodded. His fingers played idly with the hair at the nape of my neck, sending shivers of pleasure down my spine. "I wanted to be certain I'd have something to say to people at the party, and my research indicated she was particularly famous among people between the ages of twenty-five and thirty-eight."

"She is," I agreed.

His eyes fell to my lips, pupils dilated. His arm left his side and wrapped around me, pulling me closer. I could sense he was quickly losing interest in this conversation.

"It only took me two hours after you were in bed last night to memorize everything I could about her. Easy cheesy."

I smiled, and was about to tell him that the expression he was looking for was *easy peasy*—but before I could form the words he was kissing me again, his lips achingly soft against mine.

"Wait." I pulled back a little, trying to catch my breath. I inclined my head towards our driver. "Maybe we should wait until we get home."

"Why?"

"We have an audience."

"Ah." His eyes twinkled with mischief, a smug smile playing on his lips. Now it was my turn to stare at his mouth. Our faces were so close. "The driver can't see what we're doing."

I glanced at the driver. His eyes were on the road in front of him, not in his rearview mirror—which plainly showed me and Frederick tangled up in each other in his back seat.

"He doesn't see what we're doing?"

"No."

An uneasy chill crept down my spine. "Why not?"

Frederick sighed, then pulled away from me, flopping back in his seat. My body protested at the sudden loss of physical contact.

"Vampires have . . . a certain degree of magical ability." He pulled a face, then made a seesawing motion with his hand. "No. Calling it *magical ability* isn't quite it. Suffice it to say that I have the ability to do some things humans can't. The vast majority of vampires can use some degree of glamour on humans to make things appear different from how they are in reality."

"Really?"

Frederick nodded. "Our driver thinks we're each absorbed in our respective cell phones, keeping hands and all other body parts to ourselves."

I paused, processing this. What he was telling me—that vampires had the ability to make people see things that weren't there—was more or less in keeping with vampire stories I'd heard over the years. Then, suddenly, something occurred to me.

The prominent fangs I'd never noticed before I kissed him at Sam's party.

"Is that why I never noticed your . . . your *teeth* until tonight?" I raised an accusatory eyebrow. "Were you glamouring me, before?"

He looked surprised. "I didn't realize you noticed my fangs at the party."

I huffed. "Kind of impossible to miss them with my tongue in your mouth. Those things are . . . I mean, they're *massive*. And really pointy."

Frederick fidgeted with his seat belt. "It wasn't intentional, hiding them from you before. Generally speaking, humans are simultaneously a threat to us and our next meal. Using glamour to hide our fangs from humans in our midst is a self-defense mechanism. A reflex, really. When that particular glamour drops into place it's usually as involuntary as breathing." He rubbed at the back of his neck, adding, "The glamour only falls away again once we are completely comfortable in our surroundings. With people we trust."

He looked at me then, his gaze so open and guileless I understood at once the implication of his words.

He trusted me.

I could see, from my peripheral vision, that we were nearly at the apartment. A few minutes without a seat belt would be okay, right?

Before I could talk myself out of doing it, I unbuckled my seat belt and crawled onto his lap, straddling him, as the Uber guy continued driving us home, oblivious. Frederick's entire body went rigid, his thigh muscles flexing and tensing beneath me as I situated myself.

His large hands slid up to clutch at my hips, his eyes so wide with surprise I couldn't help but wonder how long it had been since he'd last been intimate with someone. He'd certainly picked up kissing quickly enough, but the little I knew about the era before he'd fallen asleep suggested he might not be used to doing much more than kissing.

Would this be an opportunity for me to teach him some of the other modern skills he may have missed during his long coma?

There'd be plenty of time to figure that out later.

For now, I simply leaned forward until my mouth was at his ear, our torsos pressed together. Frederick's breath hitched, his fingertips now digging into the soft flesh at either side of my waist.

"Do you have any other magic powers?" I pressed a lingering kiss to his earlobe, my right hand trailing down his chest until it rested over his long-dormant heart. "Or is glamouring people the only one?"

He chuckled, the reverberations of his laughter warm and gentle against my palm. "There's one more," he admitted.

"What is it?" The car was parallel parking now, coming to a complete stop in front of our apartment. I pressed a kiss to Frederick's lips; a promise of what was to come when I got him inside. "Tell me."

Frederick shook his head. "It's . . . a rather stupid ability, as these things go. But if you really want to know I'll tell you what it is when we get upstairs."

...................

WHEN WE GOT BACK TO THE APARTMENT FREDERICK grabbed my hand and tugged me along after him until we were standing in front of the hall closet. The same closet he'd made abundantly clear was off-limits to me when I'd first toured the apartment.

"The answer to your *what other powers do you have* question can be found in here." He looked at me, gauging my reaction. "If you still want to know."

He put his hand on the doorknob and a stab of panic went through me. I'd built up all kinds of possibilities for what might be inside this forbidden closet. A lot had already happened that night; I wasn't sure I was ready to find out the truth.

I put a hand on his arm, stopping him.

"You told me before there weren't dead bodies in there," I reminded him, my words coming out a little too fast.

"I did."

"Was that the truth?"

He nodded. "Yes. There's no blood in here, either. Or severed heads. Nothing that you will find unpleasant or frightening. I promise. In fact . . ." He trailed off, scratching his chin. "Maybe you'll even like what you see."

The note of hopefulness in his voice—the fact that he wanted to share something about himself he'd previously felt the need to hide—melted the last of my reservations.

"Okay," I said, nodding, bracing myself. "Open the door."

I held my breath—only to blow it out in surprised laughter a moment later when he opened the closet door and I saw what was inside.

"Frederick," I breathed, incredulous.

"I know," he agreed.

"Why are there so many pineapples in here?"

"Not just pineapples."

He pushed the pineapples—there had to be at least a dozen of them—over to one side of the shelf they rested on. Behind them were rows of persimmons, kumquats, and other brightly colored fruits I didn't even recognize.

"Some vampires have impressive abilities like turning wine into blood, or being able to fly, or turning back time," he continued ruefully. "Unfortunately, all I can do is somewhat involuntarily conjure fruit when I'm nervous."

I reached inside the closet and picked up a small, rather squashy thing that looked like a pear but smelled like an orange. "*This* is what you've been hiding in here all this time?"

"Yes," he said. "You can eat it, in case you were wondering."

"I can?"

He nodded. "It should be perfectly edible. Every week I bring whatever I've conjured to a local food pantry. Or else gift them to you."

I thought back to the basket of kumquats he gave me the day I moved in. The bowl of various citrus fruits he kept on the kitchen counter.

"Oh," I said.

"My rate of production has skyrocketed since you moved in. I seem to be nervous all the time, these days."

The idea I made him nervous was hard to believe, but I decided to let it go.

"Why didn't you tell me about this?" His eyes widened, and I quickly added, "Not that it's a huge deal, your not telling me. I'm just curious."

"It's one of the most ridiculous vampire powers in recorded history. And a pointless one, given that vampires cannot eat fruit." He rubbed at the back of his neck, averting his eyes. "By the time you knew what I really was, I wanted you to think I was impressive. Not just some clueless accidental kumquat conjurer."

A rush of warmth went through me. "You wanted to impress me?"

He nodded. "I still do."

I couldn't make sense of this. *He* wanted to impress *me*? Frederick was a three-hundred-and-twenty-year-old immortal. I was just . . . me.

I leaned back against the wall behind me for support. "But . . . *why*? I'm nobody."

His eyes snapped to mine, his gaze so intense it was like looking directly into the sun. "How can you say such a thing?"

My eyes fell to my shoes. "Because it's true."

All at once he was pressing me up against the wall, forearms bracketing my head, his gaze furious. His face was mere inches from mine. "I have never heard something *less* true in my life."

"But—"

He cut me off with his lips, kissing me with a ferocity I hadn't seen from him before. I parted my lips reflexively and he wasted no time, tongue plunging into my mouth as though he'd never be able to get enough of my taste. He kissed me like his life depended on it, like a man possessed, and I was helpless to do anything but kiss him back, wrapping my arms around him, nearly swooning at the feeling of every part of his long, hard body pressing needfully against mine.

"*You. Are. Amazing,*" he murmured, each word punctuated with hard, feverish kisses to my lips, my jaw, my throat. I melted against him, feeling in danger at any moment of slipping down the wall at my back and falling into a puddle on the floor.

"Frederick," I breathed. His hands roamed my body possessively, leaving behind trails of heat despite the chill of his touch. I felt fever-bright and lighter than air.

But he wasn't finished. "You are kind, and generous," he continued. "Even after you found out what I was you didn't abandon me, because you knew I needed your help. In all my years I have never met anyone more committed to remaining true to who they are than you are." He pulled back, looking directly into my eyes. The heated look he gave me could have melted an iceberg. "Do you have any idea how *precious* that is, Cassie? How *rare*?"

His eyes were dark, incandescent pools, pleading with me to understand.

But I didn't.

"No," I said. "I don't think there's anything particularly special about me at all."

His jaw clenched. "Then please," he began, his voice hoarse and dripping with promise, "*please* allow me to show you how wrong you are."

......................

HIS BEDROOM WAS DIFFERENT FROM HOW I'D IMAGINED IT. There wasn't a coffin, or anything else that might suggest that its occupant was anything other than a perfectly ordinary wealthy human with questionable taste in decorating.

It was much bigger than my bedroom, with a lake-facing floor-to-ceiling window that matched the one in the living room. Like the living room, it was also rather dark. Brass wall sconces ringed the room, their dim light playing with the subtle contoured colors of Frederick's hair. I wanted to bury my hands in that hair and feel the silky-soft tresses as they sifted through my fingers.

The bed was king-sized, with a thick mattress and a blood-red canopy that matched both the duvet covering the bed and the curtains covering the window. When Frederick laid me down on the mattress, as carefully as he might handle a porcelain doll, I realized the red duvet cover was made of velvet.

*This part is a bit cliché,* I thought, running my fingers over the impossibly soft material. Right from *Interview with the Vampire.* But my body was alight with anticipation and nerves, and the tender, heated way he was looking at me as he stood at the foot of the bed made it almost impossible to think clearly.

Constructive feedback on his bedroom stylings could wait.

I reached up for him, excited for the next part to begin.

The sight of my outstretched arms, however, seemed to cause the raw desire that had propelled him to bring me into his bedroom to grind to a screeching halt. He was no longer staring at me like he wanted to fuck me into the middle of next week. His entire demeanor changed, his dark eyes drifting to the wooden floorboards, the fingers of his right hand drumming a nervous staccato beat against his thigh.

I propped myself up on my elbows, concerned. "Frederick?"

"Perhaps . . ." he began, sounding pained. He sat beside me on a loud exhalation of breath, bending forward until his elbows were on his knees. He buried his face in his hands. "Perhaps we should not do this."

My heart stuttered as I tried to reconcile what he was saying now with what had just happened moments before. I pushed up on the bed until I was sitting beside him and then, hesitantly, I slid my hand up and across his broad chest, flattening my palm over the place where his heart once beat.

Every time I'd touched him in the past it had elicited an immediate, kinetic response from him. This time, he held himself almost preternaturally still.

It was like touching a statue.

"Do you . . . do you not *want* to do this?"

His breath hitched. He shifted closer to me on the bed and

then, hesitantly, he wrapped an arm around me by way of wordless response.

"That is not what I said." His voice was raw gravel, and he shifted even closer, the taut muscles of his arm flexing against my lower back. "I do want to do this. You have *no idea* how badly I want to do this. I simply said perhaps we shouldn't."

We were sitting so close it would have been nothing at all to turn my head and press my lips to his cheek. With difficulty, I stayed put.

"What's wrong?" I asked.

"I didn't plan to drag you into a romantic entanglement with . . . someone like me."

"No one is dragging me into anything."

"But—"

"I *want* to have a romantic entanglement with you."

The look on his face when he met my eyes was heartbreaking. "You couldn't possibly."

"Why not?"

"For one thing, you are human." He shook his head. "For another, I am not."

This, of course, was what had held me back until now. But none of it mattered. Frederick was kind and compassionate. He bought out an entire cookware section when I said I needed a saucepan, and said insightful, kind things about my art even though he didn't understand it.

He *knew* me, with an intuitive kind of sensitivity that took my breath away.

And, yes, okay, he was a vampire. That did present some legitimate challenges. But that didn't change how good he was—or the fact that I wanted him more than I'd ever wanted anyone in my life.

"I don't care," I said flatly. I gently took his hand and laced our fingers together.

"You should care," he murmured. But he didn't drop my hand. He was holding me so closely he could probably feel the rapid beating of my heart against his own rib cage. "You don't want the kind of half life I live, Cassie. You cannot possibly want to be what I am. For us to be together, *really* together—the *changes* you would have to undergo . . ."

I raised our joined hands until my lips met the cool, smooth solidity of his wrist, letting my mouth linger there. His lips parted, and *oh*, they had been so soft, pressed against my own lips. Even when his kisses had grown desperate. I wanted to taste them again, wanted to tease them apart with my tongue.

"I haven't thought that far ahead yet," I admitted. "All I know is that right now, I want to be as close to you as I can." At some point, perhaps I'd want to imagine what a long-term future with Frederick would require of me.

But not just yet.

We hadn't even been on an official *date* yet.

Giving in to temptation, I pressed a chaste, closed-mouth kiss to his collarbone, reveling in the feel of marble-like skin against my lips.

"Cassie," he murmured, his voice thick.

Moving a little, I touched my lips to the underside of his jaw, and then kissed my way down his neck to a spot where, many years ago, there had been a pulse. To the place I suspected another vampire once had bitten him, centuries before I was born.

"Frederick," I murmured. I opened my mouth, letting my tongue dart out to taste him. His skin was salt and musk, desire and cool night air.

He whimpered.

"If you want to do this and *I* want to do this, why shouldn't we?" I asked, though he wasn't protesting anymore. I nuzzled at the sensitive spot where his neck met his shoulder, reveling in his sharp intake of breath, in the way his arm tightened around me, the way his fingertips dug into my side.

"Cassie." His tone was half warning, half promise. On a shuddering breath his free hand came up to cup my cheek.

I sighed and leaned into his touch. Every nerve in my body was alight, sparking with anticipation. He had large, beautiful hands. Dexterous and strong. The thought of what they could do to me if he'd only let go . . .

It was a delicious torture.

"*Please*," I whispered.

With that single word it was like a switch flipped inside of him. I could see it in his eyes as the remnants of his resolve cracked and crumbled away, and then all at once his lips were on mine again, his kisses as eager and as needful as they'd been at Sam's party. He moved quickly, wordlessly, one hand at the small of my back and the other on my shoulder, gently guiding me backwards until I lay prone on the mattress once more.

"Oh, Cassie," he breathed against my lips. He loomed over me, bracing his weight on his elbows, his forearms on either side of my head. He leaned in, pressing a kiss to my temple. Then he chuckled quietly, the sound so happy and full of relief it broke my heart. "I will never be able to deny you anything you want."

When I'd imagined this happening, alone in my bedroom, I'd imagined Frederick as a quiet and tentative lover, as polite and refined with sex as he was in everyday life. But there was nothing quiet or tentative about him now. Now that I was lying beneath him atop his lush four-poster bed, his passion was a dam bursting in flood, as though until this moment he'd been holding himself back only with extreme effort. His relentless kisses left me breathless and reeling—and I welcomed it, my arms going around him as he kissed me, trying to pull him even closer.

"Cassie." This time my name on his lips was a plea. He didn't need oxygen, but he was breathing hard and fast against my neck like he'd just run a mile. Maybe it was muscle memory from the man he'd once been kicking in, now that we were here. His body lay almost entirely on top of me now, a welcome weight pressing me into the mattress. The feel of his breath on my sensitized skin made me shiver.

I wriggled beneath him, eager to feel him everywhere.

"Can I touch you?" he asked in a hoarse whisper, without lifting his head from where it rested in the crook of my neck.

I nodded, feeling like I might burst with anticipation.

His hand slid down the front of my shirt until he found my breast. I arched into his touch, and he squeezed—gently at first, and then, when he saw what his touch was doing to me, with firmer pressure. My breasts were a respectable size, but I fit easily and entirely within his large palm. My nostrils flared, my breathing coming hot and quick as sensation coursed through me.

"Frederick," I murmured, intending only to encourage him to keep going. The sound of his name must have done something to him because he *growled* his response. All his formidable powers of speech seemed to have fled as his free hand came down and cupped my other breast. He thumbed roughly at my nipples through my shirt and bra until they pebbled up into hard little sensitized buds against his palms, and then he kept going, and going, and *going*, until I was nothing but pure sensation.

"*Oh*," I said, incapable of articulate speech. The soft velvet duvet underneath me served as delicious contrast to the sharp spikes of pleasure coursing through my bloodstream, the placid and even ticking of the grandfather clock in the hallway a stark accompaniment to my uneven, rapid breaths. Frederick tore off my shirt and bra impatiently, tossing them to the floor like the hindrances they'd become. His low, desperate groan when he saw my bare chest ratcheted the coil of desire in the pit of my stomach to nearly unbearable heights.

"I want to taste you," he rasped, raising his head. His pupils were fat with desire as he continued thumbing at my pink and straining nipples. "Everywhere."

My incoherent moan was apparently all he needed by way of consent. He shoved my skirt up to my waist and then, with excruciatingly slow and careful movements, slid my underwear down my legs. Suddenly, I was half naked and splayed out before him, exposed and vulnerable. His eyes darkened further as he regarded me, his eyes trailing so hot and eagerly along my bare flesh I could *feel* his gaze.

"I've imagined this moment more often than is strictly decent." His voice was low and deadly urgent, his fingers tracing invisible patterns along my inner thigh. His touch was purposeful, moving closer to where I wanted him with every pass—but his movements were maddeningly slow.

And I was tired of waiting.

"Frederick," I urged, wriggling on the bed to spur him on. *"Please."*

But he seemed determined to take his time. "I've touched myself in my bedroom, thinking of you, just like this," he confessed against the sensitive skin behind my right knee. "I've even gone to your bed in my dreams." His hand slid higher, and higher, until he reached my aching center. He cupped me gently, reverently. I nearly arched off the bed with clawing, desperate need.

"Frederick . . ."

"Can I tell you what I do to you in my dreams?"

Finally, at last, he parted my drenched folds with one thick finger. My head fell back onto the pillow as he gently circled the place where every nerve ending in my body was centered. My jaw fell open as stars burst behind my closed eyelids, my body taut as a bowstring.

"*Oh.*" I was panting now, any pride or dignity I might have once had long gone. I needed him to touch me. *Now.* "*Please.*"

Frederick chuckled a little as the mattress at the foot of the bed shifted beneath his weight. I could almost hear his satisfied smirk when he said, "Perhaps I'll just show you instead."

He slid his large hands down my body until he reached my hips. He left them there, gripping my flesh, spreading me open as his eyes feasted on my bare flesh. I shivered at how vulnerable this position left me. The open, heated longing I saw in Frederick's eyes was almost too much to bear.

"You," he murmured against my inner thigh, nostrils flared as he breathed me in, "are magnificent beyond my wildest imaginings."

I'd done this a few times before. Mostly with my college boyfriend, someone who viewed oral sex as an obligation to be dispensed with as quickly as possible before he could move on to more pleasurable activities.

But the moment Frederick buried his face between my legs it was clear there was nothing in the world he would rather be doing than this. He tasted and licked, breathing me in as he took his sweet, deliberate time. My fingertips found purchase on his shoulders, and I clung to them for dear life as he teased me, the wool of the sweater he still wore deliciously smooth against my bare legs.

My head fell back against the pillow again and I writhed on

the mattress, bucking up towards his mouth in search of greater friction, needing *more*. But he wouldn't be rushed. His hands gripped my hips harder as my body sought to move against him, keeping me pinned helplessly to the mattress in the exact spot he wanted me. I whined in delicious agony as he traced the shape of my clit with the achingly soft flat of his tongue, dancing around the direct contact my body was screaming for. I could feel how wet I was growing, could hear the sharp keening sounds I was making as if from a distance. But he would not be rushed by my desperation as he kissed, and lapped, and tasted.

"*Frederick.*" I tangled my fingers in his soft hair and tugged, moaning. I was going to pieces. I was out of my *head* with need. "*Please.*"

At my naked plea something must have broken inside him. He groaned, long and loud, the reverberations from it sending sparks of sensation rocketing down my spine—

And then, at last, his tongue was *right there*, licking me senseless as his lips closed around my clit. He sucked gently, then with greater pressure, and the room, the bed beneath us, fell away. The world collapsed down to a pinprick, nothing existing anymore outside of Frederick and the exquisite, cresting pleasure.

"Oh, god," I moaned, bucking against his mouth. I was outside of myself, outside of reason. "*Please—*"

My orgasm came upon me like a tidal wave—devastating, and all-consuming, my toes curling with the spine-melting pleasure of it. Distantly, I could feel Frederick shifting on the bed, kissing his way up my body, whispering praise to my bare legs, my stomach, my breasts.

After what might have been a few seconds, or thirty minutes, he stretched out to his full length beside me on the bed, a crooked, self-satisfied smile on his lips.

"I want to do that to you every day for as long as you'll let me," he murmured against the top of my head.

I giggled, feeling utterly spent and lighter than air.

I rolled over and burrowed my face into his chest. "I'm so glad you've come around."

He chuckled, then wrapped his arms around me, pulling me close. "Me, too."

.....................

I STARTLED AWAKE SOMETIME LATER, NOT HAVING REAL- ized I'd dozed off. Frederick was walking towards me with a glass of water, a small smile on his lips.

He sat beside me on his bed. "Here," he said, offering me the glass. "In case you're thirsty."

I was. "Thanks." I took the water from him, taking a sip before setting it on the bedside table. "How long was I sleeping?"

"Not long. Maybe fifteen minutes."

I shifted a little beneath the duvet. The last thing I remembered before drifting off was using his chest as a pillow, his arms wrapped around me. He must have covered me with the duvet when he left the room.

Tenderness flooded me. I reached up and cupped his face in my hand. He sighed, his stubble rough against my palm as he leaned into my touch.

Only then did I notice that his jeans were tented with what must have been an extremely uncomfortable—and massive— erection.

Given his recent confession about his relationship to fruit, I was tempted to make a wildly inappropriate *Is that a conjured banana in your pocket?* joke. But I didn't. Because for one thing, he'd just given me one of the most mind-meltingly incredible orgasms of my life, and teasing him felt like a mean way to repay him. For another, I knew full well that his pants situation was due entirely to the fact that, yes—he *was* happy to see me.

I trailed my hand slowly down his chest, not stopping until I reached the waistband of his jeans. His stomach muscles rippled, tensing and flexing beneath my palm.

"Cassie," he said, hoarsely, quickly covering my hand with his own to stop me. "Wait."

Sitting up, I pressed a kiss to each corner of his mouth. He shuddered and let his head droop forward onto my shoulder.

"What is it?"

"I've never done . . . *the rest* of this before without . . ." He closed his eyes, unable or unwilling to look at me for what he was about to say. "Without blood being involved."

My heart skipped, like, five beats.

"Oh."

"Indeed." He lifted his head and met my gaze. "It's been over a hundred years since I've been intimate with someone. I'm out of practice, and I want you *so* badly. If you touch me, if we . . . continue this, I don't know if I'll have the self-control to go without once I'm . . . close to the end." He fell back onto the pillows and let out an anguished breath. "I don't know if I can do this without hurting you."

From this vantage point I could now easily see the outline of his cock, fully erect and straining hard against the front of his jeans. I wanted to peel those jeans off and get a good look at him so badly I could taste it. I felt certain he *could* do this without hurting me. If he was going to lose control and take a bite when he shouldn't, it would have happened long before now.

Suddenly, I had an idea.

"I know what I can do to help you stay in control."

He cracked one eye and looked at me.

"What?"

Wordlessly, I began to undo the button of his jeans. His hands clamped down on mine like a vise.

"Cassie, wait—"

"Shhh," I murmured, willing his panic to abate and nudging his hands away. I reached inside and gripped him in my hand, reveling in the way his breath caught and his head fell back on the pillow.

My heartbeat quickened. He was big—which, yes, I'd already anticipated. But it was one thing to see the outline and general shape of a guy's dick when he was still wearing clothes—and entirely another when you had it in your hands.

"What are you doing?" His voice was low, his dark eyes dazed and incredulous.

He was so beautiful, and vulnerable, in that moment. I wanted to make him feel as good as he'd just made me feel.

"This," I said, before leaning over and taking him into my mouth.

I half expected him to protest again, but he didn't. He fell back against the pillows with a rough groan, hands balled up into fists and pressed into his eyes.

If he was worried about losing control and biting me once he was inside me, what better way to dial things down a bit than to give him a take-the-edge-off orgasm before we did that? A pregame blow job usually helped guys I'd been with in the past last longer. And, okay, Frederick wasn't like other guys—but in this department I was willing to bet he wasn't that different from anyone else.

On instinct, I took him deeper into my mouth, enjoying the heady combination of salt and musk and Frederick on my tongue.

The helpless, pleasured sounds he made as I worked him spurred me on, encouraging me to take him deeper. Grip him tighter.

When I glanced up at his face his jaw was slack and his eyes were glazed over in pleasure. He met my gaze with a reverence and a desperation that made me eager to have him inside me, and soon.

"Is this . . . is this okay?" he murmured. He cupped my face in unsteady hands, eyes holding mine as he gently stroked my cheeks with his thumbs.

God, he was beautiful.

By way of response I snaked a hand around his body and squeezed his ass.

He gave an inhuman groan I felt more than heard as whatever fragile grip he'd still had on his self-control snapped and fell away. One large hand found its way to the top of my head, pushing me down just a little as his hips began to jerk upward in a rhythmic motion beneath me. It was hard, it was fast—and it was glorious. If the incomprehensible sounds he was making, and the way his head thrashed back and forth on the pillow, were any guide, Frederick was incapacitated from the pleasure of me taking him as deeply as I could.

"Oh, fuck," he groaned. Both of his hands were on my head now, guiding my movements as he trembled and fought for control. And for release. His thrusts were already becoming more erratic and picking up speed. My hands were growing slippery with my saliva and his own secretions. "Cassie, oh god, *Cassie*, I can't, I . . . I can't finish without—"

He cut himself off, clamping a hand over his mouth to keep from saying anything else. I looked up at his face as we moved in tandem, his eyes squeezed tightly shut, his chest heaving.

He'd said he'd never done this before without blood being involved. Was it possible that he actually *needed* blood for this?

If so, how long was he planning to deprive himself—to let me drive him to the edge like this—without asking for what he needed for release?

On instinct, I slid a hand up his chest and slipped my index finger between his lips. His body jerked beneath me. His eyes shot down to mine. As desperate with need as he was, Frederick still retained enough of his wits to know what I was offering.

"Cassie," he breathed, my name on his lips a question.

I nodded, letting him know that, yes—I was okay with it.

He made a sound that was half groan, half snarl. He bit down, and—

It didn't hurt. Not really. I'd donated blood before, and while the tip of my finger had more nerve endings than my forearm did, the bite wasn't *bad*.

Frederick lapped at the little wound like his life depended on it, licking and suckling me and . . . it was surprisingly sexy. His face was contorted into the same ecstatic, blissful expression he'd worn when he'd buried his face between my legs earlier that evening, and *fuck* if I couldn't have spent the rest of my life looking at him when he was mindless with pleasure like this.

"*Cassie*," he groaned, utterly wrecked by what I was doing to him. My finger slipped from his mouth; he greedily sucked it back in.

And then he flipped us with an inhuman speed that made me breathless, leaving me flat on my back before I'd realized it had even happened. I'd seen hints of his more-than-human strength before, but there was something primal, wild about the way he climbed atop me now.

He leaned over me, his dark hair falling into his eyes.

"Please," he rasped, his voice thick with his fraying restraint. His forearms were all corded muscle and shaking tension as he held himself perfectly still above me. My finger was still between his lips. He looked like he might die if I withdrew it. "I want to feel you."

I nodded, understanding from the desperate look in his eyes what he was asking me.

"Please," I whispered.

With a grunt and one delicious thrust of his hips he was fully seated inside me. I gasped, stunned, the sheer enormity of him stealing the breath from my lungs. My body clenched and un-clenched involuntarily, struggling to adjust to his size as he tried to hold himself back.

I wrapped my arms around him and pulled him down into a searing kiss. I'd never been with someone this big before, and the delicious way my body had to stretch to accommodate him felt *incredible*. He was *everywhere*, all at once, and I wanted him to move, to feel the glorious sensual pleasure of him sliding in and out of my body. I wanted to have him in my arms as we moved together, to fall apart in ecstasy as I held him close.

On a shaky exhale he slowly pulled out, and then thrust back into me with so much force the headboard knocked against the wall. I slid my hands down his backside, gripping the hard mus-cle beneath my fingertips as I tried to pull him even deeper in-side me.

"Is this okay?" The cords in his neck stood out in sharp relief as he fought to hold on.

"*Yes.*"

He groaned, feral, his lips so close to the overly sensitive skin of my neck I felt it more than heard it. Whatever thin filament of restraint he'd been clinging to seemed to snap with another sharp thrust of his hips. And then another. And another.

"Mine," he growled, the speed of his thrusts increasing, his voice taking on a deep rumbling timbre I'd never heard from him before. I answered with an incoherent moan, writhing beneath him, pinned to the mattress by his strong hands and the relentless pace of his hips.

He'd been a patient and giving lover earlier. Now, he was using me, my body—my blood—for his own pleasure. The realization that he wasn't going to let me out of this bed until he'd thoroughly had his way with me thrilled me. A desperate cry tore from his throat, nearly sending me spiraling straight into another orgasm.

"*Please*," I begged breathlessly, not even knowing what I was begging for. I canted my hips upward, matching his thrusts, mindless in my desperate, urgent need. My lungs couldn't pull in enough air. My body couldn't get enough friction. There was nothing in the world but his breath in my ear, the pounding, relentless thrusts of his body into mine, and the shimmering orgasm he was about to give me that still remained frustratingly out of reach.

"Frederick—"

"I . . . want . . . to . . . feel . . . you . . . ," he gritted out. I was nothing but mindless sensation. "Cassie, come for me."

When I came, Frederick quickly drew another finger between his lips, biting down and then sucking on it desperately. I was still in the throes of pleasure when his hips slammed into me one final time, my blood on his tongue, my name falling feverishly from his lips. His whole body went rigid above me, his back arching, his hands fisting the sheets on either side of my head so tightly his knuckles were white.

We were silent for a long moment after that as we lay side by side on his mattress. My head lolled on his chest, the gentle designs he was drawing on my arm with his fingertips making me drowsy. The only sounds in the room, aside from the steady rhythm of our breathing, drifted up to us from the street below. Cars honked, and people carried on, just like it was any other Friday night—even as my life had suddenly and irrevocably changed.

# SEVENTEEN

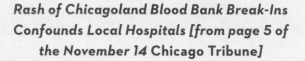

**Rash of Chicagoland Blood Bank Break-Ins Confounds Local Hospitals [from page 5 of the November 14 Chicago Tribune]**

John Weng, AP—Chicagoland hospital administrators are scratching their heads over a wave of recent blood bank break-ins among donation centers in Chicago's Near North Side.

"We expect a certain number of donations to go missing each week," said Jenny McNiven, volunteer coordinator at Michigan Avenue Children's Hospital. "Our blood drives are mostly volunteer-run, and mistakes happen. But what we have seen in the past forty-eight hours cannot be explained by simple human error."

According to McNiven, three different centers had break-ins over the weekend. In each case, volunteers showed up to their morning shifts to find refrigerators' doors hanging off their hinges and most of their contents removed. A pair of elbow-length white satin gloves left behind at one of the cen-

ters *is being analyzed by the Chicago Police Department's*
*forensics team for clues.*

"*I don't know why anyone would do something like this,*"
McNiven *said.* "*As pranks go, this might be one of the worst.*
*Blood saves lives.*"

FREDERICK—AND HIS BARE CHEST—WERE WAITING FOR ME
in the living room when I stumbled out of his bedroom at dawn
the next morning. He was on the sofa, leafing through a newspaper with a slight frown on his face.

"Good morning."

At the sound of my voice he looked up, setting his newspaper
to the side.

"Good morning." He smiled at me, a bit shy—which was a bit
ridiculous, given how we'd spent a good portion of the previous
evening. I was a little surprised to see how coiffed and put-
together he looked, given that I could tell without even checking
a mirror that I was sporting the most ridiculous bedhead in the
history of the world.

Then I remembered that he'd left the bedroom with an apology shortly after midnight and hadn't slept beside me at all.

"What time is it?" I asked. "I need to be at work at eight-thirty."

"It's just after six." He stood and walked over to me, placing
his hands on either side of my waist. Or, more accurately—on
either side of the general vicinity of my waist. I was wrapped from
chest to toe in one of his soft red satin sheets. Anatomical accu-
racy was difficult. "My bedsheet suits you."

I snorted. "I didn't get dressed again last night after . . . well."
I trailed off, blushing. "Wrapping up in this sheet was easier than
finding where you'd tossed my underwear."

He hummed, and pressed a kiss to my cheek. "You look divine."

"I do not."

"I hope you never wear anything else."

He kissed me then, chaste and tender. I placed my hands on his chest and leaned in, enjoying the soft brush of his lips against mine.

"I'm surprised you're not dressed," I mused. "It's not like you were asleep all this time."

My fingertips traced the outline of a jagged, prominent scar just below his right nipple. I wanted to ask him how he got it. If it happened while he was still human, or after. But now wasn't the time.

"Going forward I intend to spend as much time shirtless as possible."

I huffed a surprised laugh. "What?"

"You like it when I don't wear a shirt," he said, as matter-of-factly as if he were telling me rain was in the forecast. "You like it a lot, in fact. I like doing things that please you."

I hadn't exactly tried to hide how into his body I was, but the way he'd phrased this made me wonder something.

"Can you *tell* that I like it when you don't wear a shirt?" I ran my hand down his fabulous chest for good measure. "Beyond me simply telling you that you have a great body, I mean."

He smiled, bashful. "Your scent changes subtly, but unmistakably, when you are aroused."

My eyes widened in surprise. That was a new one.

"It does?"

He nodded. "Until last night I told myself I was mistaken, that it was simply wishful thinking on my part." His smile turned devilish when he leaned in and pressed his lips to my ear. "I know now, though, that I was right."

I thought back to the way he'd all but breathed me in last night, and I shivered, gooseflesh erupting on my arms. It should have weirded me out, the idea that my scent changed when I was turned on and that Frederick could sense it. But for some reason—maybe because it was Frederick who was telling me this—it didn't.

His hands started working their way beneath the place where I'd cinched the bedsheet closed around my body. "I want to be inside you again, Cassie," he whispered into my ear. He pulled me closer, until I could feel every inch of his need jutting hard and urgently against my stomach. "Last night was glorious beyond anything I could have imagined. But I want more."

I shuddered, throwing my arms around him and burying my face in his shoulder.

I mentally *screamed* at Marcie for signing me up for a Saturday morning shift.

"I want that, too," I said. "But unfortunately, I have to go to work."

Frederick groaned and pulled back from me. My body was screaming at Marcie now, too.

"Fine," he said, tersely. "I hope, however, that you are not averse to picking up where we left off when you get back home."

Then I kissed him. Because no—I was not averse to it at all.

......................

I FLOATED MORE THAN WALKED INTO THE LIBRARY FOR MY shift.

When I got there, I sat down at the circulation desk in the children's section and went through the motions of putting away my purse and logging into the station's communal desktop. But my mind was miles away, back in the apartment.

The sun had risen about an hour ago. Frederick was likely getting ready to go to sleep. This morning was another art day, and I needed to get the watercolors, canvases, and plastic floor coverings all set up. Kids had already started showing up for the event, milling around book displays with their parents until we were ready to get started.

While art days were usually a highlight for me, right now I wished I were back at home, cuddling with and sleeping next to Frederick.

"Good morning." Marcie was tying her hair back into a ponytail, rummaging around for supplies in the closet behind the circulation desk as she greeted me.

"Morning." I looked down at the plan for this morning that I'd come up with a few days ago, glad Marcie had printed it out and placed it in front of the computer. "What do you think of my idea?"

"Paint Your Favorite Book's Setting?"

"Yeah."

Marcie smiled at me. "I think it's great."

My chest warmed. "I'm glad to hear it. I'm pretty proud of it."

"You should be," Marcie said. I blushed a little at the praise, then grabbed a ponytail holder from my own bag and pulled as much of my still too-short hair as I could into a messy knot on top of my head. "We've done book characters before, and Disney princesses, but not settings."

"So many children's books take place in amazing locations," I said. I crouched down and started hunting beneath the desk, trying to find where I'd stashed the box of brushes and colored pencils. "I hope the kids have a lot of fun with this."

I didn't have to wait long to get confirmation that the event was a wild success.

"Miss Greenberg? Is it okay if I add a dragon to my castle?"

I turned away from a little girl I'd been helping who was painting a vibrant picture of the sun. She'd chosen a nearly neon shade of purple for the sun's rays. It was easily my favorite of all the projects the kids were working on.

"Of course it's okay," I said to the little boy who asked the question, who'd earlier introduced himself as Zach. "Why wouldn't it be?"

Zach gave a one-shoulder shrug. "The instructions were to paint our favorite book's setting," he said. "I already did the castle, and I thought painting a character, too, would be breaking the rules."

I crouched down so I was eye-level with Zach. His canvas was covered in shapeless swirls of browns and greens. It didn't look like any castle I'd ever seen—but then again, I'd never seen a castle in person, so who was I to judge? Maybe in his favorite book, or in his imagination—or both—this was exactly what castles looked like.

"I think a dragon would look great right here," I said, pointing to the one corner of the canvas that hadn't been covered in watercolor paint.

"But Fluffy is the main character of the book, not a setting," Zach pointed out. His tone was as serious as if he were giving a lecture on the current state of American politics, which—given that he was all of six years old—was so adorable I nearly burst out laughing.

I bit the inside of my cheek to keep that from happening and pretended to study his canvas. "I see your point," I said. "But you know—the only real rule in art is to make something you enjoy."

His eyebrows shot up his little forehead. "No other rules at all?"

"None," I confirmed. "We wanted kids to paint the settings from their favorite books today, but if you want to add Fluffy, go for it. In fact," I added, "I can't really picture a castle without a dragon. Maybe Fluffy actually *is* part of your book's setting, and not just a character."

Zach chewed his bottom lip as he considered my words. "That makes sense."

"I agree," I said. "In the end, though, this is your painting. Make something you love."

And with that, Zach dipped his paintbrush in the pot of orange watercolor in front of him, painted a giant swirl in the only spare corner of his canvas, and smiled.

......................

BY THE TIME I MADE IT BACK TO THE APARTMENT IT WAS nearly sundown. I took the stairs two at a time, grinning as I imagined throwing myself into Frederick's arms and picking up where we'd left off this morning.

When I got to the third-floor landing, however, I knew that something was very wrong.

For one thing, Frederick was shouting from inside the apartment.

"How *dare* you come to my home unannounced and behave in this way!"

For another, a woman whose voice I did not recognize was shouting, too.

"You dare to ask *me* how I dare?" the woman scoffed, the sharp click of her heels echoing so loudly on the hardwood floors I could easily hear her footsteps from where I stood. "I would have thought your manners better than that, *Frederick John Fitzwilliam!*"

I hesitated at the door, unsure what to do. The only other person who had been in our apartment the entire time I'd lived there was Reginald—another vampire. And that had ended in disaster.

From the sounds of things, another disaster was brewing in there right now. But what should I do? This argument, as bitter as it sounded, had nothing to do with me. Even inadvertently hearing what I had so far felt like an intrusion.

"Cassie will be home shortly," Frederick said. "I ask that you please leave before she returns home. I do not wish to discuss this matter with you any further."

"No," the woman said flatly. "I intend to meet this human girl to whom you've taken such a fancy."

Frederick barked a humorless laugh. "Over my dead body."

"That's easy enough to arrange."

"*Edwina.*"

"No need to get snippy with me, Frederick." The woman started pacing again, her heels clicking so loudly across the hardwood floors it sounded like she was determined to break a hole through to the apartment on the second floor. "If I cannot make you see reason, perhaps this Cassie Greenberg will be more malleable."

At the sound of my name, my heart thundered so loudly in my ears it drowned out the rest of whatever Frederick and the woman shouting at him were saying. I guess this argument concerned me after all.

Maybe I should intervene.

Before I could talk myself out of it, I threw open the apartment's front door.

The woman in the living room looked roughly my parents' age, with crow's-feet at the corners of her eyes and graying hair at her temples. Any similarities between the woman currently glaring ice daggers at me and Ben and Rae Greenberg ended there, though. Her dress was an all-black silk-and-crepe affair with velvet puffed sleeves, made in a vaguely historical mash-up of a style that would have looked right at home on the set of *Bridgerton*.

Her eye makeup, though, was what really drew my attention. The last time I'd seen face paint that dramatic I'd been in middle school, when Sam's older brother dragged us to see a KISS cover band on a night their parents were out of town. It stood out in such sharp contrast with her overall pallor it made my eyes ache to look at her.

"Is this her?" The woman pointed an accusatory finger with a perfectly manicured bright-red fingernail in my direction. But her eyes stayed fixed on Frederick. "The hussy you have thrown everything away for?"

"*Hussy?*" I couldn't believe my ears. Who talked like that? "Excuse me, but who are you?"

"*This,*" Frederick said, hissing the word, "is Mrs. Edwina Fitzwilliam." A pause. "My mother."

Time seemed to stop. I closed my eyes, trying to make sense of what Frederick had just said, and of the ridiculous situation I now seemed to be in the middle of.

His *mother*?

But how was that *possible*?

Shouldn't his mother have been dead for hundreds of years?

Then Mrs. Edwina Fitzwilliam bared a set of sharp, pointed fangs at me, and it all clicked into place.

"You're a vampire, too," I breathed, feeling dizzy and weak-kneed.

"Of course I'm a vampire," Frederick's mother said, before sauntering across the room like she owned the place. Which, I realized with a start, might be true. I didn't know anything about Frederick's finances—or really very much about him at all.

That had never been clearer to me than it was right then.

"I am not going back to New York with you, Mother. That had never been my plan." His eyes flicked to mine, filled with guilt. "Cassie has nothing to do with it. Leave her out of this."

Mrs. Edwina Fitzwilliam waved a dismissive hand at me. "Fine. In that regard at least I will do as you say. In fact, out of respect for you, I won't even eat her."

"*Mother—*"

"'There is no need to return to New York with me," his mother cut in. "The Jamesons are arriving in Chicago tomorrow evening. You will speak with them here." I had no idea who the Jamesons were, but Frederick clearly did. At her words he took a small, involuntary step back. He looked stunned, as though she'd just slapped him.

"I would have thought by returning Esmeralda's gifts both she and her parents would have inferred my lack of intent to marry her." He paused. "The last time I wrote I told Esmeralda in no uncertain terms that I would not go through with it."

It's a good thing I was standing near the couch. If I hadn't been, my legs giving out upon hearing the words *marry her* would have resulted in my landing on the floor—and would have been a whole lot more uncomfortable.

"The message was received, my dear." Frederick's mother glared at him. "You could not have been clearer in your intent if you had announced it at a dinner party full of guests."

"Then why are they coming here?"

"Because the Jamesons interpret your actions, as I have, as a clear sign that you have not been in your right mind since your awakening. They agree with me that this matter cannot be left to correspondence, and that a personal meeting is necessary."

"I am as sound of mind now as I have ever been." Frederick crossed his arms across his broad chest, adopting what he likely meant as an assertive stance. The effect was undercut by the fact that he was wearing pajama pants with Kermit the Frog on them that I *definitely* didn't buy him at Nordstrom. But it didn't matter. He was still hot.

Mrs. Edwina Fitzwilliam, however, didn't seem impressed.

"I will leave you to explain that to your in-laws directly. You and I will meet them in their rooms at the Ritz-Carlton tomorrow evening at seven to discuss your impending nuptials." Mrs. Fitzwilliam sniffed the air and cringed. "A *human girl*, Frederick. *Honestly*."

With that, Frederick's mother gave a theatrical curtsy to us both and breezed out the front door.

Deafening silence filled the room. I stared at Frederick, willing him to say something—*anything*—that would turn the chaos of the past few minutes into something that bore some resemblance to sense.

After what might have been eighteen years, he cleared his throat.

"There's more I haven't told you." He had the decency to look sheepish.

"You think?" He flinched at my hostile tone, but I didn't care. He'd promised me he would never withhold important information from me again. "Frederick, what else is there I don't know?"

He sighed and dragged a hand through his hair. "A lot." He swallowed. "Do you want to hear it, or are you finished with me?"

"Tell me one thing first," I said, holding up one hand. "Is it true that you told this Esmeralda person you wouldn't marry her?"

"Yes," Frederick said, earnestly. "In no uncertain terms, and repeatedly. This whole thing . . . all of it . . ." He trailed off and ran an agitated hand through his hair. "None of this should be happening."

He looked absolutely tormented.

"Okay," I said. "I'll hear it."

He reached for my hand, eyes tentative. "Sit with me?"

I nodded, and braced myself for the rest of his story.

......................

HE SAT BESIDE ME ON THE LIVING ROOM COUCH, HIS hands folded neatly on his lap.

As recently as ten minutes ago I'd planned to take him to bed to pick up where we left off this morning. But all that would have to wait. Right now his need to be completely open and honest with me was written all over his face.

And I needed to hear what he had to say.

"In certain segments of vampiric society," he began, eyes on the floor, "arranged marriage is still a thing. When I left England to move to America—and especially when I left where my people settled in New York and came to Chicago—I thought I had left that nonsense behind me." He swallowed hard, his Adam's apple bobbing in his throat. "My mother clearly has other ideas."

I expected him to elaborate. When several long moments passed, and he didn't, I asked, "Who is Miss Jameson?"

"Someone I hardly know." His voice was low and sheepish. "We . . . had a fling, once. Nearly two hundred years ago." He paused. "And now, apparently, we are engaged to be wed."

My heart flopped a little in my chest as an irrational pang of jealousy stabbed through me. My reaction was irrational, of course. Expecting someone to be celibate for centuries would be unfair. Whatever happened between him and this Miss Jameson more than a century before I was even born had nothing to do with me.

It still stung, though.

"Oh."

He turned to me, his eyes sad. "I haven't always lived as I do now, Cassie. In my younger days I ate as others of my kind did, and fucked anyone on two legs. Men, women, humans—everything." He looked away. "There was a party in Paris during the Regency period where Miss Jameson and I—"

"I get it," I said quickly, cutting him off. I put my hand on his. "I don't need all the details."

"Good. Because I'm not quite up to sharing them." He closed his eyes. "I am not the person I was in the early nineteenth century, Cassie. I haven't been that person in a very long time."

I had so many questions I wanted to ask him about how he became the person he was today. But there were other things I wanted to know first. "How long have you been engaged to her?"

"It happened during my coma," Frederick said dourly. "My mother never approved of the changes I made to my life when I decided to live among humans instead of viewing them as dinner. She thought that when I woke, marrying me off to someone with more traditional values would be a way to bring me back into the fold."

"Traditional values?"

"Yes." He gave me a humorless half smile. "Drinking human blood from the source, rather than acquiring it from blood banks. Or, if blood banks are necessary, leaving nothing behind after raiding them." He paused, then looked away. "Murdering humans indiscriminately."

I shivered at the thought of Frederick living that way. "But that isn't who you are."

"It's not," he said fervently. "Not anymore."

"But it *is* who Miss Jameson is," I guessed. "And your mother."

"Yes."

"And Reginald?"

Frederick paused, considering his words. "He's . . . changing. I think I've had a moderating influence on him."

I stood then, and made my way over to the window overlooking the lake. The enormity of what he was telling me was sinking in little by little. I needed space to think about what all of this meant—for Frederick, and for us.

"I don't know what to say," I murmured.

His solid presence was at my back a moment later, his strong arms going around me before I had a chance to protest. He rested his cheek against the top of my head. I breathed in his reassuring scent, wishing that everything that had just happened here with his mother had been nothing more than a nightmare.

"I'm not marrying her," he murmured fervently into my hair. He kissed the top of my head so gently it broke my heart. It felt like a promise. "I was never going to marry her, not even before I met you. That's the only reason I didn't tell you. I thought I had the situation handled. It never crossed my mind that my mother or the Jamesons would take things this far."

His assurances went a long way towards loosening the knot of pain that had settled in my chest. I sighed, turning in the circle of his arms until my head rested against his chest. His hold on me tightened.

"I made a serious miscalculation when I assumed they would drop this," he continued. "I know now that they will not take no for an answer from afar."

My mind caught on the words *from afar*. I pulled back a little so that I could look at him. "Are you planning to tell them in person?"

He blew out a breath. "The Jamesons are expecting me. My mother is here and will not leave without me. Yes, I believe I need to go to them directly. It's the only way they will understand I am serious about staying here in Chicago and living my life the way I have chosen to live it." He swallowed, and pressed a kiss to my forehead. "If I don't, it's only a matter of time until they *all* show up on my doorstep. And I will not allow that to happen. Not while you are living with me."

I tried to ignore the way my stomach sank like a stone. I had a very bad feeling about this. "So you're going to the Ritz-Carlton tomorrow night, then?"

He nodded.

"Are you sure that's a good idea?" I hated how needy I sounded. But it had been a wild twenty-four hours. I'd had myself some *glorious* sex with one vampire and an unplanned altercation with another. I got rejected from one professional opportunity and landed an unexpected job interview with another.

I probably needed to cut myself some slack.

"Yes." He brushed a lock of my hair that had fallen into my eyes behind my ear. His free hand came up to cradle my face. "All I intend to do is go to the hotel, tell the Jamesons I will not marry Esmeralda, tell my mother she can go to the devil for all I care, and then come right back."

"Somehow I don't think it will be that easy." I'd only spent a few minutes in his mother's presence, and had only known he was in the middle of a messy Regency-era betrothal situation for the past half hour. Even still, I saw at least five different ways this could end badly.

"I do," Frederick said, with a confidence I absolutely did not feel. "I don't remember Miss Jameson well, but it's the twenty-first century, isn't it? She can't want to marry someone she barely knows any more than I do."

He sounded so confident, but I couldn't shake the feeling that this was a terrible plan.

"Do you trust *any* of these people?"

At that, he paused. "No," he conceded. "But they won't take no for an answer by missive, and I'm out of options." I opened my mouth to protest, but he shook his head. "It'll be fine, I promise. And then I'll come right back home to you."

My heart fluttered at his words, despite my misgivings.

"I like that part of the plan," I admitted.

He paused, his eyes suddenly growing dark with mischief. "Since I'm not going anywhere until tomorrow evening, why don't I give you something to remember me by before I go?"

His mouth was at the pulse point of my throat, his hands tangling in my hair before I could even answer his question. All at once it was like the past half hour, and all the complications and new entanglements that came with it, had never happened.

I melted against him.

"That sounds good to me," I breathed, throwing my head back to give him better access.

He growled his approval, then carried me into his bedroom.

# EIGHTEEN

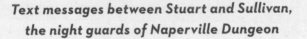

*Text messages between Stuart and Sullivan,*
*the night guards of Naperville Dungeon*

Hey Stuart

> Hey man what's up

Caught the Naperville Police Department
sniffing around this morning

> Well, fudge

Yeah

Not good

> Did you tell the boss

Not yet

I'm about to

> I tell you what, between our new prisoner,
> who's done nothing since he got here last
> night but cry and write letters to some
> human girl, and the police dropping by,
> it's been a hell of a week already

> And it's only Tuesday!

Ugh, I know

> Should I ask Mark to go take
> care of the cops?

> Actually scratch that

> I haven't eaten in a while

> I'll do it

Thanks

I owe you one

> Yeah, yeah

Meanwhile I better get some ear plugs
or else Count von Romeo in here is
gonna drive me batty

I'D BEGUN SUSPECTING SOMETHING WAS WRONG WHEN I
woke up in the middle of the night and Frederick still hadn't
come home from the Ritz-Carlton.

Now, though, fifteen hours had passed, with still no word from him. I was nearly sick with worry, and even more convinced that agreeing to meet with his mother and the Jamesons had been a terrible idea.

I hated that if Frederick were in trouble there was literally nothing I—a human—could do about it. But it was unfortunately also the truth.

And right now, I had to focus on my interview with Harmony Academy—which, through a cruel twist of fate, had been set for that afternoon. I told myself that if I could just get through this interview I'd try and find a way to reach Reginald to see if he could help me figure out what had happened. Reginald might be a jerk, but I believed he did care for Frederick on some level and would help if there were something we could do.

More importantly—Reginald was the only other vampire I knew. I didn't have a lot of options.

In the meantime, focusing on the fact that this afternoon I was interviewing for a position that could potentially change my life was a welcome distraction from how worried I was. And how powerless I felt.

I examined myself in my bedroom's full-length mirror and frowned at my reflection. The navy-blue suit I wore was the only outfit I owned that counted as business attire. I didn't know if Harmony Academy expected me to wear a suit today, and part of me hoped that they'd want applicants for this position to show up in paint-spattered overalls. But Sam told me it was better to show up overdressed to a job interview than underdressed.

Having minimal experience interviewing for jobs with benefits, and terrible job-searching instincts generally, I did what he said and put on the suit.

I still needed to fix my hair, though. It still hadn't fully recov-

ered from my haircutting experiment a few weeks ago, stuck up
in odd places in the back, and was in general extremely annoying.

I might show up to this interview looking and feeling like a
fraud, but if I could avoid *also* looking like a Muppet I probably
should.

Muttering under my breath, I stalked out of the bedroom and
made my way to the bathroom, where my hair stuff was. Just as
my fingers closed around my hairbrush handle, I heard a loud,
throat-clearing noise from a few feet behind me.

"Excuse me."

I froze.

I recognized that voice. It was burned into my memory from
the night I learned my roommate was a vampire.

"Reginald?"

What was he doing here? And *how* was he here? Hadn't Frederick said vampires needed an express invitation to enter someone's home?

But my surprise melted away when I saw his face. In the
handful of times we'd interacted, I had seen Reginald look
amused, insolent, and bored. But I had never seen him look worried before.

He looked worried now, though.

Very worried.

"I'm concerned about Freddie. He's—" Reginald broke off,
giving me a quick once-over before his nose wrinkled in disapproval. "What on *earth* is that outfit, Cassandra?"

"Cassie," I corrected. "And never mind my outfit. Why are
you worried about Freddie?" My heart rate quickened. "Has . . .
has something happened to him?"

He crossed into the living room and sat down in one of the

leather armchairs, not even waiting for me to invite him to make himself at home. "I suspect so, yes. I haven't heard from him since he left to meet with his mother and the Jamesons."

I tried to suppress my rising panic. He hadn't heard from him either, then. "And you'd expected to hear from him by now?"

"Definitely." Reggie hesitated. "We kind of hate each other—"

"I'd gathered as much."

"—but we're also really close."

I took in the worry lines creasing Reginald's otherwise ageless brow. The rigidity of his shoulders. His clenched jaw. "I'd guessed that, too."

"I don't want to assume the worst," he continued. "But I think it's time we consider that they might have done something to him."

So my worries hadn't been irrational, then. "You really think so?"

"Mrs. Fitzwilliam is a force to be reckoned with. To say nothing of what Esmeralda and her family are capable of." He paused again. "Esmeralda's actually a total bitch, if you ask me."

Normally, I hated it when men used the word *bitch* to describe women. In this case, though, it felt oddly vindicating.

"She is?"

"I don't know her well," he conceded. "Let's just say the impression she made on me in Paris in the 1820s wasn't a good one. I'm *definitely* glad Frederick's the one she's decided to marry and not me."

Every interaction I had with Reginald made it that much clearer to me why Frederick found him so annoying.

I glared at him. "You're glad she wants to marry him, are you?"

Reginald shrugged. "No offense, of course. Look her up if you like," he added. "She's got much more of an internet presence than most vampires do. Her social media accounts give a pretty good understanding of who she is as a person." He paused, then added, "She's pretty darn easy on the eyes as well, if you know what I mean."

I squeezed my eyes shut tight. I had to finish getting ready, and then I had to go humiliate myself in front of a hiring committee that would probably never give me a job. I didn't care if Reggie stuck around for a while, but I didn't have time to waste right now thinking about how attractive Esmeralda Jameson might be.

"I need to go." I gestured to my suit. "I have an interview in two hours, and it's far from here."

Reggie stood up. "Want me to fly you there?"

"What?"

"I said," he cleared his throat, enunciating his syllables very carefully. "Do . . . you . . . want . . . me . . . to . . . fly . . . you . . . there?"

I rolled my eyes. "I heard you. I just . . . wasn't expecting the offer." I paused and added, "So it's true, then? Some of you can fly?"

Smirking at me, Reginald—without warning—started to float off the ground. He rose higher, and higher, until the top of his head nearly brushed the living room's high ceiling. All at once, it felt like the room was spinning. It had been one thing for Frederick to tell me some vampires could fly. It was entirely another to actually see someone defy the laws of gravity like this.

"I try not to do this in front of Freddie very often, since his skills are so lame."

I bristled. "His skills are not lame. His pineapples are delicious, I will have you know."

He ignored my comment and began to do slow, leisurely laps

around the room, stopping only to run his finger across the top of the bookshelf. To check for dust, maybe. He was clearly showing off at this point, but I couldn't even be mad at it. It was legitimately impressive, watching him fly.

"You're wrong, Cassandra. His skills are actually deeply, extremely lame insofar as these things go. But like I said, I'm not such an asshole that I would rub my cooler abilities in his face. At least, not more than once or twice a week."

"How . . ." I watched, still awed in spite of myself, as Reginald slowly lowered himself back down to the floor. "How did you *do* that?"

Reginald shrugged. "I haven't the foggiest. How do vampires do anything? It's magic, I guess."

"Magic," I repeated, feeling stupid and slow.

"Magic," he confirmed. "So. Want me to fly you to wherever it is you're going?"

I considered the offer as much as my addled brain would allow and recognized that Reginald was being sincere in offering it. But I dismissed it as being a bad idea. I was already too distracted and worried by Frederick's disappearance to be adequately prepared for this interview. If I flew up to Evanston with Reginald—without an airplane, no less—that would likely shatter whatever remained of my focus into thousands of little pieces.

Also, it was daytime. Flying might be cool and all, but people would be able to see us in the air. And what would they think when they did?

"I appreciate the offer," I said, surprised to realize I meant it. "But I think I'll just take the El."

He raised an eyebrow. "You sure?"

"Very."

Reginald sighed. "Fair enough." He inclined his head towards me and made his way to the door. "If you do hear from Freddie, could you let him know his old pal is worried? I'm going to try and do some reconnaissance in the meantime to figure out what's going on."

I couldn't imagine what he meant by *do some reconnaissance*. Probably better that way. "I will," I said. "I promise. And if you learn anything, could you let me know?"

Reginald regarded me, as though trying to make up his mind about something. Eventually, he seemed to come to a decision and smiled at me.

"I will," he said.

......................

THE PICTURES ON HARMONY ACADEMY'S WEBSITE DIDN'T do the campus justice. It was big and beautiful, located on several wooded acres of real estate just a mile west of Lake Michigan. There was a small, half-frozen pond in the center of campus, with a paved path around it that suggested people liked walking the grounds here when the weather wasn't quite this November-y.

I decided to wear my only pair of heels for this interview. Fortunately, they mostly matched my suit if you squinted and the light wasn't too good. But I regretted this decision the second I walked under the archway that led into the administration building. They clicked loudly against the marble tile floor as I made my way towards the Head of School's office for my eleven o'clock interview, echoing loudly inside the high-vaulted atrium.

The only other noise that registered was the beating of my heart, pounding in my ears like a drum. I couldn't remember the last time I'd been this nervous. I thought back to my own serviceable, but generic, high school. There had been no marble entryways or art teachers who focused on found art back at Carbonway High.

I was as convinced as ever that any second now someone would appear in front of me and tell me they'd made a mistake inviting me here.

"Good morning." The receptionist was about my mother's age, dressed in a muted green dress that made me think of a spring day in the country. The desk she worked behind was almost as large as the bedroom in my last apartment. "You must be Cassie Greenberg."

I gripped my purse a little tighter, a bead of sweat forming at the back of my neck. "Yes."

She motioned to a pair of plush chairs at one end of the room. "Have a seat while I see if they're ready for you. Can I get you something to drink? Coffee? Water?"

"Water, please." I was already nervous. Adding caffeine to the mix would be disastrous. "Thank you."

Beside the chairs was a stack of glossy-looking brochures with smiling students in matching green uniforms on the cover. As I waited for the receptionist to return, I leafed through one of them, trying to absorb some of what I was seeing and willing my hands to stop shaking.

I pulled out my phone and reread the texts Sam had sent me this morning.

**Good luck!!**

**You've got this.**

He'd spent an hour with me last night going over possible interview questions and how I might answer them. He'd told me I hit every answer out of the park and that I was as prepared for this interview as I'd ever be. I only wished I could believe him.

"They're ready for you, Miss Greenberg." I looked up at the

receptionist, who handed me a tall glass of water. "Will you follow me?"

I took the glass from her, gripping my purse strap with my free hand so hard my knuckles hurt.

The room the receptionist brought me to was small and much more casually decorated than anything I'd seen so far this morning. There was nothing on any of the walls other than a framed oil painting of a vase of sunflowers and a large window overlooking the grassy meadow behind the school.

"Have a seat." A woman I recognized from my internet research as Cressida Marks, Head of School, sat smiling at one end of a small, rectangular table. Two other people I didn't recognize were sitting beside her. One of them looked about my age, with flaming pink hair.

For reasons I couldn't quite put into words, seeing that pink hair in a place that otherwise seemed so conventional and austere put me a little more at ease.

I sat in the chair across from them and placed my glass of water on the table.

I let out a slow breath.

I could do this.

"Welcome, Cassie," the head of school said. And then, turning to the other people at the table, "Let's start by introducing ourselves."

"I'm Jeff Castor," said the guy to Cressida's left. He looked about fifty and had on a plaid bow tie with a rumpled white button-down. The absentminded professor vibes he gave off were immaculate. "I'm the vice principal for Harmony's Upper School."

"And I'm Bethany Powers," said the pink-haired woman. "I'm the head of the arts program for the Lower and Upper Schools."

"It's great to meet you," I said.

"You as well," Bethany said. "So. Tell us a little about why you want to work as an art teacher." She was riffling through a file full of printouts of the pictures I'd sent with my application. My beach landscapes from Saugatuck. The piece I submitted to the River North Gallery art exhibition. "It's clear from your portfolio that you have a very specific vision, and that you are committed to a career in the arts. Why kids, though? That's the piece we're missing."

It was a tough question, but a fair one. My résumé was long, but my experience with kids was mostly limited to art nights in the library. If I'd been asked to interview a new art teacher, and someone walked in the door with my credentials, I'd ask the exact same thing.

Fortunately, I was ready for this.

"I work at a library right now," I began. "On Tuesday nights we have an art night, where parents drop off their kids and we spend two hours making things with them." I paused, thinking back on the last art event we'd hosted. "I've found it incredibly rewarding to help kids who might not otherwise have exposure to artistic forms of expression realize their visions through paint and modeling clay."

Bethany and Jeff each jotted down a few notes. Cressida Marks leaned forward a little over the table, hands clasped together in front of her. "Why haven't you thought of teaching art before?"

I considered that. When I'd practiced interview questions with Sam last night, we'd agreed this one would likely come up. The answer we agreed I'd give, though—that I'd just been waiting for the right teaching opportunity to come along, that Harmony Academy was the first school I thought might be a good fit—didn't feel right, now that I was here.

For one thing, it was a lie. I'd applied to several teaching positions over the past few years and was rejected by each of them.

For another, sitting there in that sparsely furnished conference room, with three people who might be my coworkers soon—if all went well—a better answer finally came to me.

"I didn't think any school would have me."

That caused Bethany to look up from her notepad.

"Why is that?" she asked.

We were off the script Sam and I had rehearsed, but that didn't matter. I knew the answer all the same.

"My art isn't conventional." I gestured to the copy of my portfolio in the center of the conference room table. "I don't paint pretty pictures or make coffee mugs on the potter's wheel that people can buy for their sisters at Christmas. I take trash, ephemera—things other people throw away—and turn them into something beautiful." I shook my head. "I didn't think my vision fit in with the kinds of things kids were taught in art classes when I was in school."

"But you decided to go for it with us," Cressida said. "What made you change your mind?"

I pondered that a moment. What *did* make me change my mind?

Suddenly, I knew.

Frederick, in our living room, telling me he could see that I brought a real, unique vision to my work. The awe in his voice as he said the words. The look in his eyes when he told me that anyone who refused to hire me was a fool.

"I realized that I'm good, actually." I smiled and sat up a little straighter in my chair. "And that Harmony would be lucky to have me."

All three of them nodded a little. The woman with the pink hair jotted down a few notes. As they continued to ask me questions about my career goals and my résumé, I started worrying whether that answer had been what they were looking for. But at least it was the truth.

And either way, there was no taking it back now.

"Do you have any questions for us?" Jeff asked, closing the folder he'd been consulting throughout the interview. He had a warm, inviting voice that put me at ease despite my roiling nerves.

I thought over everything Sam and I had talked about, trying to filter it all through the ground this interview had already covered.

"I do," I said. "I'd like to hear more about what I'll be teaching here. What can you tell me about the kinds of arts programming you have here at Harmony, and where my classes would fit into that?"

"I can speak to that." Bethany set down my portfolio and folded her hands neatly in front of her on the table. "Here at Harmony we take nurturing students' artistic expression very seriously. From kindergarten through eighth grade students are exposed to visual, musical, or literary arts every day. By the time students are in the Upper School—or high school, as it's known in the public schools—students select one of four different art tracks that they pursue all four years."

"For some students, the artistic track they pursue may be music," Jeff clarified. "For others, it may be theater, or creative writing. Upper School students who select the fourth track—visual arts—would be the ones in your classes."

"Harmony Academy is proud of all four of its artistic expression tracks," Cressida Marks said, glancing at her colleagues. They nodded. "That said, our visual arts track has traditionally had the least adventurous and diverse offerings."

I wasn't sure what she meant by that. "Least adventurous and diverse? How do you mean?"

"Historically, a lot of our visual arts classes have covered the sorts of things you said earlier that you don't do," Bethany said, glancing at her colleagues. "Painting watercolor still lifes. Art history classes covering the famous paintings you'd find in the Art Institute of Chicago or the Louvre. Lessons on the pottery wheel. And while any Upper School visual arts program worth its salt *must* cover these things, we believe we do our students a disservice if we stop there."

"And that," Cressida said, "is why we wanted to interview you for this position. We are looking for art teachers who think about art in innovative ways and are excited about sharing these innovations with our Upper School kids."

All three of them looked at me, as though gauging my response to what they'd just said. My mind was going a mile a minute trying to process everything.

What they were describing sounded . . .

Well. It sounded *perfect*. Like, too-good-to-be-true perfect.

"That sounds incredible." I didn't know if I should be playing my genuine excitement closer to the chest than this, but I couldn't help it.

Cressida smiled. "We're glad you think so."

"Let's go on a tour of the Upper School," Jeff suggested. "We can take you to the art studios and show you where you'd be teaching if you join us in the fall."

That had to be a good sign.

I grinned at them, unable to help myself. "That sounds great to me."

......................

MY EXCITEMENT OVER HOW WELL MY INTERVIEW WENT was short-lived.

When I got back home and there was still no sign of Frederick, all my worry from earlier in the day came rushing back. I checked my phone and saw I had no messages from Reginald, either, which only heightened my anxiety.

True crime documentaries weren't my favorite flavor of sketchy television, but I knew enough about kidnapping and murder cases to know that the longer you went without news, the greater the chances that the news you ultimately got wouldn't be good.

On a whim that I recognized as a terrible idea even as it occurred to me, I took out my laptop and Googled *Esmeralda Jameson*. If she had as much of an internet presence as Reginald had implied, maybe looking her up would give me some clues.

Reginald hadn't even told me the half of it. Google brought up so many search results for *Esmeralda Jameson* there was no possible way of looking through them all absent a serious obsession with her I was uninterested in developing.

The top search result was a link to her Instagram. That seemed like as good a place to start as any.

Immediately after clicking, the very-bad-idea-ness of this plan came crashing down on me like a Doberman on a plate of hamburgers. I'd been prepared for Esmeralda to be beautiful and flawless, in the same way sort-of-but-not-quite-ex-girlfriends of hot guys usually tended to be. But nothing could have prepared me for the pictures I was looking at now.

I didn't know if vampires ever worked as supermodels. If they did, Esmeralda Jameson would have been *really* good at her job. She was easily six feet tall, with legs for days and a figure that made me question my own heretofore straight sexuality. Her latest picture showed her in a bikini that was notable for what it *didn't* cover, reclining on a lounge chair beneath a beach umbrella that kept her completely in the shade. According to the caption, it had been taken somewhere on Maui. Her long, dark hair was artfully arranged, covering her bare, olive-toned shoulders and half of her angular face.

I clicked through the rest of her Instagram. There were pictures of Esmeralda being stunning in Switzerland in a ski outfit. Pictures of her prettily examining a flower in one of the largest gardens I had ever seen.

*Here I am in Costa Rica, swimming with turtles.*

*It is so beautiful and peaceful here in the Andes.*

*My garden at home needs tending. The flowers here are beautiful, but I cannot wait to be back home again among my peonies.*

There were no funny personal stories or witty hashtags. Nothing to really give me a sense of what she was like as a person. Esmeralda had over one hundred thousand followers anyway—probably people who were as captivated by her beauty as I was.

And then, I saw a post that nearly stopped my heart.

*Here I am with Frederick, my fiancé. Isn't he handsome?*

It was a grainy picture, taken from a distance and late at night. Esmeralda stood beside a black stretch limousine as she helped Frederick into the back seat. If it hadn't been for the caption, it would have been difficult to make out his features enough to realize it was him. But now that I was *really* looking, there was no question that it was, in fact, the same Frederick I lived with—and had started falling in love with. The angle of his jaw, his dark hair, the way he tilted his face away from the streetlights . . .

It was, beyond a shadow of a doubt, him.

The post was made at ten o'clock the previous night.

I closed my eyes and slammed my laptop shut. I could all but feel my heart breaking.

It was possible Reginald was right and something had happened to him, of course. But those pictures didn't lie. Esmeralda was everything Cassie Greenberg would never be. Tall, beautiful, self-possessed—and immortal.

He'd told me that he was into me. He'd acted like it, too. But what if meeting up with Esmeralda had reminded him of all he'd be missing if he stayed with a human like me? Surely someone like him—someone who wouldn't shrivel up and age and eventually die—had to be more appealing than a semi-employed artist with few skills, and with a few more decades left in her at most.

But then a moment later, my phone pinged with new texts from an unknown number.

**Cassandra. It's Reginald.**

**Frederick is in BIG trouble.**

**He needs our help.**

**Meet me at Gossamer's in an hour
and I'll tell you everything.**

# NINETEEN

**Letter from Mr. Frederick J. Fitzwilliam to Cassie Greenberg, dated November 17, confiscated and unsent**

My dearest Cassie,

It has been nearly twenty-four hours since I last saw you. In that time, I have written you three letters—though, if what the guard to my cell just told me is true, none of them have made it out of this dungeon. I shall <u>continue</u> to write you every day I remain imprisoned, however—both because it helps ground me in the here and now, in a place where time has no meaning and one hour bleeds into the next, and because who knows? Maybe eventually the courier will take pity on me and ferret at least one of my letters out of this place before it is noticed by my captors.

To make a long story short: the Jamesons have not taken my refusal of their daughter well. My mother must have warned them of my intentions, because upon my arrival at the Ritz-Carlton a pair of incredibly strong and scary-looking vampires were waiting for me. I tried repeatedly to tell them that I had no reason to believe Esmeralda was anything but a perfectly lovely woman—that the issue was with me, not her—but they didn't seem terribly interested in talking.

And now I sit, imprisoned in a dungeon in Naperville, Illinois, of all places. Every few hours one of my guards asks me if I have relented and if I will agree to marry Miss Jameson. Each time I tell them that my answer has not changed.

As you and I have discussed, I know what my life would be were I to marry Miss Jameson. It is a life I actively rejected when I came to Chicago all those years ago. My meeting you only furthers my resolve not to give in to my captors' wishes. I remain hopeful that if I see Miss Jameson again I may speak with her about the situation and convince her to come to an understanding. She was unwilling to talk last night—but then, she'd also been under the watchful eyes of her parents.

That said, all things considered I have been treated better than I expected. They do require me to eat the way those of our kind typically do (a nasty business which I try and dispense with as painlessly as possible for all involved)—but at least they are feeding me. I also have a relatively comfortable bed, as well as a few books and recordings of American situation comedies from the 1980s. I do not like those nearly as well as the programs we have watched together (several of them seem to involve a talking car, for example, a concept so ridiculous as to defy belief). But as far as I can tell this *dungeon has no WiFi, so my entertainment options are very limited.*

*I miss you more than I can adequately express in a letter. I hope that I am somehow able to tell you this in person very soon.*

*Yours,*
*Frederick*

I STARED AT REGINALD, STRUGGLING TO PROCESS WHAT HE was telling me.

"You have to be joking," I said.

Reginald shook his head. "If I were joking, I'd have said, 'A pirate walks into a bar with a steering wheel on the front of his pants. The bartender says, *Sir, are you aware you have a steering wheel on the front of your pants?* And the pirate says, *Aye, and it's driving me nuts.*'"

The room spun. My head spun. This couldn't be happening.

"I'm sorry, but . . . what?"

"Never mind," Reginald said. He picked up the decoy *We Are Lively* he'd ordered from Gossamer's barista and pretended to sip from it before setting it back down again. "I just mean that, no, I'm not joking."

His eyes betrayed no humor. For once, he was being serious. Deadly serious.

My blood went cold with fear.

"So, they've really kidnapped him?"

He nodded.

"And they're holding him inside a dungeon in . . . *Naperville?*"

Reginald gestured to the photographs he'd brought with him, which he'd apparently taken a few hours ago from a vantage point of two hundred feet in the air. They were an aerial view of a nondescript suburban neighborhood. He'd drawn a big red circle over the house where he claimed Frederick was being held against his will.

"If my contacts in the western suburbs are to be trusted," he said, jabbing his finger at the circled house, "then, yes."

I couldn't believe this. "And all because he wouldn't agree to marry Esmeralda?"

"Alas, yes. The arranged marriage thing is a big deal among the older generations." His expression became grave. "If you're unlucky enough to still have parents kicking around the way Freddie is, defying them in these matters is as close to a death sentence as you can really get in our world."

My mind reeled as I tried to make sense of this. How was any of it actually happening? This whole situation felt like a bad plotline cooked up by a Jane Austen aficionado in the seventh circle of hell.

"I just can't wrap my head around the fact that vampire dungeons are real."

"They were, for the most part, abolished among most civilized members of vampiric society shortly after the French Revolution." He shook his head. "The Jamesons still do things the old-fashioned way, though. According to my contacts, when Frederick said he would not marry Esmeralda, they tossed him into it."

"That seems a bad way to make someone fall in love with their daughter."

He snorted. "Indeed."

"But . . . Naperville? There are vampire dungeons in *Naperville*?" I thought back to the cookie-cutter suburb I'd visited once back in college when my roommate invited me home for Thanksgiving. How could a place like that have a *vampire dungeon?*

"You'd be surprised how many unassuming suburbs have vampire dungeons," Reginald explained. "Here in Chicago, the Jamesons must have had to make do with the limited options at their disposal. Though honestly, hiding him out there is kind of perfect." He gave me a sardonic smile. "Nobody expects a vampire dungeon in Naperville."

He had a point there.

"You know," he added, shooting a pointed look over his shoulder. "We should probably keep our voices down. The Jamesons have ears everywhere."

My skin prickled. "Really?" I asked, sotto voce.

He shrugged. "Probably not, but I've always wanted to say something like that. Either way, I don't think it's a good idea if we're overheard."

He had a point there, too. Nothing good would come of Gossamer's very human clientele overhearing this conversation.

"So that picture I saw on Instagram . . ." I trailed off, fidgeting with the rim of my *We Are Pulchritudinous* as I remembered the image of Frederick being helped into the back seat of a stretch limo by a gorgeous Esmeralda. "You're saying that he didn't go into that limo willingly."

"He couldn't have." Reginald's expression turned even more serious. "That man is head over fangs for you. The past few weeks have been a nightmare for me, personally, with how often I've had to listen to that goofball wax poetic about your literally everything. It's been embarrassing for both of us." He shook his head. "I have not seen the picture you are talking about, but he would never have willingly gone anywhere with Esmeralda. Especially now that he has you."

My heart soared at the confirmation that Frederick had feelings for me, even as my stomach plummeted at the thought of him being in danger.

"So what do we do?"

"We have to get him out of there. If we don't . . ." Reginald shook his head and looked over his shoulder again. "He'll be shipped back to New York and married to a woman he doesn't love before next week."

"Can they *do* that?" I asked, horrified. "Would a wedding against someone's will even be legal?"

He snorted. "We don't do things the way humans do them, Cassandra."

That had to be the understatement of the century. My fight-or-flight instincts were kicking in, the urge to go out to Naperville right that second and demand they let Frederick go nearly overpowering me. But I still had enough common sense to know that barging into a house full of angry vampires would be a seriously terrible idea.

And then, all at once, the beginnings of a plan came to me.

"I have one idea on what we could do to get him out," I said. "You may not like it."

Reginald stared at me. "That sounds ominous."

"It might be," I conceded. "Or it might just be legitimately ridiculous."

"Let's hear it."

I spun my mug of coffee around and around, just for something to do with my hands. Some of its contents sloshed onto the table, but I was too keyed up to care about that. I'd clean it up later so whoever was in charge of closing wouldn't have to.

"How familiar is vampire society with TikTok?"

. . . . . . . . . . . . . . . . . . . .

From: Cassie Greenberg [csgreenberg@gmail.com]
To: Edwina D. Fitzwilliam [Mrs.Edwina@yahoo.com]
Subject: My terms

Dear Mrs. Fitzwilliam,

I will not beat around the bush with you. You have
kidnapped someone who means a lot to me.
Specifically: your son. I insist you and the Jamesons
release him immediately from the Naperville
Dungeon. If you do NOT let him go within twenty-
four hours, I will be forced to go on TikTok and tell
the entire world that vampires are real!!

I look forward to your immediate response.

Cassie Greenberg


I reread my email to Frederick's mother, trying to work up the
nerve to hit *send.*
"Your plan isn't ridiculous," Reginald said. "It's brilliant."
"You think so?"
"I do."
"Will it work?"
Reginald hesitated. "Maybe." He stood behind me, leaning
over my chair as he read the email I'd just drafted. Around us,
Gossamer's patrons sipped their coffee and ate their muffins,
hopefully oblivious to the fact that Reginald and I were plotting
a vampire rescue in the western suburbs. "Aside from Esmeralda,
who just uses Instagram to post pictures as far as I can tell, the
social media phenomenon has passed most vampires by. A lot of

them are centuries old, after all. They don't pay much attention to current events. If they've even *heard* of social media, it's likely just that it's a tool today's humans use to spread information."

This tracked with everything I knew about Frederick's Luddite ways. But the idea that his captors might find my threat convincing was still hard to believe.

Especially since I barely knew how to navigate TikTok myself.

"I get that Mrs. Fitzwilliam and the Jamesons don't want the general human public to know that vampires are real—"

"They don't," Reginald said, bluntly. "None of us do."

"Okay," I said. "My concern is what happens if they call my bluff. I have seven followers on TikTok. I use it to watch cat videos. Even if I knew how to post something like this to TikTok—which I only *barely* do—there's a roughly zero percent chance anyone would see it."

"If they call your bluff, we'll come up with a Plan B," he said. "But I think if all we do is simply film you making a *Vampires are real!* announcement and send it with the email, it should be enough."

"I wish I believed that."

Reginald sat back in his chair and scratched his chin, pondering. "It isn't as though Edwina or the Jamesons will go on TikTok to check whether you've followed through." He regarded me before adding, "And to be honest, Frederick wouldn't *actually* want something like that on the internet anyway. Neither would I."

I swallowed down the fear that rose at the thought that this plan might endanger Frederick even as I was attempting to save him.

"Okay," I said, closing my laptop without hitting *send* on the email. "Where should we film this?"

"Freddie's apartment," Reginald said immediately. "His mom will recognize the setting, and your being there even when he's gone will send a strong message of *Back off, this man is mine*." He tilted his head as he regarded me. "Assuming, of course, that that's the message you *want* to send."

He had a knowing look on his face, and I felt myself flush under his gaze. Because it wasn't just that I didn't want Frederick to be coerced into marrying someone he did not love.

It was more than that.

I wanted Frederick to be safe.

But I also wanted him for *me*.

I needed his captors to understand that.

"That is the message I want to send," I confirmed. "Let's go back to the apartment and film this thing."

Reginald smiled his agreement. Though it's possible he was smirking at me instead.

..................

"THIS ISN'T GOING TO WORK."

"It will."

I stared at Reginald as the terrible video he'd just taken of me threatening to expose all of vampire-kind played back to us from my laptop.

"Were we convincing?"

Reginald frowned contemplatively and made a seesawing motion with his hand. "Yes? Maybe? Hard to say. Either way it's too late for do-overs. We've already emailed it to Mrs. Fitzwilliam."

I sighed and buried my face in my hands.

"*Humans of North America*," the video version of me chirped with false bravado, Frederick's creepy stuffed wolf's head with the glowing red eyes hanging just above my head. ("I got it for him at Disney World," Reginald had explained. "But I told him I chopped off a werewolf's head so I'd sound tough.") "*I come to you with news of great importance.*"

The video-me held aloft two bags of blood I'd gotten from the small refrigerator Frederick kept in his bedroom, one in each hand. I thought back to how horrified I'd been the first time I saw all that blood in the kitchen. It didn't bother me so much anymore. Frederick had kept his promise to me, never once eating in my presence or storing his blood in a place I might find it.

It was clear to me now that he'd chosen the most humane way to survive that he possibly could.

The video-me managed to keep from broadcasting any of these tender thoughts. That part had gone well, at least. Usually I had zero poker face at all. Brandishing the bags, video-me said, *"The recent rash of blood bank break-ins have all been the work of vampires living in our midst. And here is the proof!"*

Video-me pointed up to the "werewolf head" hanging above me. *"They behead werewolves for sport! They drink the blood of our children! They live right here in Chicago. In New York City. Everywhere! No corner of the earth is safe while they roam free!"*

("You're good," Reginald mused.

"You're lying," I accused.

"Maybe," Reginald admitted.)

A moment later, video-Reginald burst into the scene. *"Mwah-ha-ha!"* he exclaimed, his fangs out, his eyes wide. *"I've come to drink your blood!"* he continued in the cheesiest fake-Transylvanian accent I'd ever heard. Video-Reginald then grabbed one of the bags of blood in my hand and tore it open with a flourish, sucking it down with as much gusto as he had the night I found out he was a vampire.

Video-me screamed, and then the scene went dark.

Reginald closed the laptop and shrugged. "Okay, so I admit it's not my best work. But we're on a deadline. And as you've no doubt already noticed, hyperbole and overacting are the metaphorical bread and butter of the larger vampire community."

I thought back to my first impression of Edwina D. Fitzwilliam, in her satin-silk-velvet black mishmash of a dress and her 1970s glam-rock makeup. "I may have noticed that."

"Anyway, there's nothing we can do right now but wait," Reginald said reasonably. "If Edwina buys it, we ride tomorrow at sunset. And if she doesn't . . ."

Reginald didn't finish that thought.

But he didn't have to.

If Frederick's mother and the Jamesons didn't buy this ruse, I knew full well that neither of us had a Plan B.

# TWENTY

My dearest Cassie,

It has been more than twenty-four hours since my capture, but I believe I have made progress towards securing my release.

I have spoken with Miss Jameson. While I am as convinced as ever that a union between us would be disastrous, I am gratified for confirmation that she is not as stuck in the old ways as her parents. While my rejection has stung and offended her, she has enough self-possession and self-worth to not want any man who does not want her. I believe she will eventually become an unlikely ally in my attempts to earn back my freedom.

I hope you are faring well—and that you do not interpret my silence as anything other than what it is.

*Specifically: me, trapped in a terrifying dungeon in the suburbs with no way to escape.*

*All my love,*
*Frederick*

.....................

From: Nanmo Merriweather [nanmo@yahoo.com]
To: Cassie Greenberg [csgreenberg@gmail.com]
Subject: Your terms

Dear Miss Greenberg,

I, Mrs. Edwina D. Fitzwilliam's assistant, write you on her behalf to inform you that you have left her with no choice but to agree to your demands.

Please come to the castle located at 2314 S. Hedgeworth Way in Naperville, Illinois, at eight o'clock tomorrow evening. She will release her son to your custody *if*, and only *if*, you destroy all existing copies of your vampire exposé in her presence. The motion picture you have created has the power to destroy everything we have worked so hard to establish since leaving England—and while choosing her son's betrothed is important to my mistress, nothing is more important to our kind than to live in secret.

We will see you tomorrow evening. (Also, please do not reply to this email. Mrs. Fitzwilliam does not know how to check her email. All of her emails therefore bounce directly to me and, frankly, I have enough work to do already without also keeping up with her pettier correspondence.)

With kind regards,
N. Merriweather

"I CAN'T BELIEVE SHE'S STILL GOT NANMO DOING HER BID-ding like this," Reginald *tsked*, shaking his head. "The man is four hundred and seventy-five years old, for crying out loud. It's *embarrassing*."

"Yeah," I said, not knowing how else to respond to that. I was so far out of my element I couldn't even *see* my element anymore.

"Well, I guess the important thing is they bought it," Reginald said. "I'm at once surprised, because this really is silly, and not at all surprised. I'll fly you there tomorrow at eight."

"No," I said very quickly, holding up my hands. "I'll just take an Uber."

Reginald stared at me from his vantage point on Frederick's black leather sofa. "Don't be ridiculous. It's not safe for you to go to this by yourself."

I paled at the thought of showing up to this rendezvous with-out vampire backup. "Oh, I know that. It would be suicide to show up at that house alone."

"It would," Reginald agreed.

"I just meant if I fly there with you, I'll be too distracted by my first-ever flight without an airplane to be able to keep my head on straight for what I might have to do once we get there."

Reginald leaned against the sofa cushions as he considered that. "Fine," he said. "It's true that flying for the first time can be a lot. So sure. Take an Uber. But don't get out of the car until you see me hovering in the sky just on the other side of the basketball hoop."

I frowned at him. "Basketball hoop?"

"You'll know it when you see it," he said, before muttering something about *suburban hellscape* under his breath that I didn't quite catch. He stood up and made his way to the front door.

"I'll see you tomorrow night," I said, trying to convey a confidence I absolutely did not feel.

Reginald paused, then turned to face me, his expression unreadable.

"Please be careful," he said, his voice softer than I'd ever heard it.

My eyes felt suddenly damp. "I will."

"Good," he said. And then, in the mocking tone I was much more used to hearing from him, he added, "Because if something happens to you tomorrow night Frederick will kill me a second time."

...................

2314 S. HEDGEWORTH WAY WAS LOCATED AT THE END OF A small cul-de-sac, a beige-and-white two-story house that was nearly identical to all the other beige-and-white two-story houses on the street. It had an American flag flying from a flagpole and—yes, there it was—a basketball hoop mounted on a slightly darker beige-and-white shed off to the side.

Only the two-foot-tall stone gargoyles mounted on either side of the garage—and the six-foot-tall vampire suspended in midair about ten feet above the basketball hoop—distinguished this house in any way from its neighbors.

My eyes flicked to the airborne vampire.

Reginald had arrived before me.

That was good.

It was also my cue to get out of the car and approach the house.

"Thanks," I said to my Uber driver. My hands shook so badly I struggled to get the car door open. The night had gotten colder in the forty-five minutes since I'd left Frederick's apartment. Or perhaps it was always a few degrees colder this far west of the lake. I pulled my winter coat around myself a little more tightly as I approached the house to warm myself—and to try and settle my roiling nerves.

Reginald and I had agreed I would handle the talking at first. The video we made plainly showed that one of their own had been a part of this plot. If the vampires inside this house knew that said vampire had come with me tonight, it could complicate things in a way that could jeopardize both Frederick's safety as well as Reginald's. The idea was that he would stay safely out of sight and up in the air unless and until things went sideways— and I needed vampiric intervention.

I glanced up at him again as I approached the house. He nodded reassuringly. My stomach was in knots. A voice in the back of my head yelled at me to *run, run, get away from here* more loudly with every step I took.

But Frederick needed me.

So I kept moving forward, putting one foot in front of the other until, at last, I was at the front door.

Just as I was about to knock, my heart thundering in my chest, I heard someone clear their throat very deliberately, and very loudly, from about five feet away.

"Excuse me," the throat clearer said. "But do you know these people?" The speaker looked about fifty years old, his mouth turned down at the corners in a disapproving frown. He wore a winter coat and dark fleece pajama pants, and a red wool hat with mittens that matched.

Of all the scenarios Reginald and I had run through over the past twenty-four hours, none had included what to do in case of nosy neighbor interference. But it looked like we'd run through one scenario too few.

"I . . . I don't know them," I stammered. "Or, rather—I know who they are. But I don't *know them* know them, if you know what I mean."

"Hm." The man's disapproving frown turned into an outright scowl. "You're here to buy drugs, I assume."

My eyes widened. "I beg your pardon?"

The man pointed to the windows on the front of the house. For the first time I realized they were all covered up with dark sheets of plastic. "They've blacked out all the windows, they never come out during the day, and all manner of weirdos go in and out of this house all night long." He counted out each of his neighbors' perceived crimes against society on long, outstretched fingers. "I don't know where you come from, but around here that points to just one thing."

I paused, waiting for him to tell me what that one thing was. When all he did was look at me with a self-satisfied smirk, I guessed, "Does it mean . . . drugs?"

"It means drugs," he confirmed.

"I don't know anything about that," I said very quickly, grappling for a plausible reason for my being there that would make this guy go away. "I just . . . I'm just here because . . ." I licked my lips—and said the first thing that popped into my head. "Because of their internet bill."

I didn't have to look up to know that Reginald was rolling his eyes at me so hard they were in danger of falling out of his head.

Incredibly, the man seemed to accept my explanation. "It doesn't surprise me that people like these would fall behind on their bills," he muttered.

"Exactly," I said, trying hard to muster a laugh. It came out as more of a laugh-sob.

He clapped me on the shoulder, winked at me in a way that would in any other circumstances be the creepiest thing to have happened to me that day, and said, "Keep up the good work, hon."

As he wandered off back to his own beige-and-white two-story house, I closed my eyes and took several deep breaths. I had to calm down. I hadn't even *done* anything yet and I felt seconds away from bursting out of my own skin.

I chanced one more glance up at Reginald. He nodded and flashed me a double thumbs-up.

It was time.

"Here goes nothing," I murmured under my breath, and knocked on the door.

........................

PART OF ME HAD HOPED FREDERICK WOULD BE THE ONE to answer my knock. But when the door opened, I wasn't surprised to see Mrs. Fitzwilliam—pale-faced, with no garish makeup this time—standing on the other side.

She didn't invite me in. She also didn't mince words.

"Did you bring it with you?" She glared at me, one hand on her hip, the other fanning her face as if the cold night air that was cutting right through my winter coat was too warm for her.

Now that I was there, I couldn't help but wonder whether Edwina Fitzwilliam might have been a different kind of person before she'd turned. Had she been a good, kind parent to Frederick when he was small? I hoped so. I hated the idea of little Frederick growing up in a home with someone like this as his mother.

I patted the front pocket of my jeans, where I'd stashed my cell phone before getting in the Uber. "Yes."

"Let's see it."

I fished out my phone and pulled up the photos app. "It's right here," I said, before hitting the play button.

My voice rose tinnily from my phone, and it took everything I had not to cringe right out of my skeleton at the sight of me gesticulating wildly in Frederick's living room with a bag of donated blood in each hand. Somehow the clip looked even more ridiculous here, on my phone, in front of the very person I'd hoped to threaten with it.

But it seemed to have a profound effect on Frederick's mother all the same. She recoiled, horror-struck. Her shaking palms went to her cheeks as she watched the video of me warning everyone of the looming North American vampire threat.

I pocketed my phone when the short clip ended. Frederick's mother shrank away from me, inching her way back inside the house.

"If we agree to break the engagement and let him go," she began in a whispery voice, her hand fluttering at her throat, "will you destroy that?"

She looked terrified. Fortunately for me, though, this was the easiest bargain I'd ever made. "Yes."

"Tonight?"

"Right here," I offered. "Right in front of your eyes."

She nodded, but only appeared partly mollified. "Nanmo tells me it is possible to make copies of things like this. Do you promise to destroy all other copies if we release my son? And to not put it on the TikToks?"

"This is the only copy," I assured her. "When I delete it from my phone no one else will ever be able to see it." I paused and tried to keep a straight face when I added, "I promise you I will never put it on the TikToks."

She hesitated, as if unsure whether to believe me. And then, after what felt like entire minutes, she drew a deep breath.

"If you are lying to me," she began, "we will hunt you down like the dog you are."

The door slammed in my face.

I looked up at Reginald, who wore a wary expression.

"I'm coming down," he said, floating to the ground as though being lowered by an invisible rope. "I think she bought it, but—"

Before he could finish his thought, the door opened again.

There was Frederick, dressed in the same clothes he'd left the apartment in a few nights ago when he went to the rendezvous at the Ritz-Carlton. My eyes roved over him, taking in every inch of him—from the disheveled way his hair fell across his forehead, to the white long-sleeved T-shirt that clung to his broad shoulders like he was born to wear nothing else.

His gaze bored into mine, as though he were as unable to stop looking at me as I was to stop looking at him. He looked even paler than usual, with dark circles ringing his eyes I'd never seen there before. But he was here, and he was whole, and he was beaming at me with a look of such tenderness and wonder I felt foolish for ever having doubted his feelings.

"You came," he said, hoarsely. His eyes were wide, incredulous. "You *brilliant* woman."

Relief flooded me at the sound of his voice. I nodded, not trusting myself to speak.

"Aren't you gonna call me brilliant?" Reginald pouted from somewhere behind me. "I helped too."

"And you even had to put up with Reginald while you did it," Frederick said, ignoring him. He moved towards me from where he stood in the entryway, reaching for me. After going days without his touch, Frederick's embrace was like coming home. I felt both rooted to the spot and seconds away from falling to the ground as he held me, his broad chest steady beneath my cheek, his hands a chilly counterpoint to the warmth of my winter jacket.

His touch warmed me from within all the same.

"We should go," Reginald cut in, brusquely.

Frederick lifted his cheek from where it had come to rest on top of my head. "You're right," he agreed. He pulled back a little more so that he could look into my eyes. "They've let me go, Cassie. But it's not safe for us to stay here a moment longer."

"I'd offer to fly you back to your apartment, but I can't carry you both," Reginald said. He added, smirking, "I'd also rather not be around the two of you lovebirds right now anyway."

Frederick glared at him and was about to say something in response when I put a hand on his arm.

"It's fine," I said, very quickly. "I'll call us an Uber. It shouldn't take long for one to get here at this hour."

I programmed the pickup spot for a few blocks away from the vampire house, just in case. No need to tempt fate so soon after getting him back.

"Thank you for saving me, Cassie," Frederick murmured, his voice low and awed. "How did I ever get so lucky?"

I kissed him, unable to help myself.

"We can talk about that later," I whispered against his lips. "For now, let's get you home."

......................

WE MOSTLY KEPT OUR HANDS TO OURSELVES DURING THE forty-five-minute Uber ride back to the apartment. Frederick's eyes kept closing, and the fact that I could easily see his fangs whenever he was fully awake told me he was too exhausted to glamour us invisible to the driver. I brushed his hair back and away from his forehead as he dozed, trying hard not to imagine what he must have gone through over the past few days to make him this tired after sundown.

By the time we made it back inside the apartment, though, he seemed to have mostly come back to himself. He maneuvered me through the open doorway and into the living room, as though now that we were here he didn't want to waste any more time.

"Wait," I said, when he moved to enfold me in his arms. I *wanted* to move closer to him, to let him kiss and touch me. To kiss and touch him back. But I had questions first. "You've just been held somewhere against your will for three days, and before we do . . . anything else, I have to know. Are you truly all right?"

He nodded and closed the distance between us again. "I am now." His voice was full of so much heat and promise my knees nearly buckled. When his arms came around me and pulled me to him again, it was easy enough to tell myself this conversation could still happen while we were touching.

I rested my head against his chest again, in an approximation of how we stood when we reunited in front of the Naperville house. He started rocking me gently, back and forth. I had never been full of such utter relief, and such thorough contentment.

"Reginald filled me in on parts of what happened," I murmured, my voice muffled by the fabric of his shirt. "But I need to hear it from you. It's the only way I'll believe you're actually okay."

Frederick's arms tightened around me. He sighed, letting his head droop forward until it rested on my shoulder.

"It's just as Reggie said," he murmured. "Esmeralda's family didn't take my ending the engagement well." He stepped back and held up his wrists, which bore angry red marks I hadn't noticed earlier. "In my absence I became very well acquainted with their dungeon."

My breath caught. "They hurt you."

"A little," he admitted. "Not much. We're immortal, but because our hearts don't beat, our blood doesn't flow the way yours does. Which, in turn, means it takes an irritatingly long time for wounds to heal." He gifted me with a wry half smile. God, how I missed his smiles. "My wrists were only tightly bound for part of one day. I promise this injury looks a lot worse than it is."

He moved forward and wrapped me in his arms again. I closed my eyes, burying my face in his shoulder, breathing him in.

Somehow, I found the courage to ask the question I most badly needed answered. "So the engagement is definitely over now?"

"Yes." His deep voice was as forceful as I'd ever heard it. "I ended the engagement definitively. Ironically enough, Esmeralda helped with that. She wasn't very keen on marrying someone who would rather rot in a suburban dungeon than be her husband. She intervened on my behalf with her parents at the same time you concocted your brilliant TikTok strategy." He drew back and tucked a stray lock of hair behind my ear. "She's a reasonable woman, at least insofar as any of the Jamesons are reasonable people. She's just not the right woman for me."

The heat in his gaze was unmistakable. I blushed at the obvious implication of what he was saying and looked at the floor.

"I missed you," I admitted. It felt foolish to miss someone I'd only known for a few weeks as much as this. But it was the truth.

"I missed you, too." He paused, then added, "I wrote you." His words were a deep rumble beneath my ear. He actually *wrote* me while he was kept prisoner? I burrowed more closely into him, my heart so full it felt fit to burst. "I gave the letters to my guards and asked them to send them to you. Who knows what the Jamesons did with them, though. Did you receive any of my letters?"

My chest went tight at the hopefulness I heard in his voice.

"No," I admitted. "I didn't get anything from you." I briefly considered letting him know how I'd interpreted his radio silence at first—the irrational worries I'd harbored. But then he sighed, resting his chin on top of my head, and my concerns felt too silly and faraway to justify with words.

"I'm so sorry," he said.

"What did the letters say?"

He pulled away slightly, his eyes dark and inviting, his lashes wet with something that, if I hadn't known better, I would have assumed were the beginnings of tears. He gazed into my own eyes like he was as transfixed by what he saw in mine as I was by what I saw in his.

Then he nodded, as if coming to a decision.

"They said this," he murmured, a moment before pressing a gentle kiss to my lips.

The rational part of my mind was telling me that we shouldn't do this now. The circles he still had under his eyes belied his claim that he was fine, and I wasn't certain he was telling me the truth about those angry red marks on his wrists.

We also needed to talk about what we would be to each other now that there was no fiancée anymore, and nothing standing between us but my own mortality.

But Frederick was kissing me with so much urgency—his hands cradling my face, tangling in my hair; the evidence of how badly he wanted me already pressing hot and urgent against my hip—that I decided these conversations could wait for later.

"I thought about you endlessly while I was away," he murmured, kissing the words into my cheeks. "Your passion for what you do, your gentle spirit. Your beauty. Your kindness." His hands were growing restless, roving up and down my back as his lips found the underside of my jaw, when they latched onto the sweet, sensitive spot where neck met shoulder. I threw my own arms around him, pulling him closer, not even realizing he was backing me up against the wall until I felt it, firm and solid, behind me.

"I thought about you, too," I confessed, relishing in the way he was lavishing my body with attention. We were still fully clothed, but the touch of his hands at either side of my waist seared through my shirt as though I were wearing nothing at all. "I thought about you the whole time."

"Please tell me that you will stay with me." His words were barely above a whisper, breathed into my shoulder as he kissed me there. "With your convictions and your talents, it is only a matter of time before your financial situation improves and you no longer need to partake of our original arrangement. But—"

His mentioning what led me to move in with him in the first place broke me out of the moment, reminding me I hadn't told him about my interview with Harmony yet. Suddenly, it was important to me that he know.

"You may be right about my financial situation improving."

Frederick paused, right in the middle of doing something absolutely delicious with my earlobe.

"Hm?"

"While you were gone, I interviewed with that school." I couldn't keep the smile out of my voice. "I think it went well. Nothing's settled yet, of course. But I'm hopeful."

He buried his face in the crook of my neck and pulled me

closer. "Of course it went well. Darling Cassie—I never doubted that you would charm them utterly. The way you charm everyone." He paused. "The way you've charmed me."

I lost track of how long we stood there in the living room, holding each other. My mind spun. Maybe he'd been right about me all this time. Perhaps if I believed in myself even half as much as he believed in me, I wouldn't need a living situation with strings attached for much longer.

But that wouldn't change how I felt.

Or the fact that I would want to stay with him even if paychecks eventually became a more regular part of my life.

"I don't dare hope that someone like you would choose to stay with someone like me," he eventually continued. "But that doesn't change how badly I want you to stay with me here, all the same."

I swallowed. "Are you sure about that? I'm going to get old one day. I won't look like this forever."

"I don't care," he said, flatly. And then, with a twinkle in his eye, he added, "Besides—I will always be older than you."

I laughed in spite of myself, then put my fingers beneath his chin so he'd have to look me in the eyes. His expression was full of such painful vulnerability it stole the breath from my lungs.

I nodded. "I want to stay."

When he kissed me again, I decided that knowing exactly what came next could wait.

# EPILOGUE

## ONE YEAR LATER

I WAS JUST PACKING UP MY BAG TO GO HOME AT THE END of the day when my phone buzzed several times, letting me know I had new texts.

It took me a minute to find my purse in my art bag. Now that I was teaching full time and needed to bring supplies with me on the El every day, the bag I carried around with me was the biggest one I'd ever had. It seemed like the thing had at least a dozen interior pockets—pockets my keys and my cell phone were constantly disappearing into.

By the time I managed to locate my phone, Frederick had sent nearly a dozen texts.

> I am waiting for you outside the entrance to the Fine Arts building.

> I am wearing an outfit I selected myself this afternoon.

That green Henley you like,
paired with black trousers.

I think you would approve.

Or I hope you will approve, anyway.

But I suppose only time will tell.

I miss you. ☺

A laugh bubbled up inside of me.

Frederick J. Fitzwilliam, age three hundred and fifty-one, was texting using emojis.

It was nearly impossible to believe.

I have to put a few things away before
I'm ready to leave

We've been working on plastics this week

So my room's a mess

Give me 15 minutes

I miss you too 💜

I found him where he said he'd be, in a shady spot right outside Harmony Academy's fine arts building. He was leaning against the brick wall of the building, legs crossed at the ankle, engrossed with something on his phone.

As I approached he looked up and gave me a bright smile. "You're here."

"I am," I agreed. I took his hand and gave it a squeeze. "How was your day?"

He gave a one-shouldered shrug. "It was fine. Boring. I spent most of it tied up in communication with our realtor, who seems to think we should be able to close on our new home by the end of next month." He paused. "The rest of the day was spent listening to Reginald wax amorously about his accountant."

A group of students from my afternoon welding class passed by. They waved at me, and I waved back at them, smiling. It was still so hard to believe I was in this job, with students who respected me and wanted to hear what I had to say.

When I turned back to Frederick, he was looking at me with an expression so heated it was almost inappropriate, given that we were not only at my place of employment but also in front of a whole bunch of kids.

"Reginald has an accountant?" I asked, pushing the strap of my bag up a little higher on my shoulder. "Really?"

"So it would appear."

"Why?"

"It takes a lot of expertise to manage wealth that began accruing two hundred years ago." He gave me a lopsided smile. "Reginald has never had a head for business—that should be no surprise—but over the years he has amassed a fortune more than large enough to subsidize his lifestyle. Anyway, it appears he has become infatuated with his very *human* accountant, which has led to all the problems you might imagine and quite a few you probably cannot."

He was likely right about that. "Let's not talk about Reginald anymore," I suggested. I nodded down the hill the fine arts building perched on, towards the small man-made lake sitting in the center of Harmony's campus and the path that circled it. My impression of it when I interviewed here a year earlier—that it was probably a popular place to go walking when the weather was nice—turned out to be accurate. It was a favorite place to go walking at lunchtime, after lacrosse games, and on Friday afternoons. "Go for a walk with me?"

It was warm for early December, and I wanted to spend a little more time outside enjoying it before going back home. The overcast sky wouldn't make things too uncomfortable for Frederick, who was recovered enough from his century of accidental slumber to be able to handle daytime excursions provided there was adequate shade. Besides, it was four o'clock on a December day in Chicago; the sun wouldn't be up for much longer either way.

To my surprise, Frederick hesitated, a pained look flitting across his face.

"What is it?" I asked, concerned.

"Nothing." He shook his head, then schooled his features into a semblance of his normal expression. He squeezed my hand. "A walk around the lake sounds lovely."

......................

THE PATH WAS MORE CROWDED THAN USUAL FOR A TUESDAY, with clusters of students and even some people unaffiliated with Harmony enjoying the unseasonably mild weather with a lakeside stroll. While walking around campus was usually one of our favorite midweek activities—Frederick's ability to be awake during the day for longer stretches was something he liked taking advantage of—the walk didn't seem to have lessened his earlier agitation. He visibly startled every time a particularly rambunctious group of students passed us on the path, and the fingers of the hand I wasn't holding drummed a constant staccato beat against his right thigh.

When Frederick nearly jumped out of his skin at the approach of a duck quacking noisily at something it must have seen in the grass, I stopped walking and tugged on his hand.

"What's wrong?" I asked.

"What?" His eyes were on the duck, who was now waddling its noisy way back into the water. "Nothing's wrong. Why would you think something was wrong?"

His voice was half an octave higher than usual, the words spoken at nearly twice his normal rate of speech.

"Just a guess," I said, peering at him.

"Nothing's wrong," he said again. His jaw worked as he stared down at his feet, at the water, at the clouds in the sky. "I promise. Shall . . . shall we keep walking?"

The last time I had seen him this agitated was when we'd talked about moving into a new apartment together. One that didn't feel like it was only his. One that didn't carry with it the bad associations of the century he'd spent too incapacitated to notice the world around him.

Something was definitely on his mind.

"Whatever it is," I said in as gentle a voice as I could, "you can tell me."

He closed his eyes on a shuddering sigh.

"There's something I would like to ask you."

He shoved his hand deep into the pocket of his slacks. When he pulled it out again, in his hand was a small velvet box.

My heart stopped.

"I don't have the right to ask you to stay with me forever," he said. His voice had recovered its normal cadence and pitch. I wondered if he was starting a speech he had practiced during my long hours away from the apartment the past few months, since I started my new job here. "But I never said I wasn't a selfish man. Or that I was a good one, for that matter."

"You are *not* selfish," I insisted. "And you're one of the best people I know."

He waved a dismissive hand. "Points upon which reasonable minds can differ, I suppose. But what I want to ask you is—" He broke off. Closed his eyes. Shook his head. "What I came here today to talk to you about is—"

"You want me to think about it," I said, interrupting him.

A flock of ducks waddled across the path a few feet away from us, quacking noisily at each other as my entire world tilted slowly on its axis.

Frederick nodded slowly. "Yes," he whispered.

Then he opened the box in his hand.

I'd never given much thought to what I'd want my engagement ring to look like if I were ever to be on the receiving end of one. I'd always found diamonds to be sort of pretty, but in a bland and characterless sort of way. I'd never been able to imagine myself wearing one—on my hand, or anywhere else.

The ring that lay nestled within the black-velvet box had a blood-red ruby in its center that was the size and general shape of a dime but with interesting facets cut into it that caught the sunlight when Frederick's shaking hands jostled it a little.

I may have never thought much about what I wanted in an engagement ring, but all at once I knew I'd never see one more beautiful, or more perfect, than this.

"If I say yes," I said, my breathing starting to come too quickly, "you'll need to teach me what to do."

I chanced a look up at his face. He was gazing down at me with an expression I couldn't read.

"Teach you what to do?" he repeated.

"Yes," I said. "I've lived with you for over a year now, but you've been so careful to keep me from the . . . more *detailed* aspects of things. I'll need to know exactly what I'm in for if I . . ."

I trailed off, trying to think of how to phrase the rest of what I was thinking in a way that wouldn't frighten any passersby.

"If you . . . ?" Frederick prompted.

"If I take the plunge," I said bluntly. There. That should cover it. I raised my eyebrows meaningfully.

All at once, he understood what I was trying to say.

"Yes, of course. Darling—I'll tell you everything," Frederick promised, his words coming out in an earnest rush. "I'll show you anything you want to see. If, after you see and know what it would be like for you, if you still say no—"

"I understand," I said.

"And so will I," he vowed. "Whatever you decide. This ring is just a promise that you will . . ."

"Think about it," I agreed.

"Yes."

Satisfied, I grinned up at him. And held out my left hand.

The ruby felt cool against my skin as he slid the ring onto my finger. Once it was in place, we both stared at it, unable to quite believe what had just happened, until the sun began setting in earnest.

Still beaming up at him, I took his hand.

He took me home.

# ACKNOWLEDGMENTS

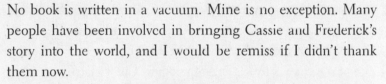

No book is written in a vacuum. Mine is no exception. Many people have been involved in bringing Cassie and Frederick's story into the world, and I would be remiss if I didn't thank them now.

First, thank you so much to Cindy Hwang at Berkley for believing in me, and for giving me the opportunity to write the kooky little vampire rom-com of my heart. Endless gratitude as well to my phenomenal agent, Kim Lionetti, who has patiently answered my countless questions, and who has been the best and fiercest kind of advocate.

A staggering amount of work happened behind the scenes at Berkley to get this book to print. I am forever grateful to my genius editor, Kristine Swartz (whose editing talents are surpassed only by her great taste in K-dramas), and to her editorial assistant, Mary Baker. Thank you to Christine Legon, the managing editor; Stacy Edwards, the production editor; and Shana Jones, the copyeditor, for their work in making this book readable and beautiful. Roxie Vizcarra and Colleen Reinhart created an absolutely perfect book cover that I've been screaming about (figuratively, but also literally) ever since it first landed in my inbox. Thank you to Tawanna Sullivan and Emilie Mills in Sub Rights; my publicist, Yazmine Hassan; and Hannah Engler in Marketing for working tirelessly to bring Frederick and Cassie's story to readers.

There are so many other people in my life I need to thank for being there for me as I wrote *My Roommate Is a Vampire*. Thank you to Starla and Dani for being the first people to ever read something I'd written and tell me that it was good, actually. Thank you to Sarah B., Quinn, Marie, Pat, Mateus, and Christa for being there when this book's concept was first conceived. (I hope you have forgiven me for ultimately taking the *virgin* out of this story's *vampire*.) And thank you to Celia, Rebecca, Sarah H., and Victoria for looking over the very first outline for this book and giving me such valuable early feedback.

Special thanks to Katie Shepard and Heidi Harper, who reviewed *every single draft* of this book as I wrote it. You are both absolute *heroes*. You provided so much helpful feedback along the way that I definitely owe each of you cake in the near future. (Possibly also ice cream and/or a six-pack of passionfruit La Croix.) A huge thank-you as well to the Berkletes, who are an absolute powerhouse of talent, and whose advice has been so impactful to me as a debut author.

"Thanks" isn't a big enough word to convey my gratitude to the Getting Off on Wacker gang, who were not only wonderful movie buddies when we saw . . . um, *Cats* . . . in December 2019, but who have become a beloved source of joy and support in the years since. Shep, Celia, and Rebecca, I don't know what I'd do without your friendship, your cat pics, your outrageous senses of humor, and your empathy. Thank you to my K-drama buddies— Tina, Emma, Angharabbit, Toni, and Bassempire—for your endless wit, and for your television recs that are always a welcome break from writing. And thank you to Thea Guanzon, Elizabeth Davis, and Sarah Hawley, whose friendship—and off-the-record conversations about writing and publishing—have been a source of much-needed validation (and laughter) this past year.

My husband, Brian, deserves special recognition for his endless support of everything I do. Thank you, sweetheart, for smiling and nodding encouragingly all those times I asked you, "Do you think my book is good?" before you'd even had a chance to read it. Thank you to my mom for teaching me how to read all those years ago while doing Muppet voices; to my dad for his blintzies and pancakes on family vacations; to my brother, Gabe, for being a wonderful headshot photographer and Instagram tutor; and to my sister, Erica, for being the kindest person I know. And of course, the world's biggest thank-you to my daughter, Allison, for being the sweetest teenager in the world (despite her not thinking I'm all that funny).

Finally, I want to give a special thank-you to my incredible online writing and fandom community. (You rats know who you are.) You encouraged me to keep going when I first tossed around ideas for this book on social media. You emailed me jokes that had me cackling in public, and you laughed at all the right places when this book was nothing but a tweet string and a prayer. To those of you who read this book in its true infancy—and to each of you who have read and given kind feedback on other stories I've shared over the past decade—it is no exaggeration to say I would not be here but for all those times you cheered me on. From the bottom of my heart, thank you.

Jenna

*Author photo by Gabriel Prusak*

By day, **Jenna Levine** works to increase access to affordable housing in the American South. By night, she writes romance novels where ridiculous things happen to beautiful people. When Jenna isn't writing she can usually be found crying over K-dramas, starting knitting projects she won't finish, or spending time with her family and small army of cats.

## CONNECT ONLINE

JennaLevine.com
JennaLevineWrites
Jeenonamit